The Investigator's Apprentice

The Investigator's Apprentice

The perpetual

Chronicles of Brother Hermitage

by

Howard of Warwick

From the Scriptorium of
The Funny Book Company

The Funny Book Company

Published by The Funny Book Company
Crown House 27 Old Gloucester Street
London WC1N 3AX
www.funnybookcompany.com

Cover design by Double Dagger.

ISBN 978-1-913383-41-1

Scriptorial appreciation is due to:
Mary
Susan Fanning
Karen Nevard-Downs
Lydia Reed
Claire Ward

Also by Howard of Warwick.
The First Chronicles of Brother Hermitage
The Heretics of De'Ath
The Garderobe of Death
The Tapestry of Death
Continuing Chronicles of Brother Hermitage
Hermitage, Wat and Some Murder or Other
Hermitage, Wat and Some Druids
Hermitage, Wat and Some Nuns
Yet More Chronicles of Brother Hermitage
The Case of the Clerical Cadaver
The Case of the Curious Corpse
The Case of the Cantankerous Carcass
Interminable Chronicles of Brother Hermitage
A Murder for Mistress Cwen
A Murder for Master Wat
A Murder for Brother Hermitage
The Umpteenth Chronicles of Brother Hermitage
The Bayeux Embroidery
The Chester Chasuble
The Hermes Parchment
The Superfluous Chronicles of Brother Hermitage
The 1066 from Normandy
The 1066 to Hastings
The 1066 via Derby
The Unnecessary Chronicles of Brother Hermitage
The King's Investigator
The King's Investigator Part II
The Meandering Chronicles of Brother Hermitage
A Mayhem of Murderous Monks
A Murder of Convenience
Murder Most Murderous

Brother Hermitage Diversions
Brother Hermitage in Shorts (Free!)
Brother Hermitage's Christmas Gift

Audio
Hermitage and the Hostelry

Howard of Warwick's Middle Ages crisis: History-ish.
The Domesday Book (No, Not That One.)
The Domesday Book (Still Not That One.)
The Magna Carta (Or Is It?)

Explore the whole sorry business and join the mailing list
at
Howardofwarwick.com

Another funny book from The Funny Book Company
Greedy by Ainsworth Pennington

The Investigator's Apprentice

Caput I: It Begins With an Argument

'**Get** him out of the workshop.' That had been Cwen's helpful suggestion after Brother Hermitage had stood at her loom for some time studying her work with interest; up close, while she was still doing it.

She was widely recognised as the most skilful of the weavers in Wat's establishment. Everyone, including Hartle, the old weaving master, the apprentices, and even Wat himself, quietly acknowledged, when pressed, and on the understanding that it would go no further, that Cwen would be the one to watch if you wanted to learn about tapestry-making.

Cwen didn't have to be pressed and made it quite clear that if the other weavers didn't learn to do as she told them, she wouldn't be held responsible for the consequences. She was very good at consequences.

Her only superior was Wat himself, but then he didn't actually do any weaving anymore, having progressed "beyond that sort of thing", as he put it. He dealt with customers, managed the production of the workshop and counted the money; after which, he hid it somewhere.

At least he had also moved on from his old tapestries, the ones that showed all the detail of life as it was lived; lived exclusively by people in private when no one should even be looking, let alone making tapestry.

One morning, Hermitage decided that he had lived here for too long without making enough effort to understand the intricacies of creating fine tapestry. And he was a learned fellow, picking it up should not be difficult. He didn't want to do it himself, but he felt it incumbent upon him to know what everyone else was doing and what their problems and successes might look like.

And he would approach this topic with all his natural enthusiasm. He would study it with the commitment he gave to the post-Exodus prophets and perhaps even write some notes for future generations. He couldn't imagine that anyone would want a book on tapestry, but if the only books written were the ones that people wanted, instead of the ones they should have, the world would be in a very sorry state.

It only took the single morning for Cwen to suggest that he replace this mission with another one; any one at all as long as it wasn't learning tapestry from her. He noticed that the large number of very interesting questions he had about every aspect of her work seemed to stiffen her resolve in the matter.

It might be a suggestion to Hermitage; it was an instruction to Wat.

They were gathered in Wat's upstairs chamber, the one in which many delicate operations took place as customers had their money removed. This one was not starting out delicately.

'He's the King's Investigator, for heaven's sake,' Cwen pointed out, which Hermitage felt wasn't really necessary, as it was the fact that loomed over his life like the tiniest apprentice in front of the biggest loom that ever there was. 'He should have his own workshop.'

Hermitage had no idea what an investigator's workshop would contain. He certainly wouldn't want anywhere that had murder victims delivered on a regular basis.

'What's King William going to think if he comes looking for his investigator and finds he's in a weavers' workshop?'

King William had frequently sent people to fetch

Hermitage, and the weaving had never seemed to bother them.

'William knows perfectly well where Hermitage is,' Wat protested. 'He knows where we all are, and what we do.'

'It's not good for the apprentices,' Cwen changed direction with ease. 'The king's men coming here all the time looking for Hermitage, disturbing our work.'

'Ah,' Wat nodded and smiled. 'They do know where he is then.'

Cwen pointed a look at him that said the next words had better be constructive.

'What do you suggest?' Wat asked with a desperate look at Hermitage.

'Build him a hut.'

'A hut?'

'Out there. Beyond the outhouse.'

'An investigator's hut?' Hermitage enquired meekly. All his enquiries were meek.

'It could be a nice hut,' Cwen offered. 'You know, like the ones old wise people who live in woods have. You could be the young investigator of the woods.'

Once he got over the idea of being despatched to a hut in the woods, Hermitage saw the attractions. His old abbot had given him his name because the life of the hermit was probably for the best; both for Hermitage and his fellow monks, whose reactions to his ever-present enthusiasm were considerably more, well, life-threatening than Cwen's.

'You could even take your books,' Cwen offered.

The hut was starting to sound quite nice.

'Have some peace and quiet to study your, erm, things.'

'My things?'

'Yes, you know. And you could have a quill and some

parchment as well.'

'Parchment?' Wat asked anxiously. 'Where's this parchment coming from? First I have to provide a hut, now I've got to fill it with parchment. Do you know the price of the stuff?'

'Hermitage has already got lots,' Cwen told them both.

'I have?' Hermitage wondered where it might be.

'All those books.'

Hermitage had to puzzle his way around that statement. 'The books are already written in.'

'There's lots of empty space,' Cwen said. 'I've seen it.'

Hermitage tried to work out what on earth she was talking about. 'Do you mean the margins?'

'That's it. Work in the margins.'

'Work in the...,' Hermitage began but couldn't bring himself to finish.

Cwen's irritation at petty objections to a perfectly good plan always swam just below the surface. 'Look, Hermitage is a monk, yes?'

There was no disputing that.

'And he is the King's Investigator. What's he doing in a tapestry workshop?'

'He lives here,' Wat reminded her, perhaps thinking that he might be the next one invited to leave his own workshop as he didn't actually make any useful tapestry. 'We rescued him from the monastery in De'Ath's Dingle.'

'You rescued him,' Cwen corrected. 'And it's fine that he lives here.'

'Very decent of you,' Wat said archly. 'We wouldn't want to send him back from my workshop, would we? Or you back to Briston, come to that.'

At the mention of her old and very disreputable master's

name, Cwen's bridling could have tied a herd of wild horses to a very small plough.

'The workshop needs to work,' she informed them. 'Hermitage needs to do what he does, and you do whatever it is that you do. The work will be done better if it is left alone.'

'Excellent plan,' Wat said quite sharply. 'We'll get on with what we do, like solve murders and sell tapestry to put food on the table. But you're right, it's probably best that you stay in the workshop and stop disturbing us.'

Hermitage had always seen Wat as an amiable fellow who was happy to let the world go by as long as it didn't disturb him. He was also very adept at persuading it to part with its money before it left. Probably holding a tapestry that it hadn't known it wanted.

When it came to them all having to investigate a murder for the king, there was nothing to be done, so there was no point complaining. Well, complaining always made everyone feel better, but they knew there was no chance of the task being taken away. Might as well just get it over with.

The world was now trying to disturb Wat and it came up against his stubborn streak. Amiability was all well and good when persuading someone that they would much prefer an expensive tapestry to a cheap one. Getting the money required a different approach altogether, and Wat could approach from two directions at once.

He and Cwen frequently had their disagreements and arguments and many of them were lively, if largely inconclusive. Most of them made Hermitage uncomfortable, but then someone saying, "how much?" when given the price of a loaf of bread made Hermitage uncomfortable.

The two weavers seemed to treat these engagements as some sort of entertainment, never holding grudges and always ending the discussion, and the day, contentedly.

Now, even Hermitage could detect a worrying undercurrent.

'There wouldn't be any tapestry to sell if I wasn't there to make it,' Cwen said plainly.

'Funny how it all seemed to work well enough before you arrived. What with all the apprentices and Hartle hard at work.'

'Ha.' Cwen's opinion of the hard work of others was summarised in two letters.

'Don't worry.' Wat's tone implied that worrying quite a lot might actually be for the best. 'We'll keep everyone out of your way. As you say, Hermitage would probably enjoy a hut of his own.'

Hermitage nodded smilingly at them both, hoping that this would take venom from the discussion.

'Well, good.' Cwen turned for the stairs and stomped down them.

Hermitage gave Wat a smile and a shrug, hoping for a reply of assurance that all would be well.

Wat sighed and drew up a seat by the fire. He then drew a mug of ale to his lips. 'Perhaps the time is coming,' he said.

'The time?' Wat's words told Hermitage that this time, whatever it was, would not be a happy one.

'It happens,' Wat explained. 'Eventually, some apprentices out-master the master, or so they think. They no longer take instruction. They think their work is so superior that the workshop relies on them, not the other way round. They think everyone should be working for them and they resent not being in charge.'

'Cwen?' Hermitage whispered.

Wat nodded heavily.

Hermitage could see that these traits were present in Cwen, but he had always taken them lightly. They were part of the lively game. Yes, she ordered everyone around and was very sure of her skill, but he naturally assumed that this was all bravado and that underneath, she was modest and self-deprecating. He started to wonder if it wasn't him who was modest and self-deprecating and he had mistakenly assumed that everyone else was the same.

'Then?' Hermitage had no idea what came next.

'Time to go,' Wat said.

'Go?' It was a very light word but squatted in Hermitage's head like an anvil.

'Start your own workshop.' Wat seemed resigned to the idea. 'It happened to me and it happens all the time; it's quite natural. The good apprentice wants to be a master and that means their own establishment.'

Hermitage was bursting to hear of Wat's history, but he wasn't the subject at the moment. 'But, but, Cwen isn't an apprentice.'

'No, she isn't, which probably makes working under my instruction even more annoying.'

'I don't think you instruct her.'

'I don't. She's good enough not to need my help, but this is still the workshop of Wat the Weaver. It's not Cwen the Weaver's.'

'Could she even have a workshop?' Hermitage knew that the workings of the weavers' guild were complex and sometimes quite bizarre, but their opinion on female weavers seemed perfectly plain;[The Tapestry of Death and A Murder For Master Wat, complex and bizarre.] they were a bad idea.

'That doesn't matter. She can have the workshop in all but

name. And she would be in charge. She'd decide what work to do, she'd supervise it and take the profit.'

'She is still young,' Hermitage pointed out. He knew that children were taken into the monastery or the convent, but trade required years of experience. Or so he had assumed. He was only twenty-something-or-other himself, (he really must work out exactly how many one day), and still felt like a novice most of the time.

Wat was considerably older, probably being over thirty, at a guess. But Cwen was the youngest of them all. Surely this was too early to be running a workshop of any sort.

'She is,' Wat agreed. 'But she's got through more in her short years than most manage in a lifetime. Starting out as a weaver under the tutelage of Briston would put the years on anyone.'

Hermitage recalled that appalling fellow with a shiver. Revolting tapestries and a revolting man.

'So, what happens?' Hermitage asked nervously.

Wat took another sup of ale. 'Either she'll come out with it calmly and carefully, explain her ideas and the urge that she has to take her weaving to the next step, or....' More ale.

'Or?'

'There's an almighty row and she storms out. Or she causes so much trouble that I have to throw her out.'

'Oh Wat, this is awful.'

'I know. I'd probably need all the apprentices and Hartle to get it done. And then we'd have to bar the door.'

'No.' Hermitage was firm. 'It is awful that Cwen should think about leaving. To think that this is not her home.'

The question of Cwen leaving the workshop was unthinkable. He could see that the organisation of the weaving might be problematic, but the three of them were like a family. And he knew that Wat and Cwen were close in more than their trade. Surely, this simple dispute could not separate them?

He shrank in his habit. He quickly concluded that if there was a cause to this, that cause should be removed. 'Have I done this?'

'You?'

'Yes. With my enquiries about tapestry.'

'No,' Wat shook his head. 'It was always coming. It could have been anything. A tapestry she didn't want to do. A customer she didn't want to work for. An apprentice who said almost exactly the wrong thing at the wrong moment.'

Hermitage quickly came to the conclusion that he should have come to a conclusion some time ago.

'We must speak to her.'

'We must what?' Wat's reaction to the suggestion seemed a bit extreme.

'Speak to her. Of course, we must. We have to have this out and see if there is not some compromise that can be reached. Find out what she is really thinking and discuss the situation. We cannot let her brood on and reach some awful answer that none of us is happy about.'

'Speak to her?' Wat seemed to be having trouble with the concept.

'Naturally. How else are we to resolve the problem? We speak to her.'

Wat folded his arms. 'We most certainly do not.'

Hermitage simply could not understand.

'She can talk to us if she likes, but we are not talking to her.' Wat seemed very firm in this opinion.

'Why ever not?'

'She's the one who wants to go. She's the one who is

difficult and rude to everyone, including you and me. She can come and talk to us and do all that discussing and compromising and the like.'

'Does it really matter who speaks first?'

'Absolutely, it does. Whose workshop is this, for heaven's sake?'

'Well,' Hermitage offered, 'I can speak to her.'

'I wouldn't if I were you. You don't seem to be her favourite monk. Just like I'm not her favourite weaver. And neither of those things are our fault or our problem. She's the problem.'

Hermitage did not like being caught between everyone like this. Cwen had made it quite clear that she would prefer him some distance away, so going to talk to her would not be well received. And Wat had told him not to even try. Perhaps leaving things alone and hoping they would all be fine tomorrow was for the best. He could do that.

With a fatalistic shrug, Hermitage shook his head. 'It would be just our luck for a murder to turn up at this very moment. Then what would we do? We can hardly investigate if we're not talking to one another.'

'Oh,' Wat said. 'There's a thought.'

'What is?' Hermitage didn't like the look in his eye.

Wat nodded slowly to himself as he thought his thought. 'She gets up to her eyes in the investigations, doesn't she?'

'I suppose she is quite, erm,' Hermitage tried to think of the right word. 'Energetic.'

'And she loves questioning people. And chasing them and threatening them and making them do what they're told.'

'I suppose so.'

'There you are then,' Wat said with a broad smile. 'She can become your apprentice.'

The Investigator's Apprentice

Hermitage's mouth fell open and he could no longer remember how to close it.

Caput II: Coming to Get You

While Hermitage fretted about the very real problems he faced here and now, something much more troublesome stirred a lot farther away.

Off in the distant east, the east of myth and legend, of wild lands and wild people, Hermitage's name was conjured in a moment of desperation. Disaster had fallen upon this place with the speed of a hawk and the mice below had scattered.

Now, out of the constant swirling mists that everyone knew hid hideous creatures and lured men and women to their deaths, a single figure staggered. The chaos that had thrown this remote land into confusion had opened the gate to escape for this one, but it was an escape that had to be taken by a strong hand and strong legs.

Pursuit was inevitable, but the pursuers themselves were pursued. If the game went well, this lone shape might slip between them all. It knew these twisting paths and tracks as well as any, and the moment had to be seized.

But if the lines were passed, if it were possible to slither from the grasp of those chasing, was the journey ahead even possible? To reach the destination from this far-flung orient might be a dream too far.

After all, Bury Saint Edmunds was miles from anywhere.

Arrival of the Normans had been foretold, expected even, but as each day went by and there was no sign, relaxation set in. Perhaps, with their drive to the north, the invaders would forget the east. Or approach it after their blood had settled and the desire for conquest had diminished.

Word had come of places that had quietly surrendered to Norman rule and, as a consequence, were living to tell the tale. The tales might not be terribly exciting, but living was preferable to the alternative.

As long as no one caused any trouble, this whole Norman Conquest business could be managed quite equitably.

But then along came Hereward. Just because his wretched brother had been killed by the Normans and his head stuck on a spike outside the family home, the man went mad and caused no end of trouble.

Killing Normans might have been fine once upon a time, but to do fifteen of them in one go was only going to annoy everyone. The eyes of King William turned east and his hand followed; the one with the sword in it.

Good Saxon families of the very finest lineage were treated abominably. Some of them were even killed while their peasants and slaves were released. Did ever such injustice descend upon a land?

And so, the Normans came to the Gudmund estate.

Lady Gudmund was of the very highest Saxon lineage in the land, being related to Harold Godwinson himself. She very wisely kept this fact to herself and sent word that the Norman commander should come forward so that terms could be discussed.

The Norman commander did come forward but seemed less keen on discussion. He appeared to be very fond of burning things to the ground, an activity he took to with considerable vigour. Tenants, peasants and slaves were scattered to the countryside, being the ones with enough sense to run away when someone set light to their hovel.

The members of the immediate family stood their ground, even if it was warming rapidly.

Lady Gudmund sent word that terms of surrender was what she had meant.

The entirely unreasonable onslaught continued unabated,

and it was suggested that this might be a good moment to leave. As quickly and as quietly as possible.

Darkness had fallen, but the light of all the things burning to the ground filled the land with a glow that was positively inconvenient to those trying to escape with their lives; along with as many purses of gold as they could carry.

Lady Gudmund herself was not one to flee her attackers in the night like some weasel. She hadn't walked anywhere at all for as many years as she could remember, and her carriage was now burnt to the ground along with nearly everything else. She would stay behind and deal with these appalling people. If they murdered her, it would only show just how far standards had fallen.

The rest of the household took to their heels, some of them wishing her Ladyship good luck as they went.

And the name of Brother Hermitage was on the lips of one.

Was it not the King's Investigator who had instigated the steps that led to this inevitable end? Looking into the death of Lord Gudmund should have been straightforward.[The 1066 To Hastings; where death was quite common.] The Normans did not need to get involved. But they had. They got involved in everything these days.

And once they were aware of the Gudmunds, their arrival to take everything that moved and all the things that didn't was a foregone conclusion. The fact that Hereward had roused them to a murderous rage made the whole process much more, well, murderous.

And so this mind turned to Brother Hermitage, even though he was as good as at the end of the earth, in Derby. It was a journey that would take days and days. Still, there was nothing to stay here for as even the ground was burning to the ground now.

Confident that any pursuit was far behind, the figure turned its back on the smoking remains of the Gudmund estate and headed west. Or should it be north? Hadn't someone said Derby was in Kent? And that was south, wasn't it? The escapee snorted and realised that he might need to ask directions to his quarry.

That first night out in open country was actually quite a crowded affair. It was hard to find a bush to hide under that wasn't already occupied by some Gudmund servant or other. Several of them had even started a fire of their own and were gathered telling sad tales; sad that they hadn't personally had the chance to set light to one of the Gudmund family.

These were people to be avoided. If Brother Hermitage were to be reached, there could be no distractions, no matter how strong the urge to stay and engage personally with those of somewhat questionable loyalty.

It was a long trek before the first vacant shelter could be found and this was simply a fallen tree that provided some protection from the wind. A tree was a rarity in this bleak and featureless landscape, and it was understandable that the poor thing had got so bored and lonely that it fell over.

Huddling in its lee and wrapping his cloak as best as he could, the man was convinced that he would get no sleep after this awful day. Shortly after that, he fell asleep.

The next day threw a still grey wash across the world that made it hard to tell land from sky. There was no movement and no sound, for which he supposed he should be grateful. No clattering of weapons or rattling of harness disturbed the peace, although a scent of things that were now a bit more burnt than they used to be hung on the air.

Cautiously raising his head above the tree, he saw nothing of concern and so pulled himself up, stretched and started to walk away from the rising sun.

The fog of the night before had lifted from his mind, and he scolded himself for not knowing which direction Derby was. He had come from there with Hermitage and those others not long ago. He simply had to retrace his steps. Thinking about this sort of thing for himself was a bit of a new experience.

He should be at Westley in an hour or so and then perhaps on to the far distant Kennet. A huge place of at least twenty households where he might be able to take his noonday meal.

Of course, Kennet could now be a Norman fortress for all he knew, and questions would be asked of a lone Saxon wandering out of the marshes. He could not let anything distract him from his goal though. Brother Hermitage would be reached come fire or high water - as they said in these lowlands where high water was a very real problem.

The day progressed and he passed through Westley without stopping or engaging in conversation. This was still too close to the Gudmund estate, or rather what had been the Gudmund estate this time yesterday. There might be Normans patrolling, and questions about his origin would be hard to answer.

Fortunately, the state of the country these days encouraged local folk to keep their heads down and avoid contact with strangers. If anyone had bothered looking up, they might have seen that he wasn't really a stranger to these parts, but it was generally best to say nothing to anyone and hope that the day turned out all right in the end.

The road at Kennet was more troublesome. The track

from the south to far-off Norwich passed by and attracted more travellers and traders. The man appraised himself and realised that he looked like someone who had just escaped a Norman attack and had spent the night hiding under a tree.

Perhaps this was not the best place to stop for food. Somewhere less busy and bustling would attract less attention.

He approached the Norwich road cautiously, trying to shrink into his cloak and pass by unnoticed. At which he failed.

'Ah, sire,' a voice called out. The voice was followed by quite a strong hand grasping his elbow. 'Heading west?'

The owner of the strong hand was a well-dressed fellow wearing a fine, bright coloured cloak, good boots and a warm-looking floppy hat. The dye for the cloak alone would cost a good penny or two. He was a mature man, and it was plain from his approach that he had something to sell; his luck was going to be out today.

The confusing thing was the woman who stood at his side. Well, it had to be assumed she was a woman and she didn't so much stand as crouch. They were obviously together, but all the money for clothes had been spent on him.

Disgusting rags hung from the woman as if they were trying to get away from someone who was making them look bad. Dirt was grimed into the face, and the hands wove in and out all the time, which was a trick in its own right, given the length of the fingernails.

The hair was long and lank and matted with something probably quite revolting. To complete the picture, a smell wafted in the air that could not possibly belong to a human and raised the question of how the well-dressed one put up with it.

Just when it was expected, the creature released a cackle of the very highest quality. This was clearly either a complete madwoman or some witch who the other witches had thrown out of the coven when they were tidying up.

'Don't go west,' the man appeared to be translating the cackle. 'At least, not without protection.'

'Oh yes?' The traveller saw the sale approaching.

'This charm for instance.'

From somewhere deep within her clothing, the mad-witch-woman produced a thing.

It wasn't clear what the thing was, and where it had come from did not bear thinking about. It might have been a rabbit's foot but the rabbit in question must have been pretty hideous, to begin with. Now it was a dark and hard-looking lump of something.

The trader leaned close. 'King Harold's thumb.'

If that had been King Harold's thumb, the rest of his hand must have been a real worry.

'It will protect you from the Normans.'

'Is that right?' Sarcasm never seemed to work on traders, but it had to be worth a try.

'Makes you invisible.'

'Invisible?' Incredulous sarcasm might be more effective.

'But only from Normans.'

'It's a very clever thumb, then.'

'The Normans can't see that Harold is rightful king, yes?'

'Because they killed him.'

'No,' the trader said confidently. 'Because he's invisible.'

'Of course, he is.' The traveller wiped a hand across his face. 'He wasn't killed near Hastings like everyone in the world says?'

'Oh, no,' the trader was confident of this. 'That's just what they want you to believe.'

'They've succeeded,' the man muttered to himself. He gave the trader his attention. 'While he was not dying, not getting shot in the eye or hacked to bits by the Normans, he found a moment to give you his thumb, did he?'

'Lost in battle. But found.' The trader tapped the side of his nose and the woman cackled again.

'The Normans managed to see him long enough to chop his thumb off, then. Why isn't it invisible?'

The trader seemed happy to ignore the practicalities. 'If you're going west, you'll come across Normans. You need to be invisible.'

The traveller nodded knowingly. 'I may have some news for you.' This appeared to give the trader some hope. 'Oh, yes?'

'The Normans are in the east as well. I've just got away from them while they ravaged the Gudmund estate. And I managed without the aid of an invisible thumb.'

The trader and his bizarre companion fell to silence for a moment before the witch/rag-display suddenly stood quite upright.

'Bugger,' she said in a voice of plain irritation. 'I told you we should have started earlier.'

'How are we supposed to know what the Normans have got planned?' the man replied. He quickly looked around as if inspiration might be sneaking up on him. 'Do you know if they've got to the north yet?'

'No idea,' the traveller replied. 'Them arriving in the east was enough for me.'

The trader nodded. 'You going north then?'

'Why?' the traveller asked very cautiously.

'Because if you are, you'll need protection.'

'You are joking?'

'The thumb works just as well wherever you are.'

'No,' the traveller replied. 'It doesn't work at all. Now, if you've got a charm to make you two go away, I might be interested.'

'There's no point staying here,' the now quite reasonable woman said to her companion as she brushed her rags straight. She even seemed to notice a spot of dirt on her front and tried to scrape it off. How she selected this one from the many was probably a sign that her madness was quite deep-rooted after all.

'We might come with you,' the man announced.

'Please don't.'

'No point staying here, is there? Where you headed?'

'Away from you.'

'Don't be like that. Never mind the thumb, three travelling together has got to be safer than going alone.'

Very reluctantly, the traveller had to admit that there was some truth in that. Never mind the Normans, the main threat in day-to-day life came from other Saxons. King Harold and the nobles had kept some measure of control and imposed the force of law, but they were dead now. Even the Gudmund estate had been bothered by wandering Saxon robbers who seemed to think that their people losing the battle near Hastings was licence to do whatever they wanted.

And then Hereward had confirmed that they could rampage through the country doing whatever they wanted, including robbing an abbey or two, as long as they called it rebellion.

'I'm going to Derby,' the traveller said, hoping that the prospect of such a great journey would put these two off.

'Are you now?' the man asked in a horribly interested tone.

He looked to his companion and gave her a gaze so knowing that it could probably read a book on its own.

'Derby, eh?' The woman too seemed inspired by this destination, which was a real disappointment. 'We might have some interest in Derby, as it happens.'

'Yes. I'm going to find King William's man.'

That dampened the enthusiasm.

'What you doing that for?' the woman asked with horror.

The traveller thought some more detail might be the dissuading factor. 'He's at the root of all this. Lady Gudmund went to him for help when her husband was murdered.' He gave the final word a delicious lick.

'Murdered?' the trader asked in a suitably worried manner.

'That's right. And once that was done, the rest was inevitable. We lived a peaceful life up until then. Nothing much good happened, but it wasn't all bad either. But then, with the King's man poking around, the Normans got involved. Naturally, they came to find the Gudmunds and that was that. Previous life over.'

'And now you're going back to find this king's man?' The woman clearly thought this was a very bad idea.

'That's right. His investigator. Brother Hermitage.'

'Funny name for a monk.'

'Funny it may be, but he looks into murders for the king.'

The two were exchanging more worried looks now.

The traveller sought to bang the final nail. 'And now I'm going to find him so I can do a murder of my own.'

Caput III: All For Nothing

Brother Hermitage approached most events in life with trepidation. He often readied his trepidation before the event in question was even in sight and knew where to get at it quickly if an event surprised him. He knew that every day would deliver several events and so prepared himself accordingly.

The noonday meal after Cwen's hut-building proposal could be seen coming from the moment of waking after very little sleep and would require more than the usual degree of trepidation. He even considered the Latin root, trepidare, to tremble, and did some trembling.

Cwen was straight off to the workshop at dawn, as was normal, and Wat was in his chamber, so there was no chance of discussing anything. They would come together for the meal and then it would all come out. The very worst kind of events were things coming out.

Which left the whole of the morning for Hermitage to get himself into a pretty hopeless condition. As the day progressed and he flitted from one thing to another without achieving anything, he fully expected to have lost the power of speech by the time it was needed.

He repeatedly told himself that Wat's apprentice suggestion was a joke and that even if it wasn't, Cwen would not be interested. She was an excellent weaver. She wouldn't give that up. She must not. She would be a loss to the world of tapestry and could not waste her talents. He would beg her to continue with the craft to which God had called her.

Then he would beg her not to be his apprentice. How could she be? He didn't know what he was doing so how could he teach anyone else?

He didn't dare go into the workshop, but neither did he want to bother Wat. He read a page of one of his books before realising that half an hour had passed and he couldn't even recall the first word, let alone what the book actually was.

He tried walking into town, but all that gave him was the need to walk back again.

Faced with the prospect of going inside once more, and it still being well short of noon, Hermitage wandered around the back of the building, idly considering where an investigator's hut might go.

There was plenty of space back here amongst the rough ground and various patches of vegetables. Wat's outhouse dominated; the place where finished works were stored and where it was rumoured Wat's treasury was hidden. Further rumour had it that the outhouse wouldn't be big enough for Wat's treasury and so some of it must be buried.

The apprentices insisted that their tending of the vegetables was so that they could be sure of the quality of food they ate, instead of relying on Mrs Grod, the cook, who tended to use things she found lying on the ground rather than growing in it. The suggestion that they were regularly digging for Wat's treasure was dismissed as ridiculous, despite the fact that a lot of their vegetables needed extraordinarily large holes, many of which had to be dug in the dark.

Hermitage considered the area and its distance from the workshop. A hut behind the outhouse would be completely invisible from the road and no one would know he was here. If he moved into a hut, the people who called at Wat's door asking for their murders to be investigated could be told that Hermitage didn't live there anymore. They needn't be told he was in a hut just around the back. Then they might simply go away.

Of course, if the king or any of the Normans turned up, he would have to be found, but being in a hut of his own appeared to have many advantages.

Naturally, trepidation wanted its say. Once word spread that the King's Investigator was living in a hut of his own, there would be no peace. Those who might have been put off by having to go anywhere near Wat's workshop would have no qualms. They could march straight to his hut, hammer on the door and demand that their murder be dealt with.

Perhaps, once that happened, he could move to another hut. He quickly saw a line of huts stretching off to the end of his days, each with a queue outside as people deposited dead bodies for his consideration.

Even so, a hut would be a good place to gather his volumes and perhaps finally organise his thoughts on the lexicography of the post-Exodus prophets to such a degree that he actually wrote something down.

He moved around to the back of the outhouse and considered the ground. This was a shaded spot and so not used for growing anything other than a few sparse weeds. If he was going to have a spot for writing it would need good light and so perhaps a little to the left.

He started to pace out the space he would need. Most of the walls would be taken up with shelving for his books, and a single window with a desk below for quill and parchment should be sufficient.

The thought of having a scriptorium without any other monks in it was shamefully pleasant.

He even wondered if the hut could be built hard up against the outhouse with the only door leading from one to the other. That way, people wouldn't even be able to find their way into his hut unless they knew to go through the outhouse.

Next, he thought that he would need a lock of some sort to stop people wandering in. Two locks, in fact; one to lock other people out and the other to lock himself in.

He now saw that this hut idea of Cwen's was a very good one indeed.

'Hermitage!' he heard a voice cry out. 'Hermitage. Where are you?'

Cwen was calling him. and he glanced up to see that the sun had ridden to its height in the sky and he had passed the best part of the whole morning in his speculative hut.

He stepped out from behind the outhouse.

'What are you doing back there?' Cwen asked suspiciously. 'It's time to eat.'

'I think I may have found the perfect spot for my hut,' he said, trepidation having been blown away by enthusiasm.

'What hut?' Cwen asked.

'What hut?' Surely, the world had not changed while he was behind the outhouse. 'What do you mean, what hut?'

'Why do you want a hut?'

'Erm, you said I should get a hut.'

'Oh, that,' Cwen gave a light laugh. 'I was just having a bad day with that wretched tapestry of saint what's-her-name. Couldn't get the nose right.'

'Couldn't get the nose right?' Hermitage couldn't believe that his world had been spun around because of a saint's nose.

Cwen's comments yesterday had been heartfelt and pointed. Was that really all down to one tapestry that didn't go quite right? Surely there was more to it than that. Some underlying unease must still fester, a deeper problem that was only expressed through that one moment but remained unresolved.

Still, she seemed happy enough now so best not to say anything.

'Our meal, eh?' Hermitage said brightly. 'I must say that I am ready for it. I wonder what Ern has brought for us today.'

'The same as every other day, probably.'

'Most likely,' Hermitage agreed. He then went into some detail about fasting and references to food in the bible; anything to keep Cwen distracted in case she had a mind to return to more difficult topics.

'Well, here we are,' he said as they arrived at the house.

Cwen simply looked at him and shook her head lightly.

In the upstairs room, Wat was already at his ale.

'Joining us, then?' he asked Cwen. 'Happy to mix with people who don't do anything useful?'

Hermitage squirmed in his habit and felt his hopes for a meal without awkwardness slipping away.

'All right, all right,' Cwen said as she took her seat. 'I told Hermitage, I was having a bad day with saint thingie's nose.'

'Saint Bibiana,' Hermitage provided the name.

'That's the one.'

'And for that, we all get told we're useless,' Wat complained. 'Including me in my own workshop.'

'It's a tricky nose.' Cwen gave a little shrug which looked a bit like an apology; a deniable one.

'I bet the apprentices were hiding under their looms.'

The shrug got a bit deeper.

Wat shook his head with resignation, but at least it looked like friendly resignation. 'What are you going to do when something really goes wrong?'

'Such as?' Cwen seemed to have trouble with the very idea.

'If you get this excited over a troublesome nose, what are you going to be like when your loom catches fire?'

'Catches fire?' Cwen was incredulous. 'How in heaven's name is a loom going to catch fire?'

'These things happen.'

'How?'

'Could be anything. A fire in the workshop. Mrs Grod's cooking gets out of control. An apprentice wants to finish a work and so takes a candle to his loom at night. He doesn't notice that the threads are a bit near the flame until it's too late and the whole thing is ruined. And then he gets the blame when he was only trying to do his best.'

Cwen frowned deeply at this, and Hermitage wondered where that tale had come from.

'This wouldn't be anyone we know, would, it?' Cwen asked.

'The point is,' Wat ignored the question. 'If you get this difficult over one nose, you haven't left yourself room to get any crosser. There could be a real disaster and everyone will think you've just done another nose wrong.'

'Hm,' Cwen considered this.

'What did Hartle have to say?' Wat asked.

Hermitage knew that the old weaving master was as calm and sensible as anyone he knew. His problem would be the opposite of Cwen's. He would mildly suggest that people might like to go outside for a moment when he should be screaming that the workshop was burning down with them inside it.

'He told me to calm down. Said it was only a nose.'

'There you are then.' Wat took a breath and there was worry in his voice such as Hermitage had not heard before. 'I thought you might want to leave.'

'Leave?' Cwen looked shocked and had gone quite pale. 'What do you mean, leave?'

'Well, you seemed so angry about being here. It's the sort of thing you see in an apprentice who is heartily sick of being told what to do and wants to be off on his own.'

'Nobody tells me what to do.' Cwen sounded quite pleading now and her voice broke slightly. 'Do you want me to leave?'

Wat jumped to his feet. 'Oh, God no. Pardon me, Hermitage. But I thought you wanted to.'

'Of course, I don't want to leave.' Did Hermitage spot a glistening in Cwen's eye? He'd never seen that before.

Cwen stepped forward and punched Wat on the shoulder. He didn't stagger backwards so it was a very friendly punch. 'This is my home. With you, and Hermitage and all the others.'

Wat simply held his arms wide and the two of them embraced, laughing with relief.

Hermitage felt a weight lift from him as this whole horrible situation had been resolved without him having to get involved.

As the embrace went on, he thought that perhaps he might go downstairs and greet Ern as their meal was delivered.

His steps on the creaking stairs were not even noticed as the embrace showed no signs of coming to a conclusion. Hermitage longed to be out of a room whenever there was a conflict; now he wanted to be out of the room for a very different reason.

At the bottom of the steps, he smiled to himself that everything was back to normal and he could relax once more. The awkwardness had dissolved, the concerns had been expressed and dealt with, Wat and Cwen had perhaps come out of it closer than they had been, and Hermitage had reached a very important conclusion; he would really like a hut.

He stepped out of the door to take a breath of fresh air and saw Ern walking up the track bearing his basket of provisions. The landlord was making the most of being away from the toil of his tavern for a while and was ambling along quite contentedly.

He always spent quite a bit of time at the workshop when he delivered their food, staying to talk with them about the gossip of the town and the goings-on of the workshop. Hermitage thought him a very sociable fellow, which was probably good in a landlord. Cwen said his wife was back in the tavern, which was why he tried to spend so much time away from it.

As he strolled along, his bald head covered in a simple straw hat, he had the look of a man who was at ease with the world.

Which was just how Hermitage felt at the moment. 'Good day, Ern,' he called.

'Brother Hermitage,' Ern replied. 'You seem in a jolly mood, if I may say so.'

'I am going to have a hut,' Hermitage explained, not wanting to go into Wat and Cwen's personal lives.

'Oh, ar?' Ern said, looking as if he would quite like to put his basket down on the ground and walk slowly backwards.

'For my work, you understand. Somewhere I can have my books and parchment and not disturb the workshop. And they can't disturb me,' he added honestly.

'Oh, right. Someone annoyed Cwen, have they?'

'A nose,' Hermitage said, acknowledging Ern's

understanding of the workshop's complexities.

'A nose and a hut, eh? Quite a day.' Ern arrived at the door and Hermitage stood before him.

'All is well now, though. Wat and Cwen have sorted things out.'

'And in time for a good meal,' Ern tried to step forward.

'Just so.' Hermitage didn't move. 'They are, erm, just addressing the final details.' He couldn't stop his eyes wandering towards the upstairs chamber. 'So perhaps I can take the basket?'

Ern looked up as well. 'About time those two sorted out their details if you ask me.' He winked.

Hermitage thought for a moment before he looked shocked at the suggestion. The very same idea was in his own mind, but it shouldn't be winked at by landlords.

Ern put the basket down between them.

'Why don't you come into the kitchen?' Hermitage asked.

'God no,' Ern shied away. 'Mrs Grod'll be in there.'

'Well, yes.'

'So I'm not coming into the kitchen,' Ern explained the facts of the situation. 'Might never get out again. At least, not with all my bits and pieces intact. She's mad, that woman, you do know that?'

'She does have her idiosyncrasies.'

'And she's not going to surprise me with any of 'em.' Ern turned his nose up.

Hermitage gestured that they could simply sit on the front step and watch the world go by.

Ern did so with a snort. 'Front step,' he coughed. 'Whoever heard of a front step? Ridiculous thing.'

'Wat saw some at an old Roman house, apparently. Along with the upstairs.' Hermitage tried very hard not to look upstairs this time. 'Thought it was a good idea. Stop the rain washing in.'

'Rain washing in is how you freshen the floor.' Ern explained the basics. 'How else you going to get a good new coat of mud?'

'Wat has wood on the floor.'

'He's as big an idio-thing as his cook.'

Hermitage simply moved his head around in a non-committal sort of way.

Ern looked up and down the path and saw nothing to spark a conversation. 'This hut of yours then?'

'Ah, yes.'

'You going to do the murder in it?'

'Murder?' Hermitage almost jumped off the step.

'Yes. You know. Like all the other ones you've done.'

'I haven't actually done any murders.' Hermitage said quickly. He thought it important to make this point clear.

'Well, no, not done them like done them. You haven't murdered anyone, I know that. You wouldn't, not with being a monk and everything. But you investigate them, we all know that. King's Investigator, that's you.'

'Don't remind me. And no, I do not plan to investigate murders in the hut.'

'Wouldn't be enough room, I imagine,' Ern speculated strangely.

Hermitage was starting to regret mentioning the hut, particularly to Ern. Word would be all over the town in an hour and then his privacy would be gone before the first wall was up.

'I shall use it for Biblical research. My work on the lexicography of the post-Exodus prophets, you know.'

'Oh, ar,' Ern shifted away from Hermitage a little.

'So, if you hear of anyone who has references or information that might be pertinent, you send them along so we can have a good long discussion and really get to the bottom of things.'

'Er, right you are,' Ern confirmed vaguely.

Hermitage felt bad about being so devious about this. He knew that his request was a certain guarantee that no one would come anywhere near his hut.

'Just a moment,' he said as a horrible cold washed through his soul making his shoulders shiver. 'You didn't say murders or a murder, you said the murder. What do you mean, the murder?'

Caput IV: Companions Without Company

'I don't think you can actually stop us going to Derby if we want to.' By this very annoying argument, the ragged woman and her charm merchant accompanied the traveller on his journey.

They walked far enough behind to avoid accusations of being with him, but close enough to be considered a group by anyone of ill-intent.

'It's you who needs us, really,' the merchant argued from a distance. 'Man on your own on the road could come to an awful fate.'

'It's pretty awful at the moment,' the traveller turned his head and replied.

'I'm Marcus, by the way,' the merchant introduced himself when he hadn't been asked. 'And this is Aurelius.' His companion nodded her head in a very normal manner while retaining her completely abnormal looks.

'Marcus, Aurelius?' The traveller asked without giving his name in return. 'Where have I heard that before?'

'We read it on a rock. Sounds nicely mysterious.'

'Read it on a rock?'

'Well, someone read it to us. And it was a Roman rock. You know, the sorts with heads on them.'

'A statue?'

'That'd be it.'

The traveller nodded to himself. 'Lady Gudmund had one.'

'Did it say Marcus and Aurelius?'

'Do I look like a reader?'

'You look like a man who could be on his own in Norman country in a moment,' the merchant said, finally losing some of his annoying patience.

The traveller sighed. 'All right, you're Marcus and Aurelius. Now, if we're ever going to get to Derby and you insist on coming, we need to get on. I'm not slowing for you two.'

'Or us for you,' Marcus retorted as the three of them walked more closely together now.

'What's your name, then?' Aurelius asked. 'We can't spend days on the road without knowing.'

'We could give it a try.'

'What if we need to call out to one another when we're attacked?'

'A simple, "look out, we're being attacked" will do.'

Aurelius stared at him, making it clear that the stare would continue until she got an answer. Despite the fact that he knew these two to be frauds, this stare from a woman who did a very good impression of a witch had disconcerting power.

'Very well. My name is, erm, Edgulf.'

'Edgulf?' Aurelius did not sound convinced.

'That's right.'

She scowled. 'I'm not sure that's your real name.'

'Well, I'm certain that Aurelius isn't your real name so we're all happy.'

Aurelius grumbled but said no more as they walked along.

'I need something to eat,' so-called Edgulf told them. 'I thought Kennet would be a good spot but unfortunately, you two were there. Fordham's probably best.'

'Fordham?' Marcus didn't sound keen on that idea.

'What's wrong with Fordham?'

'Nothing with Fordham itself, but it is on the road to Ely.'

'Don't worry, we'll keep clear of that place.' There were many people to blame for Edgulf's current circumstances and Hereward the Wake was up there with the Normans. And

Hereward had a close association with Ely; so close that he used the town for all his pillaging practice.

There was no certainty about where the man was hiding, it could be anywhere in these marshes and drains. However, if anyone wanted to be sure of keeping out of his way, they would keep out of Ely. Resistance to the Normans was all well and good as long as someone else was doing it. Being too close to Hereward meant being too close to all the people who wanted to kill him.

'We'll have to keep well to the south,' Marcus cautioned. 'The Normans will be keeping a close watch on all comings and goings around Ely.'

Normans keeping a close watch on something usually led to its untimely death.

'Stop worrying about Fordham,' Edgulf said. 'Anyway,' he continued thoughtfully. 'You've got Harold's thumb. You'll be fine.'

Marcus and Aurelius shared a glance that said they may have over-done the effectiveness of the thumb.

'Here we are anyway.' Edgulf gestured towards a humble building squatting in the field ahead and to the right of the road. 'Must be one of Fordham's out-lying farms.'

The construction was so humble it looked like it was out lying in the field because that was where it was going to collapse and die. Like all good Saxon dwellings, it was sunk partly into the ground with a thatch roof dropping almost to the floor. In this case, it looked like it was only the thatch propping the place up.

A wisp of smoke emerging from a hole in the roof was the only indication that this conglomeration of mud and thatch in a hole was someone's home.

'I don't think we're going to get much of a meal here,'

Marcus observed. 'At least, not one any of us would want to eat.'

'We don't need to bother the farmer,' Edgulf said. 'But the rest of Fordham won't be far now.'

As they walked by, Edgulf couldn't help but wonder what sort of farmer occupied such a place. A very bad one, probably.

Leaving the home to sink further into its decline, and into the surrounding countryside, the triumvirate pressed on.

'Oh, yes,' a loud voice called from behind. 'And where do you think you're going?'

They all turned slowly back to the decrepit dwelling.

Standing at its door, a large and well-armed Norman soldier stood with his hands on his hips.

Edgulf's first reaction was to wonder how such an imposing figure had fitted inside the tiny and frankly horrible Saxon hut. His wonder increased as three more Normans emerged to stand at their leader's side.

He half-expected the building to collapse now that the Normans weren't in there holding it up.

'Oh, erm, nowhere really,' The look on Marcus's face said that he knew this was a stupid thing to say even as he said it.

'Nowhere, eh?' The Norman didn't move but beckoned that they should come and join him to discuss the question in more detail.

Only for a foolish moment did Edgulf think that he had a choice in this matter.

The three Saxons tried to saunter over to the Norman in a manner that said they'd be delighted to explain as there was really nothing to hide.

'Nowhere?' The Norman repeated the question when they were up close.

'Well,' Edgulf started. 'We're not going nowhere, obviously.' He scowled at Marcus and tried to draw himself up to exude some authority. As he had none, it wasn't easy. 'I am on my way to the king's man in Derby.'

'King's man?' The Norman seemed to suffer a moment of doubt. 'What king's man?'

'His investigator. And it is important business. I cannot afford to tarry.'

'His what?'

'Investigator.'

The Norman turned up his nose. 'Our king wouldn't do anything like that. You Saxons are disgusting.'

'It means someone who looks into murders.' Edgulf gave the word a growling horror.

'He can look into yours in a moment,' the Norman suggested, clearly being someone quite comfortable with murder.

'It's a monk, Brother Hermitage, you may have heard of him from the king?'

'Funny name for a monk. And it's also funny that King William didn't happen to drop the name of this monk in my ear.'

The other Normans guffawed at this for their own reasons.

'They're all on the way to Ely, by the look of it,' one of them suggested.

'Ely?' Marcus asked as if he had never heard of the place.

'And what's wrong with her?' the Norman leader asked, nodding his head towards Aurelius who was looking at them all intently.

'She is touched by mysteries,' Marcus said as if starting the sales talk for the thumb.

'She'll be touched by something a lot more dangerous if she doesn't stop staring.' The Norman rested his hand on the pommel of his sword.

Aurelius nodded to herself as if she had got all the information she needed and started to dart her eyes back and forth for no obvious reason.

'Hereward's men, then.' The Norman said while his look strayed to Aurelius in a slightly nervous manner. Not nervous that she would do him any harm but that she might do something revolting.

'Hereward?' Marcus asked.

'Don't be stupid,' the Norman instructed. 'And don't think I'm stupid. Hereward is in these parts somewhere and is using Ely for supplies. Anyone travelling nearby is with him. And if they're with him, they're against us. And if they're against us, we get to kill them.'

'We are not with Hereward,' Edgulf said as honestly as he could manage. 'In fact, we're trying to keep away from him. It is as I said, we are travelling to the king's man in Derby. We have to avoid any trouble.'

'Not doing very well so far, are you?' the Norman observed.

'We're heading south of Ely, not going anywhere near it,' Marcus put in.

'You're already anywhere near it.' The Norman gestured to the tower of Ely abbey that could be clearly seen in the distance.

Aurelius now gave them all as mysterious a look as was possible in the circumstances. 'We are going to Derby.' She intoned this as if it were a magic spell to transport them somewhere just beyond the end of the world before you get to all the dragons.

The Norman stared back with a lot less mystery. 'No,

you're not,' he said without any intonation at all. 'Put them in the hut with the others,' he instructed his men.

'Look..,' Edgulf began again but was bundled into the hut before he could recap the subject of the King's Investigator. As he entered the space, he wondered how on earth there could be more people inside this hovel.

Marcus suffered the same fate, while Aurelius was herded with Norman swords, no one being willing to get too close.

Inside, the hut was naturally dark and it took a few moments for their eyes to adjust. The faint glow of a dying fire in the middle of the space was the only illumination of a scene that would be much better appreciated in complete darkness.

A gathering of Saxons huddled around the walls and into the middle of the single room. Edgulf counted eight of them straight away but thought there might be more off in the gloom.

Naturally, they were a miserable band, which was quite understandable, but it was the looks they gave the new arrivals that disturbed the soul.

Even Aurelius seemed disconcerted.

No one said a word but the messages in the faces were as clear as a babbling brook that has forgotten how to babble. "Welcome," they said. "Welcome to the room you're going to die in."

'I've got you now,' the lead Norman said with some pride. 'Hereward the Wake's forces captured.' He folded his arms and appraised his conquest.

'His what?' Edgulf had to question this conclusion.

He directed his glance at the assembly of bedraggled and hopeless Saxons. He saw that at least three of them must be over sixty, three more were children and one woman was so heavily pregnant that the ninth Saxon could arrive at any moment. Only the final one, a hulking man of some thirty summers or so, looked capable of being a force for anything at all. His rugged and weather-worn face said that his main talent lay in persuading oxen to plough in a straight line. Probably because they thought he was one of them.

'Hereward's forces,' the Norman confirmed.

'This lot?' Edgulf asked in a quiet voice.

'Threat to Norman rule.'

'These people aren't a threat to a Norman donkey. Look at them.'

The Norman did look at them and obviously couldn't see a problem.

'Can I ask?' Edgulf spoke as politely as he could. 'Were you, erm, at the battle? You know, the one near Hastings? When William arrived?'

The Norman soldier lowered his head. 'I was not, to my eternal shame. I came on a later boat.'

'So, you've probably never seen any real Saxon forces, the like of which Harold had at his command.'

'I've heard all about them.' The Norman was clear that hearing about them was all the motivation he needed.

Marcus picked up the line of questioning. 'Have you ever actually engaged with Hereward's men? In a fight or a skirmish?'

'They keep slipping away,' the Norman complained.

'And did it take much effort to capture these particular, ah, forces?' Edgulf enquired nodding sideways at the Saxons.

'Found them in here,' the Norman said proudly. 'Hiding.'

'Right you are.'

'And now I've got you too.'

'Stopping us on our way to the king's man.' Edgulf stated

this as a fact. 'And how do you know we're anything to do with Hereward at all?'

'I've told you,' the Norman growled his impatience. 'You're Saxons and you're near Ely.'

'And that's it, is it?'

That seemed to be it as there was no further comment.

'Any Saxon near Ely must be with Hereward?'

'That's it exactly.'

Edgulf nodded as if this made perfect sense, which got a frown from Marcus.

Beckoning the Norman to draw close, Edgulf lowered his voice and imparted vital information. 'Ralph the Staller.'

'What?' This clearly made no sense to the Norman.

'That's who you want. Ralph the Staller.'

'Do I?'

'Oh, yes. Hereward's uncle, so they say.'

'His uncle?' The Norman sounded quite excited at this prospect.

'That's right. So he must be Saxon and he's near Ely. What more do you want?'

'Staller, eh?'

'Important position under King Harold, being a staller. In charge of a whole area, he was.'

The Norman did now consider his captives with a fresh eye and started to look a little disappointed. 'And where will I find this Ralph?'

Edgulf opened his mouth to speak and then stopped. He held up a finger. 'I've just remembered.'

'Where he is?' the Norman asked.

'No. I've just remembered that Ralph the Staller is a good friend of, what's his name? King William, that's it. And before I left home, I'd heard he was going to be made Earl of

East Anglia.'

'So, he'd probably be in charge of these Normans?' Marcus suggested.

'You could be right,' Edgulf agreed. 'But if our friend here wants to go and capture him because he's a Saxon and near Ely, I suppose that's up to him. After all, everyone near Ely is in Hereward's forces, even children, old men and the unborn. And people on their way to see king's investigators,' he added pointedly. He clicked his fingers. 'I've just remembered something else.'

'Something else?' The Norman asked rather disconsolately.

'Ralph isn't even Saxon. He's a Breton. Whatever one of those is'.

'From Brittany,' the Norman explained with a sigh.

'Sounds a bit French to me,' Marcus observed.

Aurelius released a perfectly timed cackle to accompany the Norman's discomfort.

Edgulf decided the risk of driving the nail home might be worth it. 'So. You've captured a hovel full of Saxons who weren't going anywhere or doing anything. You've delayed me attending upon the king's man and now you want to capture his favourite Earl of East Anglia.'

A low groan came from one of the other Normans. 'It's Cabourg all over again,' he muttered.

'Shut up,' his commander ordered. 'That was completely different.'

The subordinate did not shut up. 'It explains why William didn't want us on his boat with him though, doesn't it? Probably thought we'd sink it.'

'Right!' The commander commanded. 'I've had enough of this.'

'That's what William said,' an impudent Norman

muttered quite loudly.

'If you're going to the king's man,' the Norman addressed Edgulf, 'we're coming with you.'

'Oh, erm,' Edgulf couldn't immediately think how to refuse this kind offer.

'I thought we were commanded to stay here and harry Hereward's forces?' one of the Normans asked.

'That's, erm, what we were doing. Now we're doing this.' The commander didn't sound too sure.

'Just a moment,' one of his other men enquired suspiciously. 'Did anyone actually give us this command?'

'We act on our own initiative,' the leader said proudly.

'No, then,' the other Norman concluded wearily. 'Does anyone, in fact, know that we're here at all?'

'These people do.' The commander took in his captives with a sweep of the arm.

'I mean any other Normans?'

The leader gave no reply to this, which brought a muttered, 'Oh God,' from his men.

Striking a commander-like pose, the man addressed his disappointed force. 'We go to Derby and the king's, erm..,'

'Investigator,' Edgulf prompted.

'That's the fellow.' The Norman turned from his men and spoke quietly to Edgulf. 'Derby, eh?'

'That's right.' Edgulf could see no way of getting out of this. At least being with some Normans should stop them getting attacked by Normans. Although with this lot, he wasn't even too sure about that.

The commander nodded to himself. 'It's not in Scotland, is it? Only I'm not allowed in Scotland.'

Caput V: Ern Spills The Wrong Beans

'A murder, the murder, what's the difference?' Ern shrugged.

'There is a world of difference. A murder could refer to any murder at all. One that has been done, one that has yet to be done, even one that never has been and never will be done.'

'There you are then.'

'There I am, what?' Hermitage told himself that Ern was the alehouse landlord and so might not be fully conversant with the more subtle features of language, but the difference between a and the should be clear enough to anyone.

'A flagon of ale and the flagon of ale. See the difference?'

Ern screwed up his eyes and tipped his head on one side as he considered this complex question.

'A customer comes in and asks for a flagon of ale. Up until that point, the particular flagon of ale in question doesn't even exist. Then you fill a flagon with some ale and it becomes the flagon of ale that you hand over. It has come into being, yes?'

'Has he paid?' Ern enquired.

'It doesn't matter whether he's paid or not,' Hermitage said with some exasperation.

'He's not getting any ale at all if he hasn't paid.'

'With a coin?' Hermitage latched on to a new proposition.

'Or something worth a flagon of ale,' Ern specified.

'So, in his purse, he has a coin. He hands it over to you and it becomes the coin with which he paid for the ale.'

Ern seemed to follow this.

'There's a pile of coin on your table,' Hermitage developed the proposition.

Ern smiled and nodded.

'Give me a coin, you would say.'

'I would.'

The ale drinker selects one of the coins and gives it to you. It's now the coin. The specific coin.'

'I'd have to check it,' Ern said.

'Check it?'

'Bite it, look at it, make sure it's not just some lump of metal. And if it's a cut penny, I have to make sure it's a whole half.'

Hermitage didn't want to start exploring the contradiction in the concept of how something could be a whole and a half at the same time, tempting though it was.

'So it is with murders.'

'You bite them?'

'No, of course not. Do try to follow. I could have a pile of murders on my desk.'

'I told you that hut was too small.'

Hermitage pressed on. 'And I look at my pile and think, over there is a murder, just here is a murder and one might have fallen on the floor. Then I select one to investigate and it becomes the murder.'

'Clever,' Ern commented.

'So,' Hermitage approached his conclusion with little confidence. 'You said the murder. You didn't say a murder, you said the murder. The specific murder.'

'If you say so.'

Hermitage released a sigh and thought that perhaps he was reading too much into the statement of a man who was simply careless with his words. The struggle to get to this point indicated that Ern might well not know the difference between a and the.

'Hello, you two.' Cwen's voice surprised Hermitage as his

head was slowly sinking in a bog of his own devising.

He turned and saw Cwen and Wat standing on the threshold. They were both smiling and holding hands. As Ern turned to see, they quickly let go of one another.

'About time,' Ern commented.

'What are you talking about?' Wat enquired curiously.

'Coin,' Ern said quite proudly.

'No, we aren't,' Hermitage corrected. 'We are talking about murder.'

'Hermitage, really,' Cwen chided gently. 'You've got to think of other things once in a while.'

'I am desperately trying to think of other things.' Hermitage thought the criticism most unfair. 'I wasn't thinking about them at all until Ern asked if I was going to investigate the murder in my hut.'

'There's been a murder in your hut?' Wat asked. 'We haven't even built the thing yet, don't get ahead of yourself.'

'Oh, for goodness' sake,' Hermitage complained. 'I mentioned to Ern that I was going to have a hut in which to work.'

'Well...,' Wat sounded as if this wasn't actually agreed yet.

'And he asked me if I was going to investigate the murder in it.'

'I said it would be too small,' Ern said. 'But I suppose you could build him a big one.'

'Hold on a moment...,' Wat cut in.

'The point is,' Hermitage said, quite loudly for him. 'The point is that Ern said the murder, not a murder.'

'So?' Cwen said. 'The murder, a murder, what's the difference?'

'Don't you start.' Hermitage ran his hands over his head. 'He said the murder, so the question is, what murder?'

'Any one you like I suppose.' Cwen said.

'No,' Hermitage insisted. 'Exactly not any one I like. That would be a murder. This is the murder. One specific murder. A definite murder, you might say, as opposed to an indefinite murder, which would be a.'

The three listeners exchanged looks that said they had better humour Hermitage as he seemed to be getting quite excited, which was never good for him.

'Who has been murdered, Ern?' he asked the direct question.

'Who?'

'Yes. Who is the victim of the murder that I am going to investigate in my hut?'

Ern looked to the others for some help. There was none.

'You're the investigator, don't you know?'

'I only investigate murders I'm told about. And you're the one who told me about this murder.'

Ern did look slightly uncomfortable now. 'I was only asking. Being polite, like.'

'A strange thing to say just to be polite.'

'Don't know what else you'd say to someone who does murders all the time.'

'He's right there,' Wat commented. 'It's either murder or your posted prophets.'

'Post-Exodus prophets,' Hermitage corrected. He turned his attention to Ern and tried one last time. 'Ern, who has been murdered?'

Ern looked bewildered. 'Lots of people, I should think. King Harold. All them Saxon nobles who went with him. Anyone done by the Normans, I should say.'

'Anyone in Derby?' Hermitage asked.

'There was Agnes,' Ern said.

'We know about Agnes. I've already dealt with Agnes. You're hardly likely to suggest I investigate her murder again.[The 1066 via Derby; poor Agnes]'

Ern didn't have anything further to offer.

'Who has died, then?'

'Died?'

'Yes, who was alive and isn't now?'

'Well, again, I'd say lots of people. In fact, apart from the ones who are still alive, it'd be everyone.'

'Who in Derby has died recently?' Hermitage tried to make the question piercing and insistent.

'I suppose there was Athlot.'

'Athlot, eh?'

'That's right. He was alive and now he's not.'

'Hermitage,' Cwen spoke up. 'You can't just assume that people who die have been murdered.'

'Ern said the murder,' Hermitage insisted.

'I wouldn't rely too much on the actual words Ern uses, if I were you,' Wat cautioned.

Hermitage was thinking the same but had to get to the bottom of the question. 'And this Athlot died suddenly, did he?'

'Most people do,' Ern commented. 'I mean, it can take a long time to get there, but in the end, it's sudden. Be the same for all of us. Take sixty years dying and then it happens in a moment. Funny, when you think about it.'

'Athlot,' Hermitage muttered. 'And why do think he was murdered?' he sprang the question on Ern.

'I don't,' Ern insisted with a hint of panic in his voice. 'You asked me who died and I told you.'

'I wouldn't get your hopes up about Athlot,' Wat said.

Hermitage gave him an enquiring look.

'He was an old man when I came here, I'm surprised to hear he was still alive at all.'

'Ninety years old, they say,' Ern told them. 'Mind, Athlot couldn't count so that's probably not right. Claims he saw King Aethelred though.'

'And there are no other suspicious deaths?' Hermitage asked.

'Athlot wasn't suspicious,' Ern replied. 'Shouldn't have been on the roof at his age.'

'On the roof? What was a ninety-year-old man doing on the roof?'

'Trying to fix his thatch, I imagine. After that wind we had.'

'Did someone see him fall from the roof?'

'No, but he was lying next to a fallen ladder, covered in fresh thatch.'

'Hm.'

'Hermitage, give it up,' Cwen said. 'You always say you don't want to be investigator and never want to look into a murder again. Ern tells us that there has been no murder, but you want to find one anyway.'

'He did say the murder,' Hermitage argued rather weakly.

'Hardly reason to go assuming anyone has been murdered at all. If you're going to take Ern's word for things, we'll all be believing that the little people are living in holes outside town and come out just to make his ale go off.'

'You shouldn't mock the little people,' Ern cautioned.

'Perhaps one of them has been murdered?' Wat suggested.

Well, that was it. If Hermitage was being dragged into the realms of investigating the murders of fairy-folk, it was time to give up. 'All right, all right,' he sighed. 'It was just Ern's way of talking, no one has been murdered.'

'There you are,' Cwen said. 'Happy now?'

Hermitage knew that he should be happy with no one being murdered, but a rankle of dissatisfaction still shivered through him. Perhaps it would be resolved by teaching Ern the difference between a and the.

Ern took this as his permission to leave; quickly. He handed his basket over to Wat. 'I'll pick it up later, goodbye.'

'You've scared Ern away,' Cwen observed. 'All your talk of murder.'

'It was his talk of murder that started the whole business,' Hermitage complained, feeling quite aggrieved that he was being given the blame. He had spent most of his life being blamed for things that weren't his fault; it was time that he registered a modest objection.

'Come on,' Wat said. 'The food's here now, so let's eat.'

Hermitage followed the others back into the workshop, at least grateful that the awkwardness between them all had dissipated. There was now a new awkwardness as Cwen and Wat were obviously on very good terms once more, and he felt like the extra monk at mass. At least this wasn't the sort of awkwardness that would keep him awake at night.

As was normal practice, Ern's food was spread out on the floor in Wat's upper chamber and they all helped themselves. This was usually the time for lively chatter but Wat and Cwen seemed very quiet and kept looking at one another.

Hermitage knew that he was very uncomfortable with any sort of conflict. He now knew that he was very uncomfortable with the opposite as well.

'It is still a concern, isn't it,' he mused.

'Hm?' Wat hummed with profound disinterest.

'Ern,' Hermitage pressed.

'It looks all right to me,' Cwen said, addressing the food

but not looking at it.

'Not the food. What he said.'

'What did he say?' Cwen asked vaguely.

'The murder,' Hermitage insisted.

'You're not still going on about that?' Cwen now dragged her attention away from Wat. 'For heaven's sake. Someone tells you there is a murder and you get all worried and fretful. Someone tells you that there is no murder and you get all worried and fretful.'

Hermitage didn't like to explain that he spent most of his life worried and fretful for one reason or another. And if there were no reason, he would worry and fret that he'd simply forgotten what it was.

'You had better investigate then, hadn't you?' Wat suggested amiably.

'Investigate what?' Hermitage couldn't see how you could investigate a murder if there wasn't one. That really would be frustrating.

'Whether there's been a murder at all or not.'

Hermitage considered the proposition as he took a handful of nuts to go with the cheese.

'It would require a number of specific steps,' he mused. 'First of all, find out if anyone else in town is talking of murder. If they are, that would be a good indication and we could progress accordingly.

'If they aren't, perhaps it would be best to compile a list of all those who have died recently, including Athlot, and record the circumstances of each situation. From that, we may be able to discern any suspicious features or recognise similarities.' A horrible thought crossed his mind. 'What if there has been more than one murder? What if they're connected?'

'Hm.' It wasn't clear whether Wat was commenting on the plan or the ham.

'Although Ern did say the murder,' Hermitage reminded himself. 'It wasn't the murders.'

'There you are then,' Cwen said without listening at all.

'Sounds wonderful,' Wat dreamily commented.

Hermitage nodded. Compiling a list, if not several; comparing information from a number of sources and across a number of events. Identifying patterns or features of interest; it did sound wonderful. The only problem would be if there really was a murder at the end of it all.

Caput VI: Ill Intent

'You would think that being in the company of a band of Normans would help.' Edgulf muttered to Marcus as they all strode along.

The Norman leader, who announced himself as commander Fortmain, had insisted that they travel so far south of Ely that they walked directly away from Derby before eventually turning north once more.

By this time, it was dark and Edgulf concluded that they had spent the day making very little progress towards Derby at all. He had reassured Fortmain that the town was not in Scotland, but the Norman was not entirely convinced. He seemed to think this might be some devious Saxon trick to get him over the border.

It was impossible to guess why a Norman would not be allowed in Scotland, but from the performance of this band so far, it could easily be that the Scots simply had standards.

Edgulf wondered about trying to find out from one of the other Normans, as none of them appeared to hold their leader in great regard or any regard at all. That could be rash, though. These Normans may not think much of one another, but that wouldn't stop them doing something horrible to an impudent Saxon.

As a result, Edgulf, Marcus and Aurelius said nothing and settled for the night as best they could. The result of them being with a cohort of Normans, albeit a small one, was that they were both comfortable and uncomfortable at the same time.

Comfort came from the fact that they had found shelter in the shape of a very modest Saxon longhouse and so had a fire, some food and drink, and a roof over their heads.

The discomfort came from the fact that the Saxons who had been in the house with the fire, the food and the drink had been escorted into the dark at sword point by the Normans.

The three Saxons grimaced as their countrymen, women and children filed out in the cold and dark while the Normans chortled over the pot of stew that they had done nothing to deserve.

Edgulf shrugged an apology to one old man who limped out with a thin blanket around his shoulders. He got a very dirty look in response.

Fortunately, the Normans located a small barrel of mead, which they quickly devoured. After that, they sang two songs, hurled some insults in Norman French and fell asleep.

Soon after that, Edgulf sneaked the evicted Saxons back into their home to tiptoe to the back where they slept behind a pile of hay. That didn't stop the old man glaring at Edgulf as he noticed the empty mead barrel.

The next morning, Edgulf made sure the Normans were roused at dawn and hurried from the house while their heads were still bleary from the mead before.

'What's the rush?' Fortmain complained.

'The king's man,' Edgulf reminded him.

The Norman appeared to momentarily think even a king's man wasn't worth this trouble. Instead, he grumbled and complained as he and his men stole everything that moved and could be carried, before setting off on the road once more.

Edgulf chanced a glance back at the longhouse as they left and saw three or four Saxons peering out to make sure they had been left alone. He thought they should be grateful to still have their lives, but they didn't look very grateful.

'This king's man, then?' one of the other Normans asked. 'What's he all about? And why does he want you?'

Fortmain nodded at this with a slight look about him that said he probably should have asked that yesterday.

'King's Investigator,' Edgulf explained. 'Looks into murders. Tries to find out who did them.'

'Bit of an odd thing to do,' the Norman commented. 'I mean, if you've done a murder, you don't want to be found out, do you?'

His companions nodded and muttered their agreement to this.

Edgulf tried to understand that statement. 'It isn't the murderer who asks for the investigation,' he pointed out unnecessarily.

'Oh, right. That makes sense.' The Norman understood now and considered the idea carefully. 'So, if you've got someone who's been murdered and you don't know who did it, you could ask this Brother Herbiflage.'

'Hermitage, yes.'

The Norman now gave his commander a very piercing look. 'He might even find out who accidentally killed someone close to the king years ago. Someone who's never had it proved but everyone knows he did it.' The rest of the Normans chortled at this idea.

'I suppose he might,' Edgulf acknowledged.

'Are we sure we still want to meet him?' One of the other Normans asked with a snort.

Fortmain stared ahead along the road and ignored the chatter. 'Why are you going to him, then? What's a Saxon doing going to the king's man about a murder? And what are these two here for at all?' He gestured towards Marcus and

Aurelius who were keeping their distance.

'Ah, well,' Edgulf said as nonchalantly as he could manage. 'It's a long story.'

'I don't think we're in a hurry.'

'Right,' Edgulf nodded slowly. 'Well, I lived on the Gudmund estate and Brother Hermitage investigated the murder of Lord Gudmund.'

'And did he find out who did it?'

'In a manner of speaking.'

'He spoke about it?'

'He worked something out.' Edgulf frowned at Fortmain's understanding if there was any.

'Why do you want him now, then? Is this Lord Gudmund not dead anymore?'

'No, he's still dead,' Edgulf tried not to gape. 'He didn't get better.'

Fortmain nodded thoughtfully as if recovery from death was a common occurrence.

'There have been, erm, more deaths.'

'Not surprised.'

Edgulf's urge was to ask why Fortmain was not surprised, but his sense told him not to go down that rabbit hole.

'And you want this king's man to interpret them.'

'Investigate,' Edgulf corrected. 'I'm going to, erm, discuss them with him, yes.'

Fortmain appeared to think that this was a reasonable explanation. 'Dead Saxons?' he enquired lightly.

'Well, yes.'

Fortmain now shook his head slowly and breathed in slowly through his teeth. 'Don't know if you'll get a king's man to look into Saxons. I mean, they're Saxons, aren't they?'

'I suppose they would be.'

'King's man will be busy with Normans. That's the priority.'

'Murder Normans?' Edgulf tried to sound surprised. 'Who would dare murder a Norman?'

'Good point.' Fortmain complimented the argument. 'And these two?' he tipped his head towards Marcus and Aurelius.

'Just going to Derby,' Edgulf reported. 'Safer to travel together. It's dangerous on the road alone these days.'

'Aye,' Fortmain agreed sombrely, clearly not recognising that he was one of the dangers.

Edgulf chanced a question but made it sound as light and uninteresting as he could. 'So, erm, why do you want to go to the king's man? What with Hereward running abound Ely?'

Fortmain's men seemed to draw closer at this as if they'd be quite interested in the answer as well.

'Service to the king,' Fortmain announced blankly. There could be no questioning that.

'Well, yes, I suppose so. But the investigator already has help.'

'Oh, dear,' one of the Normans at the back said in a very pointed manner.

'A force of Normans?' Fortmain asked very carefully.

'Not exactly.'

'Exactly who, then?'

'Two Saxons.' Edgulf knew there was no point trying to hide the fact, it would be pretty obvious when they arrived.

'Two Saxons?' Fortmain couldn't believe this. 'What are Saxons doing with the king's man?'

'Well, Brother Hermitage is a Saxon.'

'He's a what?'

'Saxon. He's a Saxon monk.'

'The king's man is a Saxon monk?'

'Yes, didn't I mention that?'

'No, you did not. You just said he was called Brother Hertigore.'

'Hermitage.'

'Which could be a good Norman name for all I know. Why in God's heaven does this monk think he's the king's man?'

'Because the king appointed him, I suppose.'

Fortmain shook his head at this nonsense as if Edgulf was trying to tell him that William was fond of children. He stated the plain fact. 'The king would not do that.'

Edgulf shrugged. 'Obviously, I've not met the king, but that's what I was told. And it's what Lady Gudmund knew, which was why we went to Derby. And everyone there knew he was the king's investigator.'

Fortmain was looking quite smug and superior, for once. 'I can see that we're going to have to sort a few things out in this Derby place. King's man, indeed.' The Norman now strode ahead with renewed confidence, plainly anxious to get to Derby and start sorting things with some vigour.

Edgulf blew out slowly. What had been a perfectly reasonable plan was now descending into chaos. First, two strange Saxons, now four unwanted Normans; not that he could think of any Normans who were wanted. His encounter with Brother Hermitage was going to be a lot more complicated than was necessary and might not lead to the desired end at all.

He felt a movement at his shoulder and was surprised to see one of the Norman soldiers walking at his side.

The Norman gave him a short nod of acknowledgement. 'Fortmain, eh?' the man said in a very heavy Norman accent that was clearly new to the Saxon tongue.

Edgulf could only agree.

'Don't, erm, worry. Yes. Don't worry.'

'Don't worry?'

'Fortmain.' The soldier waved a hand towards his leader; a rather contemptuous hand, somehow. 'He will not sort things out.'

'No?'

'No. Why do you think we are here?'

That seemed a bit of an odd question. 'King William won the battle?'

'No, no. Us, Fortmain, us. Why are we here? Why are we in a hut in a bog with old men and children?'

'Looking for Hereward?'

'Pah. Because no one else wants us.'

'Really?' Perhaps Edgulf was going to get to the bottom of Fortmain's situation after all.

'Fortmain sorts things out.' The Norman made it sound as if sorting things out was a very bad idea.

'He sorts out at the wrong time. He sorts out the wrong people. He sorts out and someone ends up dead.'

'No!'

'Not his fault, of course. Never him. Always someone else. No proof, so he goes away and is told not to sort things out anymore.'

'Why are you with him?'

'No choice,' the Norman shrugged. 'We are his men and are stuck. But we make sure he doesn't sort out. Not this king's man of yours. Fortmain sorts out another king's man and we're all dead.'

'Why does he want to go to Derby, then?'

'He thinks he will be back in favour. One smell of a position is enough.'

Edgulf longed to know more of this history, but the Norman was trying to help, so best not to risk antagonising the man. 'What do we do when we get to Derby?'

'We will watch. It is not good this monk is Saxon, Fortmain does not like the Saxons.'

'I'd noticed that.'

'And he may do something stupid. Again.'

Edgulf would just have to wait and hope that more might be revealed.

'This monk?' the Norman asked.

'Yes?'

'He deals with murders, yes?'

'That's right.'

'For the king?'

'So it seems. The murder of Lord Gudmund was not investigated for the king, but for Lady Gudmund. I'm told that he was the king's appointment though.'

'Hm.' The Norman was thoughtful as they walked along. Eventually, he seemed to come to a conclusion and nodded towards Fortmain. 'Do you think he does murders as well?'

'Does murders?' Edgulf tried to keep his voice calm.

'Yes. He must know a lot about them.'

'I, erm, think he just finds out who did them.'

'Pity.' The Norman sighed.

'And he is a monk,' Edgulf pointed out.

'I've met some monks in my time,' the Norman said, which did not want pursuing.

'Ah,' was all Edgulf felt comfortable saying.

'We would not do Fortmain harm,' the Norman assured him. 'We are his sworn men. It would be very bad.'

'I see.'

'But if we could find someone else.'

'Surely, not?' Did this man really mean to suggest they would gladly have their leader killed?

'It could be a, erm, what is it? Accident, yes.'

'An accident?' Edgulf knew about murderous Normans, but he'd never thought they did it amongst themselves.

'A big cliff. Mad dog.'

'A big cliff or a mad dog?' Edgulf wanted to move away now.

'Or both. Mad dog at edge of big cliff.'

'I don't think the King's Investigator is the man for you.' Edgulf tried to sound very firm on this. He was alarmed that this Norman soldier was prepared to discuss murdering his commander with a complete stranger. It sounded as if plans were already well developed, particularly if mad dogs and cliffs had already been considered.

'If we go to this murder monk, there will be a murder, yes?'

'There will be one?' Edgulf asked with mounting panic.

'Yes. He finds murderers, he will be finding one when we get there.'

'Oh, I see,' Edgulf breathed again. 'I suppose it is possible that there may be an investigation going on.' It hadn't occurred to Edgulf that Hermitage could be away investigating somewhere and might not even be in Derby. That would stop his plan dead.

'Good.' The Norman nodded and smiled. 'When the murderer is found, we can have a little word with him.' He then tapped the side of his nose. He even winked at Edgulf as he slipped back to talk to his fellows.

Edgulf was grateful that he couldn't understand a word they were saying, although the cackling laughter was rather disconcerting.

He wondered about sharing all this with Marcus and

Aurelius but quickly decided not. He had personal business with the King's Investigator and if these Normans were planning their own murder, he might never achieve his goal.

Caput VII: Murder, Anyone?

Brother Hermitage's expedition into Derby the next morning to search for death sounded perfectly sensible when he explained it to himself in theoretical terms.

As he walked along the track from the workshop, he started to wonder what on earth he was doing. And only now did he question how he was actually going to do it.

Was he to knock on every door in town asking if anyone was dead? That seemed heartless, to say the least. Would he then progress to enquire as to whether the deceased might have been murdered at all?

And what were those he spoke to going to say? "Funny you should ask, Brother but yes, my husband/wife/son/daughter was murdered as it happens, but I forgot to mention it"?

No, of course, they wouldn't. If there had been a murder it would be the talk of the town and Ern would have said. But Ern had talked about the murder, so perhaps the town did know all about it, they just wanted to keep it from him.

Why on earth would they do that? Surely, if someone in town had been done to death, they would want Hermitage to investigate. He could make his usual enquiries as to method, motive and opportunity, and would question everyone closely about their involvement in the matter.

Wat and Cwen would do their bit as well, them being much better suited to questioning people than he was. He had a tendency to accept the first answer given as the truth, and still struggled with the fact that killers were frequently dishonest. The killing shocked him, naturally, but the dishonesty was more disappointing somehow. Murder might be the act of a moment, but lying was a way of life.

Ah, Wat and Cwen. Perhaps that was the root of the

problem.

Wat's reputation was a trouble to the town, or rather the reputation of the tapestries he used to make. Having now seen one in all its horrible and intimate detail, Hermitage could see the problem.[Murder Most Murderous is revealing in this regard.] He had seen several things he'd never seen before in that tapestry and hoped never to see them again.

And Cwen could be a little, what was the word? Energetic wasn't quite right on this occasion. Alarming? The business of the saint's nose had shown how excited she could become over small matters. When it came to people being difficult about a murder, she promised all manner of personal retribution.

It could be the case that there had been a murder in Derby, but the people didn't want Wat or Cwen disturbing the place. It was a most unreasonable position to take in the face of such a fundamental sin, but on his own, he might be able to make some headway.

But then he had been on his own with Ern, although that was at the workshop with Wat and Cwen close at hand. Perchance Ern said the murder on purpose, to get Hermitage's attention without alerting the others. A trip to the alehouse was in order as Ern might reveal all and Hermitage could make some progress.

He nodded to himself that this was already a good step forward and he hadn't had to speak to anyone.

Then he fretted that he might be enjoying investigation a little. That would never do.

The preferred conclusion was that it was a slip of Ern's tongue and there was no murder at all. A simple enumeration of the dead, and a brief examination of the circumstances of each should put the whole matter to rest.

Unless, of course, someone had been murdered but no one knew. What if everyone assumed old Athlot fell from his ladder when in fact, he'd been pushed?

He tried to tell himself to stop looking for murder where there was none.

Ern would be the first stop.

The alehouse was quiet at this early hour of the morning, as was right and proper. Ern and his wife were up and about preparing the place for the noonday meal, when those who were not out in the fields, might stop for a tankard to go with their food.

'Good day Ern,' Hermitage called as he approached and saw Ern outside, making repairs. A pile of wet daub was on a board on the ground at his feet and a rough wooden trowel was in his hand. 'Trouble with the wall?'

Ern turned and considered Hermitage with some surprise. 'Brother Hermitage? Yes, the rain yesterday softened things up a bit, and then last night, young Wilfrid and Edgar got in an argument and fists were thrown.'

'Oh, my. Was anyone injured?'

'Who cares about them?' Ern asked with some annoyance. 'They punched a hole in my wall.'

'Are they not here to repair it?'

'Wouldn't trust either of those two to put mud in a mudpile.' Ern scooped up a trowel full of daub and skilfully laid it in a neat layer across the exposed wattle. 'Made them fetch the dung though.' Ern sniffed at the daub as if checking the quality of its ingredients. 'Anyway, what brings you into Derby this time of day?'

'Our conversation.' Hermitage didn't like to say "death", or "murder" straight out.

'Which one's that then?' Ern asked as he examined his

handy work.

'The one yesterday. At Wat's workshop.'

Ern winced at the name. 'Quietly.'

Hermitage frowned as Ern drew close. 'Don't mention that place,' he whispered.

'But you were there,' Hermitage whispered back. 'You delivered our food like you always do.'

'Not so loud,' Ern urged, even though Hermitage could barely hear his own words. 'As far as anyone is concerned, I take the food up the lane where I meet one of the apprentices who takes it on up to the workshop.' He gave a deliberate look towards his alehouse where his wife could be heard humming as she worked. 'I never go there myself, yes?'

There was no question that Hermitage would cooperate in any sort of deception, but if the opportunity arose to say nothing at all, or not answer a question if he was asked, he would do his best.

'But,' Hermitage talked in a breathless hiss. 'You were there for quite a while yesterday.' He too glanced towards the alehouse. 'What were you doing all that time?'

'I'm bone idle and lazy.' Ern nodded and smiled.

They hardly seemed qualities to boast about but Hermitage thought there was no need to speak to Ern's wife, so he wouldn't be asked to confirm any of this.

He could only shrug an acknowledgement that he understood the words, while not approving of their intent.

'The murder,' he whispered.

'You're not still on about that?'

Hermitage nodded. 'I wondered if you said the murder to me, in order to get my attention?'

'I wouldn't have said the word at all if I'd known it was going to get this much attention,' Ern complained.

'There really has been no murder?'

'Really,' Ern said sincerely.

'Are you sure?'

'It's the sort of thing that does get talked about,' Ern said. 'Particularly in the alehouse of an evening.'

'Perhaps there has been one, but no one has noticed?'

'Not noticed? How do you not notice a murder?'

'Oh, there could be many ways.'

Ern looked as if he were desperately avoiding asking Hermitage about any of them.

'I was only asking about your hut,' Ern said with some desperation. 'Being polite, like. Making conversation while Wat and Cwen were, you know,' he winked.

'But murder?' Hermitage asked.

'It's what you do, isn't it? We all know that. King's Investigator. What else are we supposed to talk to you about? Every time you come and go there's been some murder or other.'[Hermitage, Wat and Some Murder or Other, for example.]

Hermitage had to accept that was true, sadly.

'I'm mean,' Ern went on, 'I'm no churchman, am I?'

He certainly wasn't.

'I can't talk to you about God and stuff. The weather will only take you so far, so murder it is.'

It could be that Hermitage was simply going to have to accept this. 'You mentioned old Athlot.'

'The ninety-year-old Athlot who stupidly tried to repair his own thatch and fell off the roof? That old Athlot?'

Put like that, it didn't sound like much of a murder.

'Is there anyone else in town who has died recently?'

'Where do I start?' Ern asked.

That sounded ominous.

'We live in troubled times,' Ern stated the obvious. 'People die all the time; doesn't mean they've been murdered.'

'Of course, not. But it does no harm to be sure.'

'You want to be sure that everyone who died has not been murdered? That's going to take a while.'

Hermitage was thinking that he really should stop fishing for a murder. Ern had confirmed that he knew of none, so why could he not give up?

It was that business of the letter e in the gospel again. Some Brothers had told him that the letter a had been miswritten as an e in one word of a very large gospel at the monastery. Well, he had read it over and over again. He'd even gone forwards, backwards and upside down to try and spot the thing. Then they'd told him it was a joke and had laughed heartily. He said there weren't any jokes in the gospels, at which they laughed even louder. Then he got it. And he still worried about e's in Gospels to this day.

Details such as this were like fleas in his habit. He had to find them and would pull the fabric apart thread by thread if necessary.

Ern had said the murder, and despite the protestations of the man who had used the word, he had to satisfy himself that there wasn't one.

'I suppose the priest would know all the names,' Ern offered.

'Really?' Hermitage asked in some despair. That priest was a troublesome fellow and seemed not to care much for his priestly duties, or even know what most of them were.

'Perhaps not,' Ern accepted. 'Come on,' he nodded towards the tavern. 'I've got to put the inner coat of daub on before the outer dries too much.'

He went over and picked up the board of daub and his

trowel and carried them into the alehouse.

'You need to get the inner coat of daub on before the outer dries too much.' Ern's wife, the somewhat optimistically named Mistress Angel announced as they entered. 'Oh, hello Brother,' she said as she noticed Hermitage.

'I was just telling Brother Hermitage here as how I need to get the inner coat of daub on before the outer dried too much,' Ern said as if he hadn't heard a word. 'Him not being familiar with daubing, I imagine.'

Hermitage smiled and nodded that this was indeed the case. He recalled that his father had tried to teach him once, but as Hermitage ended up more daubed than the wall, it was taken no further. He was eight at the time and had already stated a preference for the monastic life over becoming a dauber.

'What brings Brother Hermitage here at this time of day?' Angel asked Ern quite piercingly. 'Have you been up that workshop again?'

'Course not.' Ern said brightly. 'Here,' he added. 'You'd know.'

'I'd know what?' Mistress Angel asked as she very slowly returned to sweeping the floor of the single room that constituted the alehouse.

'Dead people.'

'Dead people? What do you mean, I'd know dead people?'

'You'd know who's died recently. Brother Hermitage was asking.'

'Asking who's died?'

'That's right.'

'Why do you want to know who's died, Brother? Oh my, it's not murder is it?' Angel put a hand to her mouth.

Hermitage despaired. Did everyone only associate him

with murder now? He knew it was mainly King William's fault for making him investigator, but he didn't help himself. If the only topics of conversation with him were the weather and murder, what hope was there?'

'Not at all,' he assured her.

'Apparently,' Ern began as if sharing a juicy piece of gossip. 'Brother Hermitage is having a hut built. The apprentice from the workshop told me.'

Hermitage was grateful that Ern was taking the lead in the lying.

'A hut?' Angel asked.

'So he can investigate away from that disgusting Wat, I imagine.'

Angel frowned a deeply suspicious frown at her husband. 'What's a hut got to do with dead people? You're not having dead bodies in this hut, are you?'

'Oh, Lord, no,' Hermitage confirmed.

'You know what monks are like,' Ern continued. 'Mysterious ways.'

Angel looked very much as if she didn't believe a word of this, but had no argument to offer, monks being odd people at the best of times.

Hermitage's urge was to point out that it was God who worked in mysterious ways, not him. Over the years of investigation, he had come to recognise that this was one of the moments when silence was a virtue.

Mistress Angel leaned on her broom. 'Well, there's old Athlot.'

'Yes, we covered him.'

'Then there's Mistress Alodie.'

'Mistress Alodie?' Hermitage asked. 'How did she die?'

'Oh, plague,' Angel said nonchalantly.

'Plague?' Hermitage asked in some alarm.

'That's right. Her and her husband. And her parents. And his parents. And three of the sheep. Lucky the children had moved out, I reckon.'

'Has it spread?'

'No,' Angel dismissed the concern. 'We all rubbed ourselves with onions, so we'll be fine.'

'Didn't Maynard the Mighty go?' Ern asked.

'Oh, yes, he did,' Angel was grateful for the reminder.

'Maynard the Mighty?' Hermitage knew of Maynard but had never known he was called mighty.

'Always covered in mites, he was. Didn't do to get too close.'

'He died of mites?' Hermitage found that hard to believe.

'Oh, bless me, no. It was the sweating sickness took him.'

'So, that's Maynard, most of Mistress Alodie's family and old Athlot.' Hermitage thought that was a very high number of deaths for one town.

'This week, yes,' Angel confirmed.

Hermitage decided that he didn't want to enquire any farther back. 'One sweating sickness, several plagues and a ladder, then.'

'Sounds about right,' Angel agreed. 'Mind you, I always wondered about old Athlot and his ladder.'

'Oh, yes?' Did Mistress Angel have something to offer?

'Well, he was a modest fellow. Had been something in his younger years but now had a tiny old hovel like most people.'

'I see.'

'And he was fit for his age, very active still.'

'Hence the climbing on the ladder,' Hermitage nodded sadly.

'Well, no. He was a lanky old boy, not stooped at all. Must

have been five foot nine if he was an inch.'

Hermitage was impressed by such height but didn't know how it helped. 'I'm not sure I see the problem?'

'Tiny hut, tall man?' Angel asked. 'He could have reached the top of his thatch in his bare feet. What was he doing up a ladder at all?
'

Caput VIII: Interruptions

'Horses?' Edgulf gaped at the animals.

'Of course,' Fortmain said. 'Normans don't walk.'

'We just walked from south of Ely.'

'Only because we couldn't find any horses.'

'We're not finding these horses,' Edgulf pointed out. 'We're stealing them.'

Fortmain shook his head sadly at this lack of understanding. 'This is now a Norman country and so everything belongs to the Normans. We are Normans, these horses are in this country, so they belong to us.'

'What about the man they currently belong to?' Edgulf gave the poor Saxon stable master and his lad a sympathetic look.

Fortmain barely glanced at them. 'Not Normans,' he concluded. 'And don't you want to get to the king's man as quickly as possible?' He peered at Edgulf.

'Well, yes, of course.'

'After all, there is a murder to be dealt with, isn't there?'

'Absolutely. A murder, that's right.'

'So what are you complaining about?'

They had found this place once they came upon the main Roman thoroughfare heading north. It was obviously a stopping off spot for those travelling to and from London. Somewhere they could refresh horses. Unless all those horses were stolen by Normans, of course.

'You're simply going to take all the horses and leave the man with nothing.' The journey to Derby would certainly be a lot faster on horseback, but simply taking horses from a fellow Saxon was unfair.

'Not nothing,' Fortmain said. 'We don't want that one.' He

gestured towards an old and decrepit horse.

'No one would want that one,' Edgulf replied. 'It's probably only here to keep passing horses company.'

'I do know how a stable works,' Fortmain sneered. 'It'll just have to wait for some new friends, won't it? Not that these beasts are up to Normans standards anyway.'

'Good enough to steal, though,' Edgulf muttered. 'Anyway,' he added, 'there aren't enough for us all.'

'Those two can share.' Fortmain nodded to Marcus and Aurelius. 'If they have to come at all. Perhaps it's best to leave them on the road,' he mused. 'After all, they're nothing to do with us.'

'Happy to share, sire,' Marcus smiled and bowed. 'Not a problem at all.'

The stable master sidled up to Edgulf and whispered in his ear. 'We've got a cart.' He nodded his head over towards a cart that was sitting in the stable yard. It wasn't much of a cart, just some planks fixed to the top of two wheels.

Edgulf could see that it would be better for the stable if these Normans took fewer horses and the cart, but he wasn't confident that those wheels would make it as far as Derby.

Nevertheless, he had to try. 'Perhaps we could take just two horses and a cart?' he suggested to Fortmain with a nod towards the cart.

'That thing?' Fortmain asked in disbelief. 'First of all, Normans do not travel in carts, and secondly, that's barely even a cart.'

Edgulf couldn't believe that no Norman ever travelled in a cart, but Fortmain's mind seemed made up. 'Going in a cart wouldn't be much faster than walking anyway. No, it's the horses we're taking.'

Edgulf shrugged his apologies to the stable master. At least he had tried.

'Fetch saddles,' Fortmain commanded.

The Saxon looked as if he was longing to say, "fetch them yourself", but managed to contain himself. He waved a hand to his lad, who went off to fetch the saddles.

'And we'll need food and drink,' the Norman added.

'Why not take my head, while you're at it?' the stable master grumbled quietly in the old Saxon tongue, guessing, correctly, that the Normans wouldn't understand. If they did, they might really take his head as well.

It wasn't long before six horses stood saddled and ready in the stable yard. Of course, Fortmain had complained that the saddles weren't good Norman saddles; that the tack was not good Norman tack, and that the animals probably didn't even understand Norman French.

A muttered, "go back to Normandy, then," was only heard by Edgulf.

Raising himself up in his saddle, Fortmain commanded departure.

The stable master and his lad shook their heads at the instantaneous loss of all their business, while Fortmain's own men shook theirs in apparent amusement at their leader's pretension.

Edgulf had to admit that the horses were going to speed his way to Brother Hermitage. They appeared to be in very good health and kept up a good pace, much to the discomfort of Marcus and Aurelius.

They had been given the largest wooden saddle, but even then, they did not look as if horse-riding was something they'd done very often, if at all. Instead of moving in rhythm with the trot of the horse, they bounced around looking as if they were going to fall off at any moment.

Edgulf had ridden, but not often, and tried to demonstrate how they should move. Eventually, they got themselves in better order, but if this trot broke into a gallop, they would be on the floor in a moment.

And if that happened, it was almost certain that Fortmain would leave them behind.

The horses seemed happy to trot on for some time before Fortmain slowed them to a walk to recover their strength. After a few more miles, the Norman decided it was time to stop and eat, and found a field edged with a small stream where the horses could water and graze.

Edgulf pointed out that the horses were grazing on this field of oats, which was probably what the locals were relying on to eat. Fortmain showed little interest. Once again, he embarked on his explanation that everything belonged to the Normans anyway. He even suggested that the Saxons shouldn't plant oats if they didn't want them eaten.

When one of his men said that letting a horse fill its stomach with oats was not good for them, Fortmain blamed the Saxons for deliberately planting oats to sicken his horses. He instructed one of his men to move the horses though and they were taken across the track to some rough grass; from which they almost immediately took themselves back to the oats.

Taking their stolen supplies, the Normans devoured their meal and drink quickly, only Fortmain complaining that the food he had stolen from Saxons was all Saxon.

Marcus and Aurelius only ate lightly, neither of them looking very well at all.

'Are you sure you still want to go to Derby?' Edgulf asked them.

'How long is it going to take on horseback?' Marcus asked

in the manner of one asking how long it will take to pull his rotten tooth out.

'A full day, I reckon.'

'A full day?' This was clearly the equivalent of an eternity of torture. 'Last time I went to Derby it took days.' Marcus grumbled. 'I think I prefer that.' He looked to Aurelius, who gave a pained nod.

'Try to sit more forward,' Edgulf suggested. 'Keep your back straight.'

'Can't we have a softer horse?' Aurelius asked.

'It's the saddle,' Edgulf explained. 'They're all the same.'

'Why do people do this?'

'Much faster than walking.'

'But not much good if you can't walk when you arrive.'

Without further time to recover, Fortmain gave the order to mount up.

As they went to get their horses, a disturbance on the track made Edgulf look around in alarm. He quickly reasoned that he was in the company of a band of Normans and so didn't need to run away and hide.

Down the road, another mounted group could be heard approaching and it had to be assumed that these would be Normans as well.

A moment later, some half dozen Norman soldiers appeared, travelling quite quickly and looking to have some fearsome purpose to their journey. Their leader reined in, and the new arrivals came to a halt.

Fortmain raised a fist in greeting.

'Good God,' the new Norman leader said. 'It's Fortmain.'

There was a muttering amongst the fresh crop of Normans that sounded something like amusement.

Fortmain's own men said nothing but seemed to be

keeping their heads down.

'What's happened, Fortmain? Been captured by some horses?'

At this, the new force burst into laughter.

Fortmain's face was serious. 'We are taking these Saxons to the king's man in Derby, so you can be on your way.'

The Norman looked down from his horse. 'We're commanded to make all speed to London,' he said. 'There's rebellion afoot.' The man considered the Saxons with narrowed eyes. 'You and your men can come with us. Bring the Saxons as prisoners.'

Edgulf hoped that his despair at this didn't show. If these Normans took him to London, he might never get to Brother Hermitage; or even survive at all. He was in no position to argue and had no idea whether Fortmain was simply going to obey orders.

'I did say the king's man,' Fortmain said in what Edgulf thought was a dangerously patronising tone.

'What king's man?' the leader asked from his saddle. His was a serious and suspicious question, although his men were still chortling.

Fortmain drew himself up straight. 'The King's Estimator,' he announced.

'Estimator? Do you mean investigator?' the other Norman corrected with a wry smile and a shake of the head.

'Ah, you know him, then.'

'I know of him. I don't know what business you think you've got with him.'

'I am taking this Saxon there about a murder.'

The Norman considered Edgulf with a look that was worryingly sympathetic. 'You don't take people to the investigator to be murdered, you know.'

Fortmain didn't grace that with an answer.

'And what about the other two?' The Norman nodded towards Marcus and Aurelius.

'Camp followers,' Fortmain replied.

'We are not,' Aurelius shouted over. 'How dare you?'

'They'd have to be pretty desperate to follow your camp,' one of the Normans in the band called out. His commander waved him to silence.

'Be careful, Fortmain,' another called. 'Three Saxons and only four of you? It could end badly.'

Fortmain simply tutted and shook his head as if in disappointment at his compatriot's poor understanding of a simple situation.

'Fighting off rebellion is more important than some Saxon's murder,' the Norman said. 'You come with us.'

There was a noticeable grumbling amongst the man's own band.

'What?' he demanded, turning in his saddle.

After an exchange of looks and some quiet cajoling, one of the number appeared to be nominated to speak.

'Well?'

'It is Fortmain,' the nominee said pleadingly.

'So?'

'He's not really going to be much help, is he? Him and those three? Fighting off a rebellion?'

'Some rebellious sheep?' one at the back suggested to a smattering of laughter.

'And, be honest, he's more likely to make things go wrong,' the spokesman continued.

'I don't want him anywhere near me,' another called out. 'I'd like to see my home again.'

'He is more likely to get us killed instead of the enemy.'

The group's representative seemed to be treating this statement as a fact rather than an argument. 'Don't forget Cabourg.'

The leader took a deep breath and blew it out slowly before addressing Fortmain. 'I suppose the king might rest more easily knowing that you're miles away. And if you're never seen again, I can tell everyone where you went.'

Fortmain looked as if he wanted to protest this unjust treatment but could see that he was getting his way.

'Do the Saxons think they're going to make it, Fortmain?' One of the Normans said. 'Have you warned them there's a good chance they'll be dead when they arrive?'

With more laughter, the leader gave Fortmain a dismissive and quite rude gesture, before galloping off in a cloud of dust.

Fortmain turned back to his men and indicated that they should be ready to go. No one said a word, but the silence was pretty loud.

'What was all that about?' Marcus asked Edgulf as they readied to depart.

'I don't really know. From what one of the other Normans was saying, this Fortmain got something wrong somewhere and someone died. After that, they got sort of cast off from the rest of the Normans.'

'Oh, wonderful,' Marcus complained. 'We're not even in the company of a proper Norman.'

'I can't move my legs,' Aurelius complained as she stood by the side of their horse.

To moans of pain and vocal objections at her treatment, Marcus lifted her up and placed her onto the back of the saddle.

'Oh, God,' she moaned.

'If it gets too bad, take turns to stand up in the stirrups for a few moments,' Edgulf suggested. 'Take the weight off.'

'Stand up in the what?'

'These things you put your feet in. They're called stirrups,' Edgulf held the stirrups out from the side of the horse.

'We put our feet in them?' Aurelius asked with horrible anger. 'And who's had their feet in them up until now. She clipped Marcus round the back of the head.'

'How did you get on the horse in the first place?'

'The stable master had a stool.'

'Ah. Yes, you, erm, put your feet in the stirrups. You have to, really. Otherwise riding would be very difficult.'

'And painful, I imagine,' Aurelius added with a very hard stare.

Marcus said nothing as he was helped up.

'Right,' Fortmain called. 'Onwards.'

'I don't know if we're even going to make it to Derby.' Marcus moaned as he and Aurelius rode alongside Edgulf.

'It's not that bad,' Edgulf chided. 'Anyway, after a couple of days you'll be used to it and your legs will toughen up.'

'If the horse doesn't kill us, the Norman might. If he's got a bad reputation amongst other Normans, he must be a complete disaster.'

'He doesn't wish us any harm. I was told that he wants to see the king's man to help him get back into favour.'

'He may not wish us any harm, but he sounds like the type who causes it without wishing. A walking bad omen. I've met them before. You know, best will in the world but if anything's going to go wrong, it happens to them.'

'Let him ride ahead,' Aurelius said. 'If something horrible is going to happen, we just need to keep far enough away.'

'He's obviously survived this far,' Edgulf pointed out.

'It's not him surviving I'm worried about,' Marcus replied.

'He's already proved his worth. If we'd been on our own on the road when that other lot turned up, it could have been our end. You saw what they were like.'

'Real Normans.' Marcus seemed to reluctantly accept that there might be some truth in this.

'Anyway,' Edgulf continued. 'You've still got Harold's thumb. How come those Normans could even see us?'

Neither Marcus nor Aurelius seemed keen on exploring the fickle qualities of the thumb.

'Just put up with a bit longer in the saddle and we'll be safely in Derby. Then you can get on with whatever is so important.'

'Nothing, really. Just got some interest there, like we said.'

'So interesting that you'll put up with horses and Normans to get there, eh?' Edgulf held his hands up. 'I'm not interested in prying into your business, but if you really do want to go to Derby, you could stop moaning about getting there all the time.

'Besides, what could go wrong now? We've got horses and food, both stolen, obviously. We've survived an encounter with a band of Norman soldiers, and we've got one of their own to protect us. We just have to keep going and it'll all be over.'

'Stop right there,' a strong voice called out of the trees to the left of the road; a strong voice with a very strong Saxon accent. 'No Normans pass this way without paying the price.'

From the trees, a band of six Saxons emerged. They looked reasonably young and fit and longbows hung in their hands, arrows just waiting to be nocked. Knives were at belts, and one even had a sword.

'We're not Normans,' Aurelius called out. 'We're just with them.'

'Then you are worse than Normans,' the lead Saxon cried. 'And you shall all die.'

Caput IX: The Athlot Mansion

'I must see old Athlot's home,' Hermitage said.

'He's not there anymore,' Mistress Angel informed helpfully. 'The priest buried him.'

'Erm, yes,' Hermitage said, wondering why she should even think otherwise. 'But if the home is as you say, there could be some suspicion about his death.'

'Suspicion?'

'If he did not fall, perhaps someone pushed him?'

'Who would want to kill Athlot?' Ern asked.

'We don't know,' Hermitage said. 'But if he had no need to be up the ladder..,?'

'Maybe the ladder didn't kill him?' Ern suggested.

Hermitage raised an eyebrow.

'Maybe he was a ninety-year-old who happened to die next to a ladder? I should think he was going to do it pretty soon anyway. We've never had anyone that old before.'

Hermitage had to admit that was a possibility. And he reminded himself once more that he should not go hunting for a murder when a natural death was perfectly reasonable.

'I mean,' Ern continued. 'If he died next to his cooking pot, would you think the pot hit him?'

'Well, no, of course not. But it was you who said he was lying at the bottom of the ladder covered in thatch. And if he didn't need a ladder, why did he even have one?'

'People have things,' Ern explained in all seriousness.

'Looking at the home can do no harm,' Hermitage said. 'If there is nothing to be seen then we can rest assured that Athlot died because his allotted span had come to its end.'

Ern shrugged. 'Come on then,' he said and started to lead Hermitage along the road.

'And where do you think you're going?' Mistress Angel asked.

'To look at Athlot's home,' Hermitage said apologetically, not realising that Mistress Angel wanted him.

'Not you, Brother. Him.'

Ern gave a weak smile.

'He's not the King's Investigator. He's the alehouse dauber. And he's still got an alehouse with a hole in it.'

'It's up the lane and on the left,' Ern explained. 'Behind the smithy.'

Hermitage nodded and set off up the lane while Ern returned to his daubing.

The smithy was not far, being central to the town, and was already at work, the overnight fire having been brought to life before dawn.

As he approached, Hermitage's pace slowed a little. There was no need to stop at the smithy, after all. Athlot's home was behind it, but it would mean he had to go past.

The smith himself was a fine fellow, as strong and robust as a smith would be. He was looked up to in the town as a dependable man who worked hard and was skilled at his trade. His knowledge and understanding of smithing and metalwork could not be challenged; his knowledge and understanding of anything else were a little more sparse.

He was also looked up to because he was tall and strong and could see off trouble if it came knocking. Several times, the smith had been called upon to deal with young troublemakers who came into the big town from nearby Marcheaton simply to fill themselves with ale and have an evening of mischief.

Ern usually made sure they were full of as much ale as they could pay for before he sent for the smith.

It was even a common sight to see the town headman standing slightly behind the smith when dealing with the more difficult residents.

Hermitage would be happy to exchange some words with the smith, he just hoped that the apprentice wasn't about.

That young man was a most difficult boy; argumentative, rude and self-important, all with no cause. He was an apprentice, for heaven's sake, what made him better than others? Nonetheless, he behaved as if born to arrogance; neither his elders nor his betters being spared.

For some reason, the smith seemed blind to his apprentice's behaviour, which was a common topic of conversation.

It was widely assumed that if the smith ever died or moved on, Derby would rather cope without a smith than let the boy take over. In fact, some detailed plans were in place to chase the apprentice out of town; preferably towards Marcheaton.

The smith treated his behaviour as an amusing distraction as if the boy were playing a part and wasn't really as unpleasant as he made out, even when other people told him quite explicitly.

Hermitage thought he was significantly more unpleasant than he made out.

'Ah, good day, master smith,' Hermitage called happily as he saw the man outside his workshop. He was considering the state of a large cartwheel that had obviously been left for a new metal band to be fitted around the outside. Clearly, this was a wheel belonging to one of the more wealthy inhabitants of the town who could afford such luxury.

The impressive thing was that the smith was holding the wheel up to his eye, rather than bending down to look at it.

He put the wheel down with a thump and beamed a smile at Hermitage. 'And good day to you, Brother.'

'Oh God, it's the monk,' a younger voice sneered as the apprentice appeared.

'Now then, Grimulf,' the smith chuckled. 'You show Brother Hermitage respect.' He winked at Hermitage. 'He is a little horror, isn't he?' he asked lightly.

Hermitage thought, yes, he is.

'What does he want?' Grimulf asked rudely.

'Get back to that scythe,' the smith instructed gently. 'It won't temper itself.'

Hermitage was ashamed to wonder whether there might soon be an accident involving Grimulf and a hot scythe.

'What can I do for you today, Brother?' the smith asked once the apprentice had slunk back into the dark interior. 'Some loom part from Wat for repair?'

'Oh, no, nothing like that. In fact, it's not you I've come to see. I'd like to have a look at old Athlot's home.'

'Old Athlot?' The smith looked confused. 'He's dead, you know.'

'Yes, I know.'

'You thinking of moving out of the workshop, then? Ern said you were going to get a hut, but I think you'd want something better than Athlot's place.'

Hermitage was surprised to hear that talk of his hut had already reached the smith. He supposed that he shouldn't be, really. There was very little to talk about most days and so something as exciting as a monk in a hut would liven any evening. He imagined there would not be a person in town who didn't have an opinion on the matter by now.

'Not that either. I was simply concerned about the circumstances of Athlot's death.'

87

The smith nodded seriously at this.

'You have your own doubts?' Hermitage asked. He was still torn between needing to find out what happened and hoping that nothing happened at all.

'Of course,' the smith said. 'Stands to reason.'

'What does?'

'You do know how old he was?'

'Ninety, they say.'

'There you are then.'

'There I am, what?' Hermitage was now recalling how difficult it could be to have a conversation with the smith that did not involve metal.

'Not natural, is it?'

'Isn't it?'

'Man lives to that age, he's up to something.'

'Up to something?'

The smith looked around and up and down the lane. 'Of course, he never said. Went on about leading a good life and being rewarded, but I don't know.'

'Don't you?'

The smith spoke quietly and carefully, making sure no one could overhear. 'Magic.'

'Magic?' Hermitage relaxed as he saw that the smith had no serious or useful information about Athlot.

'Live to ninety you'd need magic of some sort. Witches, probably.'

'There are no such things as witches,' Hermitage said plainly. 'The Church is quite clear on that.'

The smith did not look as if he considered the Church to be a reliable source of information when it came to witches. 'He'd probably made a pact.'

'A pact?' Hermitage was just going to have to hear this out.

'A pact to live to ninety. Then, when he got there, they came to take him.' The man looked quite confident that this was a perfectly reasonable explanation.

'Did you notice anyone come to take him?'

'Well, no, but then I wouldn't. Not if they were magic.'

Hermitage quickly decided this was a difficult question to pursue as it wasn't a sensible question in the first place. 'Did you know him well, after all, he lived behind your workshop?'

'Oh, yes.' The smith smiled and nodded at the recollection. 'We'd have long talks when the time allowed. I liked to make sure he was well. And young Grimulf was always round there helping him out with this and that.'

'Really?' Hermitage found that hard to believe.

'He's a good boy,' the smith assured him. 'Just likes to appear gruff and fierce. And old Athlot knew a bit about smithing, you know.'

'Did he? Didn't mention magic at all?'

The smith seemed to suddenly realise that this might be an impediment to his assumption. 'No, he didn't.' He frowned hard.

Hermitage moved on. 'Ern said he was found on the ground by a fallen ladder.'

'That's right.' The smith seemed quite happy with the idea of a ladder; something you could get hold of.

'But he was a tall fellow who probably didn't need one.'

'That's right,' the smith said, before seeing that there was something wrong about that.

'Which is why I would like to look at his home. Just to see for myself.'

'Good idea,' the smith nodded. 'Just round the back, it is. You help yourself. I've got this wheel.' He lifted the wheel once more.

'Thank you.' Hermitage gave a little bow and then moved around the side of the smithy onto a path that led to the rear. A large tree grew close by the smithy wall and narrowed the way. He thought that this would be ripe for felling, as many trees were when they got in the way of the town's growth.

He thought that once upon a time, the smithy may even have been outside of the town, but Derby had expanded with trade and travel.

Now that the Normans were in charge, he supposed it might start shrinking again.

He quickly came upon what must have been Athlot's dwelling, and it really was humble. The old folk tended to stick to their ways and have as little to do with modern ideas as possible. Athlot would doubtless have been horrified at Wat's workshop with its wooden floors and front step. This place was as traditional Saxon as it was possible to get.

A simple rectangular hole had been dug into the ground some two feet deep. Into this, wooden posts had been driven and the walls constructed between them. The place did look in reasonably good repair and Athlot had clearly been conscientious about maintaining his home.

The daub walls were complete and solid, looking quite capable of keeping out the wind and rain. The thatch overhung the walls and came down to within two or three feet of the ground, so there would be no need for any ladder to reach these lower levels.

Most interesting of all, the roof looked fine.

Hermitage was no expert in thatch, but this roof seemed to be complete and of a good thickness. There was some moss growing in parts, but nothing to be of any serious concern. He couldn't see that it needed any repair at all.

There was a bundle of reasonably fresh-looking thatch

piled up towards the back of the house, but this could be simple spare material kept for emergencies. Or it could have been put there by the people who found Athlot. There didn't seem to be any thatch missing from the roof.

Hermitage knew there had been some wind that might have caused damage, but any repairs seemed to be complete. Hardly the time to fall off a ladder when the job has been done.

He stepped up to the front door and peered inside. As expected, there was nothing of particular interest. A simple fireplace occupied the middle of the packed-earth floor and a hole in the thatch above would take the smoke away.

The biggest risk to the roof in any such home was fire. A stray spark could see the whole roof gone in a few moments, but most people kept a bucket of water close by, just in case.

If Athlot had had any possessions, they were gone now and there was nothing to show that anyone had lived here at all.

As far as he knew, the old man had no relatives to pass his goods on to, even if they were simple and of little value. He would have to find out who had been here and taken things away and hope that they had done so with the best of motives. To simply take the dead man's property would be disgraceful.

Hermitage stepped back from the door and quickly answered the most pressing question of all. He lifted his arm and easily touched the apex of the roof.

He went around to the side and, by laying on the roof where it dropped low, he could also reach the top. And if Athlot was taller than him, why the ladder?

He did know enough about thatch to be aware that it needed pinning in place, and that getting up above it would make the task easier, but would a ninety-year-old man really attempt such work himself?

The questions had not gone away and as the smith was the nearest neighbour, perhaps he could supply some further details of Athlot's life.

Making his way back around the path, Hermitage, unfortunately, found Grimulf instead of the smith.

'Ah, Grimulf,' he tried his best to sound pleased, but it wasn't easy.

The apprentice looked up from the scythe he was sharpening but said nothing.

'Is your master inside?'

Grimulf sighed at such a stupid question. 'Funny that. Asking whether a smith is in the smithy,' he sneered.

'Then I would speak with him.' Hermitage said as firmly as he could manage.

'He's dealing with a wheel,' Grimulf said as if Hermitage should be perfectly aware of this.

'Then you can tell me about Athlot,' Hermitage said bluntly, his irritation at Grimulf getting the better of his natural reticence.

'He's dead.'

'We all know he's dead. The whole town knows he's dead. That comment is of no help at all. I want to know about him when he was alive.'

'Bit late now,' Grimulf grumbled, but at least he seemed to respond to Hermitage's annoyance.

'Who found him?' Hermitage asked.

'The smith.' Grimulf coughed as if that was just the sort of ridiculous thing that man would do.

'When was this?'

'Few days ago, I suppose.'

'You suppose,' Hermitage sighed. He longed to say that he was King William's investigator and that Grimulf had better start cooperating. Unfortunately, Cwen was better at that sort of thing, but he thought going back to get her might be a distraction.

'What were the circumstances?'

Grimulf looked up from his scythe. 'The smith went round there at noon, like he usually did, and came rushing back to say he was dead. Fell off the roof.'

'What was he doing on the roof?'

'How should I know? Liked it up there?'

'Was it the sort of thing he normally did?'

'What, climb on his roof?'

'His home is only just behind here,' Hermitage pointed out. 'You must know how he lived.'

'I didn't want anything to do with him,' Grimulf sneered. 'Boring old man.'

'How do you know he was boring if you had nothing to do with him? And the smith said you were always round there helping him out.'

'Made to go round there, more like,' Grimulf complained. 'And he kept coming 'round here bothering us when we were trying to get on with work.'

'He probably welcomed someone to talk to.'

'He could talk all right. On and on about all the people he'd met. Where he'd been, what he'd done. Who wants to hear that?'

'It was his life and he was long-lived,' Hermitage said. 'I'm sure it was a comfort to him and an interest to those a bit older than you.' He was quite shocked to hear himself criticise the boy so explicitly.

'Please yourself,' Grimulf said. 'You might want to hear endless tales about the Duke of Normandy, but I don't.'

Caput X: The Battle of, erm..,

The four Normans on their horses appeared to be frozen by this attack, in which no one had actually attacked anyone else yet. None of them drew their swords, shouted cries of defiance or leapt into the fray.

From Fortmain's gentle tugging on his reins, he appeared content to simply move on and pretend he hadn't seen anyone.

One of the Saxons stepped forwards and did nock an arrow onto his bowstring. 'A sorry band,' he commented, looking them all up and down. 'What are Saxons doing in the company of these?' He didn't even name the Normans, just sneered in their direction.

'They're more in the company of us, actually,' Marcus offered.

'An explanation is needed, or death shall come your way,' the man announced grandly.

Aurelius coughed. 'It didn't come the way of the band that just passed by, did it?'

'What?'

'The previous band of Normans. You know, rather fearsome looking bunch. Well-armed, travelling fast. How come you didn't tell them that they've all got to die?'

The Saxon sighed as if weary of explaining the fundamentals of resistance and rebellion to people who weren't involved. 'We have to pick our fights. There's no point us going against a far greater force, is there?'

'Only smaller ones, then?' Aurelius asked with considerable contempt. 'Women and children, that sort of thing.'

'Normans and their Saxon collaborators,' the Saxon spat.

'Only fight people you know you're going to beat before

94

you start.'

The Saxon was sounding annoyed. 'If we lost our lives in a futile cause, who would there be to drive forwards and ultimately win our struggle against the Norman oppressors? No, we must make sure that we remain an effective fighting force.'

'Effective against people who don't fight back,' Aurelius continued. 'You're not going to win your struggle against the oppressors if you keep avoiding them. Somewhere out there is King William himself, the biggest oppressor of the lot. How are you going to get rid of him? Ask nicely?'

The Saxon pointed a gloved finger at Aurelius and issued his response. 'Shut up.' He had clearly had enough of Aurelius's battle strategy.

'You,' he turned his back on Marcus and Aurelius and addressed Edgulf. 'Explain.'

Edgulf glanced over at the Norman commander, wondering for a moment if he might like to engage with this armed Saxon, which was supposed to be his job, after all. Fortmain was trying to look as if he was appraising the situation in order to determine the perfect moment for his decisive move. There was no telling which direction that move would be in.

Edgulf sighed. 'I have come from the Gudmund estate.'

'Gudmund, eh?' The Saxon knew it and said the name with some sadness.

'And I am simply seeking a monk.' He really didn't want to go into any more detail than that.

'A monk?'

'That's right.'

'What do you want a monk for?'

'It's a particular monk.'

'Oh yes?' The Saxon sounded suspicious and a little concerned.

'Brother Hermitage,' Edgulf specified.

The Saxon leader turned quickly to his men and then back to Edgulf. 'The King's Investigator?'

'You know him?'

'Of course.' The Saxon smiled broadly. 'Brother Hermitage has been a good friend to us.'

'Oh, has he?' Fortmain now spoke up with a hard look for Edgulf.

'Silence, Norman,' the Saxon instructed. 'Why do you seek Brother Hermitage?'

Edgulf leaned forward in his saddle as if imparting a confidence. 'Murder,' he said in a low voice.

The Saxon glanced over at Fortmain and frowned. 'Brother Hermitage doesn't do murders, you know. He finds out about them.'

'I know that,' Edgulf replied sharply. 'I have business with Brother Hermitage. Arising from the Gudmunds. And I really need to get on with it.' He gave the Saxon a pleading look that they should be released.

'What are you doing with them?' The head was nodded to the Normans as contemptuously as a head could be nodded.

'Protection,' Edgulf winked. 'They helped us get past that earlier band of Normans. They'll be useful until we get to Derby. And they want to meet the King's Investigator. Offer their services, I think.'

'Oh, he won't like that,' the Saxon said but he nodded slowly as if he understood. 'You don't need all of them, though. One would do. We could have the rest.'

'Have them?' Edgulf didn't understand.

'We are fighting the Normans, you know. They always go

around in big groups and there's only six of us.'

'So, you haven't actually fought any oppressors at all,' Aurelius piped up.

'There's plenty of time,' the Saxon snapped back. 'And this lot's just the right size. Come, we'll take you to our camp and sort them out.'

'I really need to get on,' Edgulf pleaded. Honestly, if it wasn't the Normans stopping him reaching his goal it was his own people. He half expected the next interruption to be a roaming band of Celts. If he got as far as the next interruption.

'It won't take long,' the Saxon assured him.

'What are you going to do?' Edgulf asked in some alarm. He didn't like the Normans but thought this band such a particularly useless example of their people that they probably didn't deserve this fate.

'Oh, nothing like that,' he was assured. 'Hostages.'

'Hostages? This lot?' Edgulf didn't like to say that no one would want them back at all, let alone pay for the privilege.

'Oh, yes. Very popular, hostages. You can get a lot for a good hostage.'

Edgulf could only hope that one day they might find a good hostage.

The Saxon gestured his men to round up their captives and lead them off into the woods. Four well-armed Normans on horseback were herded with considerable ease, resistance obviously being kept in reserve.

'I'm Scemund, by the way,' the Saxon said as he led Edgulf's horse.

'Edgulf. And those two are Marcus and Aurelius.'

'Really?' Scemund didn't sound too sure.

'I doubt it, but that's what they say. Are we going far, only I really do need to get on? I don't want Brother Hermitage going off on business and I miss him.'

'No, not far. We'll just sort this lot out and then you can be off. We'll keep the Normans and the horses, obviously.'

'The horses?'

'Of course. A horse is worth a lot more than a Norman. This has been a great victory for us.'

As there hadn't been any fighting, Edgulf wondered about that.

'I've got to get to Derby,' Edgulf pleaded.

'Oh, you can have yours. We'll just keep the Normans'.' Scemund appraised the animals. 'They look like local beasts.'

'They are,' Edgulf said. 'The Normans stole them from a stable master back down the road.'

'Did they now?' Scemund obviously held Normans in very low estimation, but they had now sunk further.

'I expect he'd be glad to have some of them back.'

'I expect he would,' Scemund said, the intention to return the horses clearly being nowhere in his thinking. 'He'll be pleased that they now support the fight.'

'I suppose he might.'

They walked on through the woods for some while, Edgulf growing increasingly concerned that this camp might be miles away and he was losing time.

'So, you will let me keep one of the Normans?' Edgulf asked lightly.

'Hm.' Scemund seemed to be having second thoughts.

'Yes. It's just that I really do need to get to Derby, and you know what it's like on the roads these days.'

'Ha,' Scemund agreed. 'Full of robbers willing to stop anyone and whisk them away. No one's safe.'

'Well, quite.'

'Of course, I blame the Normans.'

'Well, yes. But if this lot did have a use, it was giving us safe passage. If we're on our own again, goodness knows what might happen.'

'They'd fetch better ransom if I had the whole lot. I assume they go together?'

'I think so. We found them all in a hut in the marshes.'

'Looking for Hereward, no doubt,' Scemund said with some amusement.

'I suppose so.'

'They'll never find him.'

'Is he not there then?'

'Oh, he's there. But he is like a spirit on the wind.'

'That's nice.'

'Here we are then,' Scemund announced as they entered a simple camp of cloth tents hung between tree branches. A fire burned in the middle of the space and two much older men and women were sitting by it. One of them stood occasionally and stirred the contents of a large pot hanging from a frame over the flames.

Scemund strode ahead into the camp at the head of his great booty.

The four by the fire stood and faced the returning band.

'What's this then?' one of the women asked, sounding rather disappointed at the haul.

'We have captured a band of Normans without losing a drop of Saxon blood,' Scemund announced proudly. 'Hostages and horses to boot.'

The woman stepped forward and turned her nose up as she peered at the captives. 'This isn't the band who were travelling south,' she said. 'There was a good dozen of them.'

'There was,' Scemund agreed, sounding a little cautious

now. 'And we took these.'

'They don't look much.'

Scemund breathed deeply. 'They look like four mounted and armed Normans with Saxon captives who we have rescued.'

'Didn't put up a fight, then?' the woman was now positively sneering.

'What's he done?' An old man asked as he joined the conversation.

'Invited some Normans to stay,' the woman replied.

'I have captured four Norman soldiers,' Scemund insisted.

'The wrong ones,' the woman concluded. She looked at the Normans again. 'Some easy ones, by the look of them.'

'Mother!' Scemund burst out. 'For God's sake. Will you please acknowledge that this is a triumph?'

'Pah,' old mother Scemund turned her back on her son and headed back to the fire.

'Father,' Scemund pleaded to the old man who simply waved a disinterested hand and followed his wife.

The rest of the Saxons were looking quite embarrassed at what seemed to be a regular scene. They looked away, found reason to attend to their bows or kicked at pieces of earth that appeared to be in the wrong place.

'I am the leader of this band and I have captured Norman hostages,' Scemund was insisting loudly as he followed his parents back to the fire.

'Some leader,' his mother scoffed as she returned to the pot. 'Weeks, we've been here and nothing.'

'Do you call them, nothing?' Scemund pointed over at the Normans. 'Look at them.'

'I can see them,' the mother said without looking. 'Mistress Opie's son is dead, you know.'

'I know he's dead. You tell me every day.'

'Dead fighting off the Normans. And what do I have to say for myself? Scemund? Oh, he's fine. Yes, still alive. No, not even wounded. I know, it is a shame isn't it? You're an embarrassment to your poor mother.'

'You'd rather I was dead, I know.'

'And young Mathew has gone off to join Hereward.'

'That's what he said,' Scemund muttered. 'Funny how he went in the opposite direction.'

'Still got all your arrows, then?' Father Scemund observed contemptuously.

'We took the Normans without firing a shot.'

'In my day we didn't take people without firing a shot. In my day we had a pitched battle just to eat at night.'

'Oh, God, here we go,' Scemund sighed. 'Vikings as big as houses.'

'They were,' his father insisted.

The band of Saxons had now taken to actively avoiding any of this awkwardness and were sidling over towards their various tents.

Edgulf could only watch with a mixture of disappointment and disbelief. He glanced over as he felt Fortmain's horse shift next to his.

'Now look what you've done,' mother Scemund's diatribe continued at volume a moment later. 'You've let them escape.'

'These horses do run fast, don't they?' Marcus panted as his animal kept pace with Edgulf's as they spun and sprinted through the woods. He had to shout over the screams of Aurelius as she was bounced around on the rear, sometimes rising out of the saddle completely before crashing down again.

'They do when the need arises,' Edgulf shouted back. 'But then that's how they defend themselves from danger, they run away. Looks like it's how Fortmain does it as well.'

At least the Norman had seen an opportunity and taken it. While the Saxons were having their little family dispute, he had slowly worked the horses together, before giving the silent command to run for it.

Before an arrow could be notched, Fortmain had urged his horse onwards and away through the woods. His men had followed suit with such alacrity that one might assume they did this sort of thing quite frequently.

Edgulf thought that he heard an arrow fly, but it was nowhere near them by the time it landed.

He did feel bad about escaping from his countrymen, and particularly for leaving Scemund to his fate, but the horses were simply following one another. When one ran, they all ran.

After a headlong rush, considerably longer than that required to escape some Saxons on foot, Fortmain brought the group to a halt. Not only had they escaped the woods, but they'd gone a good half mile farther up the road, just to be on the safe side.

Edgulf watched as the Normans gathered around and appeared to be congratulating themselves on a magnificent victory against overwhelming forces. Considering they'd had their backs to the overwhelming forces, he wondered at their behaviour.

'Well done, lads,' Fortmain praised his men for their headlong escape.

'We showed them,' one of the others called out to much-relieved laughter.

The Saxons looked at one another with bemusement.

Obviously, whatever happened at Cabourg was only a taste of what these men were capable of. It was no wonder their fellows didn't want them.

'They might have known where Hereward was,' Marcus suggested mischievously. 'I thought you were supposed to be hunting him.'

Fortmain turned to him with some anger. 'We have a new mission now; the king's man. We will let nothing divert us.'

His men all seemed in accord with him, grumbling their complaint at the Saxon's comment.

'Come,' Fortmain instructed. 'To the north.'

Edgulf looked over his back to see if the Saxons were following, but as they had all been on foot, it seemed unlikely. They'd probably never seen any Normans run away so quickly.

He could only hope that there weren't any more obstructions on his way to Brother Hermitage. If they came across a real force of some sort, he didn't rate their chances. And with Fortmain in the lead, a couple of fighting badgers might be enough.

Caput XI: Well Connected

'What do you mean, the Duke of Normandy?' Hermitage asked with the usual nervousness that title imbued.

'I don't know, do I?' Grimulf retorted impudently. 'I don't listen to what old men go on about.'

'Perhaps you should. You might gain some wisdom.'

'Wisdom? Pah.' Grimulf clearly wanted nothing to do with wisdom. Hermitage strongly suspected that the boy's life would not be troubled by it.

He tried to calm away the irritation that arose whenever this lad opened his mouth. 'Grimulf,' he said quietly. 'You mentioned the Duke of Normandy and indicated that Athlot would talk of him. When did you hear the name mentioned?'

'I don't know,' Grimulf complained. 'He was always here talking. I don't remember every time he said anything. I try to forget.'

'But he mentioned the Duke of Normandy,' Hermitage pressed.

'Why do you keep going about him? God, anyone would think we lived in Normandy.'

'The king,' Hermitage said simply.

Grimulf shook his head. 'No, he never went on about the king to me. Went on about lots of other kings. Way he talked, you'd think he knew them all.'

Hermitage took a breath. 'Grimulf,' he said to get the lad's attention.

'What?' Grimulf did not look up.

'Look at me.'

'What is it?' the boy whined, but at least he glanced at Hermitage.

Holding his eyes and speaking very slowly, Hermitage explained. 'The Duke of Normandy is the king.'

Grimulf scowled at such nonsense. 'What, King of Normandy? They should call him king, then.'

'No, King of England.'

'You're daft, you are.' Grimulf returned to his scythe.

'You have heard of the Normans, presumably?'

'Of course. I'm not stupid.'

Hermitage seriously doubted that. 'And the king is now called William. King William? He defeated Harold.'

'God, you monks do go on. You're as bad as Athlot.'

'King William is the Duke of Normandy.'

Grimulf's face said that he was working hard to follow that. 'He can't be,' he said with confidence.

'What do you mean, he can't be?' Hermitage's reserve of patience, probably the largest in town, was running dangerously low. He was willing to take learning on history from any expert on the topic; Grimulf was not one.

'That's two people,' Grimulf pointed out. 'You can't be two people at the same time. Everyone knows that.' He turned up his nose at Hermitage's obvious stupidity.

'It's a title!' Hermitage heard his own voice raised and struggled to calm himself. 'One person can have two titles. You are Grimulf the apprentice. You could also be Grimulf the, I-don't-know,' he longed to say, "fool". 'Grimulf the tall. If you were tall, that is. You see. Grimulf the tall and Grimulf the apprentice, all at the same time.'

Still Grimulf didn't seem to get it.

'William, the Duke of Normandy came over from Normandy, which is part of France, by the way. He battled and killed Harold and was made King of England. It's the same person.' Hermitage had an unfamiliar urge to clip

Grimulf round the ear. Naturally, he controlled it.

Grimulf shrugged with little interest. 'If you say so.'

'If I say so,' Hermitage breathed heavily. 'I do say so. And Athlot mentioned the Duke of Normandy, who you now know is King William.'

'Could be.'

'Could be?' Hermitage wanted to jump up and down on the spot and turn the clip into a slap. He had come across some recalcitrant novices in his time, but Grimulf would try the patience of a whole host of saints. 'Did Athlot say that he knew William? King William, Duke of Normandy?'

'Hmm.' Grimulf gave a half-hearted hum that sounded like, "I don't know."

'Oh, for heaven's sake,' Hermitage's persistence collapsed in the face of this uncooperative wall. 'I shall have to speak to your master, wheel or no wheel.'

Grimulf did seem to become more alert at the mention of his master and cast his eyes towards the interior of the smithy. Perhaps the threat of reporting his behaviour had got into his head. It was the only thing that had. 'Athlot is dead, though?' he said.

'He is,' Hermitage confirmed, wondering why there was any doubt. 'But if he had some connection to the Normans and the king, his death may be of import. It could be suspicious that someone known to the king falls off a roof. Or it may simply be that the king should be informed. Until I know more, I can't tell.'

'Hm,' Grimulf nodded with a look that probably passed for thought. 'And he's been buried.'

'Naturally.'

'And all his things have gone.'

'They have,' Hermitage agreed. 'And that is something we

may need to look into.'

Grimulf gave one more quite positive nod before coming to his conclusion. 'Is his hut going spare then?'

'Is? What?' Hermitage had dealt with killers, heartless nobles and the downright evil, but this level of nonchalant self-interest was so unexpected he didn't know what to say.

'I mean, he won't need it anymore. And no one else has moved in.'

'I have no idea,' Hermitage said as plainly and firmly as he could manage. 'There are more important things to consider than who gets Athlot's hut.'

'Might be to you,' Grimulf muttered. 'You don't have to live with the smith.'

'What's this then?' the smith called cheerfully as he stepped out to join them.

Hermitage felt a huge relief that he might be able to have a sensible conversation at last. If it was with the smith and it wasn't about metal it might be hard work, but it would be better than Grimulf.

'Ah, master smith,' Hermitage said. 'I was just talking to young Grimulf about Athlot.'

'Is that right?'

'Erm, yes. He said that old Athlot talked about the Duke of Normandy.'

'He did,' the smith confirmed. 'He had lively tales of kings and adventures the like of which you wouldn't believe.'

'Really?' Hermitage gave Grimulf a sharp glance at this, but the young lad only shrugged his disinterest.

'Oh yes. I mean most folk's talk is about crops and weather and animals and the like. Things they've seen and done, which the rest of us have already seen and done for ourselves.'

Hermitage knew that most tavern conversation was

extraordinarily dull and repetitive.

'Take me, for example,' the smith went on. 'I can talk about smithing for as long as you like.'

Hermitage knew that.

'But old Athlot had wild tales.'

'I see.' Hermitage didn't want to press too quickly, in case the smith started to get confused. 'Including the Duke of Normandy, William.'

'That's him,' the smith said. 'And Athlot would make up the most fanciful tales about how he'd been to Normandy. How he knew old King Aethelred. Made me laugh, he did.'

'You think he made the tales up?'

'Well, of course. That's what old folk do, isn't it? They make up tall tales to keep people interested. No one would talk to them otherwise. Anyway, who in Derby has ever met any kings?'

'I have,' Hermitage said.

The smith and Grimulf looked at Hermitage with wide eyes.

'So have Wat and Cwen.'

'Never,' the smith breathed.

'Of course. I am the King's Investigator.'

'Well, yes, but the old sheriff said he was the king's sheriff, but he'd never met the king.'

'I expect he might have done when he went off to Hastings with him.'

'Oh, ar.' The smith sombrely acknowledged that that meeting might have been a brief one. 'But you've met the king?'

'I have. Several times. He has summoned me to investigate on too many occasions and has given me his own instruction.'

The smith closed one eye and looked sideways at

Hermitage. 'Oh, really?' he asked in the manner of one accusing another of ridiculous exaggeration.

'Yes,' Hermitage said firmly. 'But it's not my meetings that are in question, it's Athlot's.'

'He never really met no kings,' the smith dismissed Athlot's storytelling.

It was clear that the smith was going to treat any detailed information as fanciful nonsense. Hermitage needed to find out Athlot's true history. If he had had dealings with kings and courts, he could well have been a marked man. With William's conquest of England, Athlot's life may have been put in danger.

While knowing that William and the Normans were ruthless killers, he thought that pushing an old man off a roof would not be their chosen method. A simple sword would do the job; preferably several. Still, it was a horrible connection that had to be considered. How was he to find out more, though?

'Did Athlot share his tales around town?' he asked. Perhaps there was a more reliable source than the smith and his horrible apprentice.

'Didn't get out much,' the smith said. 'He was ninety, you know.'

'Yes, I suppose so. But you looked after him. Checked he was well, as you said. And you listened to his tales.'

'That I did. And young Grimulf went round regular like.'

Hermitage thought that if he was ninety, the last thing he would want was young Grimulf coming round.

He wondered where to start. Wat had said that Athlot had been here when he arrived, but perhaps the old man had told the smith more. 'Had he been here long? In Derby, I mean.'

'Oh, yes, a good many years. Long as I can remember.'

'And how long have you been here?'

'All my life,' the smith said proudly. 'I went away as apprentice, but soon came back. Don't think much of away. There's funny people away.'

'I'm sure,' Hermitage smiled. 'And Athlot was always here?'

'Oh yes.'

'How many years is that?'

'Years?' the smith sounded puzzled.

Perhaps the man wasn't as familiar with counting time in years as a farmer might be.

'How old are you?' Hermitage specified.

No, that didn't help.

'How many summers?' he tried.

'Well, my old mother says it's twenty-seven.'

'Twenty-seven, eh?'

'Ar. But she can't count. Sounds about right, though.'

'Which means Athlot was already sixty-three when you were born.'

'Good God.' The smith seemed genuinely taken back by the calculation. 'Isn't that a thing?'

Hermitage would have to ask Wat how long he had been in Derby, but he was sure it would be less than that. Wat himself could only be thirty, or so, and had established himself in the tapestry trade well before he built his workshop.

'So,' Hermitage reasoned, mainly for his own benefit. 'How did Athlot spend his younger years? It is perfectly possible that he was not in Derby at all. He may well have been out in the world as a young man, travelling and meeting kings.'

'Well, I never.' The smith shook his head, seemingly not so much at the possibility he might have been wrong about Athlot, but that someone might have willingly spent their life away from Derby.

'After all,' Hermitage said. 'He would have been born around the year nine-hundred and eighty, give or take. Assuming he kept good count of his years, that is.'

'Nine-hundred?' Grimulf was disbelieving. 'There ain't no such year.'

Hermitage didn't want to delve into that particular aspect of the apprentice's ignorance.

'So,' Hermitage thought and spoke to himself. 'That would have been in the reign of Aethelred. The first one.'

'The first Aethelred?' the smith asked.

'No, the first reign. He was made king around nine-seventy-eight, if memory serves, but was only a child at the time.'

Smith and apprentice appeared to be genuinely interested in all of this.

'I need to refer to a history, but there was an invasion about the year ten-thirteen or so.' Hermitage was quite excited at the thought of having to refer to a history. 'King Sweyn Forkbeard, the Dane, ruled while Aethelred was in exile, but that only lasted a month or two, I think. Then Aethelred returned for a second reign until he died.

'I believe he was about fifty years old at his death, which would have given time for Athlot to grow and be engaged in the king's service in his youth. After all, the king would only have been some twelve years older.'

Having reached his conclusion, he knew what he had to do. 'Is there anyone in town who might have been here before Athlot arrived?'

'Oh, well,' the smith was thoughtful. 'I suppose old Jacob.'

'Old Jacob,' Hermitage checked.

The smith tutted at himself. 'But then he's dead. Has been

for a while.'

'Someone alive?' Hermitage managed to ask without sounding too incredulous.

'Hm,' the smith had to give this some serious consideration.

'Your old mother, perhaps?'

'That's an idea. She's pretty old.'

'And alive?'

'Oh, yes. She is that.' The smith didn't sound too happy about this, but it was a start. 'And she says she's fifty if you can believe that.'

'It sounds about right.'

'Been fifty for many years now as well,' the smith added.

'Erm, right. Perhaps you could direct me to her home?'

'I can.' The smith sounded quite proud of knowing where his mother lived. 'Are you saying that some of what Athlot said might be true? That about the kings and all?'

'It is possible. He was certainly old enough. And if we can find out that he came to Derby and did not live here all his life, it may make it more certain.'

'What's it got to do with him falling off his roof though?' the smith asked. 'That's the question.'

'It is,' Hermitage agreed. 'And it could be nothing. But if he was a man with high connections, someone may have wished him harm.'

'An old man in a hovel? What trouble could he be?'

'It may have been revenge,' Hermitage said. 'For something Athlot did in the past.'

The smith and his apprentice clearly thought that was very exciting.

'Oh, my,' Hermitage expressed shock at his recollection. 'I've just remembered.'

'Who revenged on him?'

'No, I've just recalled where Aethelred went into exile. Normandy.'

'Where the Duke comes from?' Grimulf checked.

'Exactly,' Hermitage confirmed, his horrible sinking feeling girding itself for action.

Caput XII: The Smith's Mother

The smith, explaining that his wheel was only resting before the next stage of the process, instructed Grimulf to take Hermitage to his mother.

Both monk and apprentice clearly thought this a tiresome suggestion. Grimulf simply had to do what he was told, even if it was with bad grace, while Hermitage didn't want to cause any trouble, which he did with good grace.

'Come on then,' Grimulf complained as if he were being asked to carry a monk to London.

'Is it far?' Hermitage asked as they walked down the lane towards the centre of the town. He wondered if the smith's mother might be on a farm somewhere. After all, it would be more normal for the smith's family to all live with him in the smithy. If his parents had their own trade, it would explain why they were elsewhere.

'Here we are,' Grimulf announced when they'd only walked for a couple of moments. He gestured with little interest towards a neat-looking home set on the side of the road.

It too was a traditional Saxon dwelling, although it showed considerably more signs of life than Athlot's silent hut.

'Are you coming in?' Hermitage asked.

'God, no,' Grimulf said with a genuine shock at the suggestion. Hermitage couldn't quite tell if it were disgust or fear, but he didn't like either.

'You just tell her the smith sent you,' Grimulf said as he turned back to the smithy. Hermitage did not like the way the young man was sniggering as he went.

'Erm, hello?' he called into the dark interior of the place. He couldn't imagine this woman called herself mistress smith, so didn't know what else to say.

'Hello?' a voice called back from within, and the call was quite alarming to Hermitage's ear. He had read ancient tales of sirens singing men to their deaths, but he knew that they didn't live in Derby. Nonetheless, he declined to enter the room, telling himself that it would be rude without a formal invitation.

A movement on the border between light and dark even prompted him to take a step back.

A woman appeared in the entrance and leant nonchalantly, and very deliberately against the doorpost.

'Oh,' she said in plain disappointment. 'It's a monk.' It sounded as if she were complaining about people who left monks at her door.

'Brother Hermitage,' Hermitage announced with a bow.

'Get in here,' the woman instructed, grabbing him by the habit and pulling hard. 'We don't want anyone to see.'

'We don't?' Hermitage managed to ask as he found himself inside the hut.

His eyes quickly grew accustomed to the gloom, and he took in his situation. The home was very neat and well ordered, and showed signs of considerable comfort. A good chair sat against one wall while a bed of fresh straw lay at the back. Over the fire in the middle of the room, a fine set of irons hung, and the smell of the cooking was quite wholesome.

Either the smith's parents were rich enough in their own right, or their son provided well for them.

He turned to his host and gave a smiling nod to the smith's mother. He had to assume this was she as Grimulf had brought him to this very house. However, if this woman were fifty, someone had invented a new system of counting.

He could tell that she had once been fifty, after all,

everyone over fifty had been fifty once. But only the once. He simply assumed that in her case, she could remember that far back. Why she would claim to be an age she most assuredly wasn't, was not something Hermitage could fathom.

'Erm, the smith sent me?' Hermitage suggested. Could it be that this was the smith's grandmother and he had the wrong person altogether?

'He's a good boy,' the woman said. 'I had him very young before you ask.'

Hermitage hadn't been going to ask. 'Yes,' he was very confused, 'I suppose he would have been.'

'Not him, silly, me.' She smiled. 'Wassa,' she introduced herself.

'Mistress Wassa,' Hermitage nodded but found that the smile made him very nervous for some reason.

'But his father went and died,' she explained for no obvious reason.

'I am sorry,' Hermitage said.

'Left a real mess behind.'

'Ah, I see.' Hermitage didn't see and didn't really want to.

'Silly man, he was.' Wassa now beckoned that Hermitage could take the chair and make himself comfortable.

Hermitage felt that sitting in the chair, so far from the door, would not be very comfortable at all, but he couldn't be rude. He sat carefully while the woman turned to her pot.

'A farmer,' she went on.

'Was he?' Hermitage had to assume she was still talking about the dead husband.

'Owned his own land and everything.'

'Really?' Hermitage asked. That was unusual. If this husband had been a landowner, what was Wassa doing in this situation?

'Fought for the king, he did.'

'Which one?' Hermitage asked with interest.

'Why, Edward of course. There's only been three, haven't there? Edward, Harold and now William.'

'Only three,' Hermitage nodded. 'Well, if you like.'

'And the king rewarded him with a bit of land. Not a lot, but enough.'

'Very good. He must have been well-thought-of.'

'Oh, he was. And it was good land. Served us well. Bought the land for this house and everything. But then he went and came down with the droops, he did.'

'The droops?' Hermitage hadn't heard of that before. Probably some local name for a perfectly normal disease.

'Everything drooped until he could do no more.'

Hermitage just nodded, not really having anything to say.

'And before he drooped his last, he went and did a very silly thing,' Wassa laughed a tinkling laugh; tinkling like a bell falling from a church tower. 'He left all his land to the town to look after unless I married again.'

'Did he?'

'He was always looking out for me, bless him.'

The words "bless him" were said with quite inappropriate vindictiveness.

'Of course, my son takes care of me, and the town pay me something for the crops they grow on my land, but it's not right, is it?'

'Erm.' He hoped she wasn't going to ask about the price of crops. He knew nothing of such matters.

'Him leaving his land like that. It should have come to me.' She got to the nub of her question and was suddenly very plain speaking.

'Well, yes, I suppose it should have,' Hermitage said as he

gave the matter some thought. It was a more comfortable problem to consider than finding a husband for mistress Wassa.

'You agree?' the woman sounded quite surprised.

Hermitage tipped his head from side to side as he went through the process. He was not an expert in this area at all, but he had dealt with donations to one or two of his monasteries, frequently being the only one who could reliably read and write and not simply copy the shapes of letters.

And the families of those who had died were as pleased with part of their inheritance going to a monastery as Wassa was losing her land to the town.

'Did your husband write down this arrangement of his?'

'Write it down? Lord no. He could make his mark, but that was about it.'

'Did someone else record it and he made his mark?'

Wassa shook her head, 'Not that I know of.'

'Who told you that it was the case, then?'

'The headman.'

'Your husband never even mentioned it?'

'Not to me,' Wassa snorted and spat in the fire, all pretence having been abandoned.

'Is it not the sort of thing he would discuss? It is quite common for men to die before their wives and preparations have to be made.'

'Spent all his time in Ern's alehouse,' Wassa complained.

'Did you challenge the situation?'

'I did, and I do. I complained to the headman, but he said there was nothing to be done. Unless I married again and my new husband straightened everything out.'

'The headman being the one who told you about it in the first place,' Hermitage pointed out. 'And none of the men of the town have shown any interest in wedding you, even though they would get the land?'

'Men,' Wassa grunted.

'Indeed,' Hermitage could only agree. He frequently found it hard to raise his sense of suspicion, even when he was dealing with a murder. Now, it was positively racing all on its own. 'Then how do we know it's true?'

'Beg pardon?' Wassa asked.

'You may have heard that I am the King's Investigator?'

'Oh, is that you?' Wassa seemed surprised. 'Yes, I suppose it would be, now you come to mention it.'

'In that role, I mainly deal with murder, but I have to consider situations such as this.'

'My husband was murdered?' Wassa was horrified.

'No, no,' Hermitage assured her. 'I have no reason to think he didn't die of the droop, whatever it is. No, I mean dishonesty. People perhaps hiding the truth or giving only part of it.'

Wassa frowned.

Hermitage laid it out. 'It seems to me that there are two possibilities. First, your husband did make this bequest, but there is no record of it. He didn't write it down and no one else did either. In that case, I can't see how it can be enforced. The inheritance should come to you, as you say.'

Wassa grinned broadly. 'And the other?' she asked carefully.

Hermitage didn't want to cause trouble without evidence; he didn't really like to cause it when there was evidence, but somehow it had to be said. 'What if there is a, erm, misunderstanding? Your husband actually made no such bequest, but the headman thinks he did?'

'Why would he think that?'

'You'd have to ask him.'

'I have tried,' Wassa seemed crestfallen.

'Your son?' Hermitage suggested.

Wassa sighed. 'If it's not made of metal, he doesn't understand it. He's a good boy, but this is beyond him.'

'Then you need some help,' Hermitage said.

'Really?' Wassa was almost tearful. 'Dear Brother, you are the first person who has ever listened to me, let alone taken my side and said what can be done. How can I thank you?'

'Oh, er, well, I wasn't really thinking of me dealing with the headman.'

Wassa sagged.

'I can look into the matter and find what authority I can,' Hermitage thought quickly. 'But there is perhaps someone who could take your case to the headman in a very direct manner.'

'Really?'

'Yes,' Hermitage said. 'Have you ever met Cwen the weaver?'

'No.' Wassa looked rather alarmed. 'But I've heard about her.'

'I shall talk to her, but I think she could be just the person.' He was already feeling quite sorry for the headman.

'Bless you, Brother, bless you.' Wassa left her pot and came over to give Hermitage a hearty hug, which was quite uncomfortable. She even kissed him on both cheeks, which was even worse.

'Oh, this is a wonderful day,' Wassa said and did a little skip back to her pot. 'Brother, you shall eat from my hearth.'

'That is very kind,' Hermitage said, happy to stay now that he understood the situation. 'There was actually something I wanted to ask you,' he said as she busied herself finding bowls and bread.

'Anything, anything at all.'

'It's about old Athlot.'

Wassa instantly stopped being quite so cheery. 'Athlot.' She said the name as if she'd just found some Athlot at the bottom of her pot and it had ruined the stew.

'Erm, yes. Your son said he had been here as long as he could remember, but that you might know more.'

'Oh, I know about Athlot,' Wassa said, it being plain that she knew very little that was good. 'He was one of the worst.'

'The worst? Worst at what?'

'Him and that alehouse and my husband. Always leading him astray. Giving him ideas.'

'Ideas, eh?'

'That's right. Scheming and plotting. It was all right for old Athlot, he'd made his fortune, didn't need to work. But my husband had the farm to run and money to make.'

'I'm not sure I follow?'

Wassa explained. 'Athlot could afford to do nothing and spend his time chatting in the alehouse.'

'He had money, then?'

'He did. Came into Derby with it, what, forty years ago, probably.'

'When he was fifty,' Hermitage said. He didn't like to add that Wassa would have been ten by her own reckoning.

'And my husband looked up to him and listened to all his nonsense. Put ideas in his head, he did. And he followed him around like a dog. Spent all our earnings on a life he could ill afford.'

'Athlot's home showed no signs of wealth,' Hermitage said.

'No. Said he'd been a soldier all his life and that was how he liked to live.'

'But he had money somewhere if he was spending it at the alehouse.'

'I suppose he must have done.'

'You don't know where it went?'

Wassa was firm and clear. 'I had no interest in Athlot when he was alive and even less now he's dead. He was a bad lot and good riddance. Begging your pardon, Brother.'

'Your husband spent a lot of time with him?'

'Too much time. Every waking minute. You'd think he was married to Athlot instead of me.'

'So they might have discussed any plan your husband had for the farm?'

'I suppose,' Wassa admitted. 'But we won't know now, will we?'

'No, I suppose we won't,' Hermitage said, a new suspicion coming horribly quickly after the last one. He glanced around the comforts of Wassa's home once more; her own home. The one she kept instead of living with her son, the smith. The smith behind whose workshop, Athlot lived with his secret wealth and perhaps knowledge of Wassa's inheritance. Before he apparently fell off a ladder, that is.

Caput XIII: Final Approach

$\mathfrak{F}$ortmain had driven the pace of the rest of the day as if the mother of Scemund herself were on his tail.

'The horses will not keep this up,' Edgulf warned him when they stopped briefly for water.

'Then we shall have fresh horses.'

'Steal fresh horses,' Edgulf corrected.

'How much farther is it?' Fortmain asked. 'This Derby place?'

'I don't know,' Edgulf replied.

'What do you mean, you don't know? We're travelling the country looking for the king's man and you don't know where he is?'

'I just don't know how much farther it is,' Edgulf explained. 'We didn't come this way last time. Nor on horses and it took us ten days.'

'Ten days?' Fortmain was horrified. 'It is in Scotland.'

'It is not in Scotland. We travelled on carts before. They don't run away from danger like horses.' Edgulf felt he had got the measure of this Norman and was prepared to risk issuing the occasional challenge. He did recognise him as one whose favoured opponents were the defenceless, though, so had to be a little careful.

'Do you even know where we are?'

'We took the north road after Ely. Briefly captured by the Saxons in the woods...,'

'Distracted,' Fortmain corrected.

Edgulf bowed his head sarcastically. 'Distracted by being captured by the Saxons in the woods. And since then, we've been riding like the devil for the best part of the afternoon.' He glanced up at the sky. 'It wants an hour of sunset now, so we must have come about fifty miles, I reckon.'

'And how many miles is Derby?'

'I don't know,' Edgulf said rather more forcefully than he intended.

Fortmain drew his sword. It took a bit of fiddling about as he was sitting on his horse and he had to slip over to the side a bit which diluted the impact considerably, but when he eventually got the thing out and untangled it from his cloak, he brandished it at Edgulf. 'Perhaps we'd better find someone who does know.'

His men looked over with little interest.

'All right, all right,' Edgulf surrendered.

'After all,' Fortmain said thoughtfully. 'once we're there, what do we need you for at all?'

'I'm coming for Brother Hermitage,' Edgulf reminded him.

'Yes, but I'm not interested in you, am I? You're only the means to get me to the king's man. Once we're there you're no longer required. In fact, when we find the place, we can leave you in a ditch while I go and offer service.'

'Why would I find the place, then?' Edgulf challenged. 'In fact, why should I tell you who the King's Investigator is once we get there. Only I know him.'

'We can ask,' Fortmain said with a horrible wave of his sword. 'We Normans are good at getting people to tell us things. And how many monks are there going to be called Brother Hermitage? Stupid name for a monk anyway.'

Edgulf worried that Fortmain was getting quite decisive. It probably wouldn't last.

'We shall ask the next peasant we come across, then you can be gone.' The Norman wheeled his mount away so that he could try to put his sword back without falling off.

Marcus and Aurelius walked their horse up to Edgulf.

'I know where Derby is,' Marcus said quietly.

'God,' Aurelius moaned to herself. 'I won't be able to walk for a week.'

'You do?'

'Interests there,' was all Marcus would say.

'Are we close?' Edgulf asked in a whisper.

Marcus nodded once while looking sideways to check there were no Normans in earshot.

Edgulf gave it a moment's thought. 'Do you think we'll arrive tonight?'

Marcus nodded again.

'Right. We say nothing then. If we simply ride into town and Fortmain discovers we've arrived, it'll be too late to leave us in any ditches.'

'I think it was only you he was going to put in a ditch,' Marcus pointed out.

'Thank you very much,' Edgulf hissed. 'I can always ask to have you for company.'

'Only saying,' Marcus shrugged.

Edgulf looked up and down the track. 'No one about, so hopefully, he won't find any peasants to ask.'

'Right,' Fortmain called everyone to order. 'We ride on for half an hour or stop at the next village, whichever comes first. Then we'll have directions to Derby for ourselves.' He gave Edgulf an unnecessary look; a look that said the Saxon would soon be unnecessary.

The pace was a little slower now, but the horses were still trotting along, even if they did need more encouragement than earlier.

After a while, they came to a bridge. It was a large bridge and spanned quite an expanse of water, which was something to be thankful for. But it wasn't a good bridge.

The wooden piles looked like they'd been driven in by someone who thought the benefits of a level surface had been exaggerated. On top of the piles, wooden planks appeared to have been scattered at random and there was no telling if they'd been nailed down at all.

Nonetheless, there were people on the bridge and no one floundering about in the water.

'We have to cross that?' Fortmain asked. He sounded contemptuous of the Saxon idea of a bridge and fearful of the Saxon water that flowed underneath, even if it did not look too deep.

In fact, this place appeared to have once been a ford, but a bridge had been put up for the convenience of travellers, if not as an exemplar of bridge construction.

'That wasn't here last time I came this way,' Marcus whispered to Edgulf.

'Doesn't look like it's been up long,' Edgulf observed. 'Nor that it's going to stay up much longer.'

'Come on, then,' Fortmain ordered with profound resignation.

'There will be a toll,' Marcus warned.

'We're Normans, we don't pay tolls.'

A couple of miles beyond the bridge, with Fortmain still trying to work out why he'd parted with the toll to a very persuasive Saxon standing at a table, the first simple Saxon home appeared on the side of the road.

They had been promised they were nearly at Derby, but the toll man very strongly implied that only another toll would get them clear directions. Fortmain refused to pay that one.

'We'll ask here,' Fortmain announced.

The Saxons said nothing as they let the Norman dismount,

secure his horse, walk over to the place and peer through the hole where the door used to be. The complete absence of thatch on the roof, animals or any other sign of life made the chance of getting directions remote.

'There's no one here,' Fortmain called over.

'Really?' Marcus asked, containing a smirk very poorly. 'Perhaps they're out.'

'Places with roofs tend to be more popular,' Aurelius suggested.

Fortmain looked at the house, then at each of them and pointed that finger of his. 'You are all at risk of not making it as far as Derby,' he growled.

The next place along the track came quite quickly and this was occupied. In fact, there was a woman outside tending to vegetables and pulling weeds.

'You there,' Fortmain called.

The woman looked up and considered the arrivals with serious concern. The Saxons tried to give her comforting glances, but the presence of the armed Normans was a major distraction. She stood up straight and appeared to be waiting for instructions.

'Where is Derby?' Fortmain asked.

The woman did not reply.

'Derby,' Fortmain repeated much louder.

The woman smiled.

'She must be an idiot,' he said to his men. 'Do you understand me?' he mouthed and shouted. 'Can you speak?'

The woman nodded.

'Well, do so. Where is Derby?'

'Where is it?' the woman asked. 'How do you mean?'

'How do I mean? It's a simple question. Where is Derby?'

'Where is Derby?' The woman seemed to be considering

the question carefully. 'It's in England,' she said.

'Gods above. I know it's in England. Where is it? Which way?'

The woman scratched her head. 'Which way is Derby? Which way is it supposed to be?'

'Oh, Lord. They're all idiots. Come on, we'll ask someone else.' Fortmain gestured and the Normans followed him up the road. Edgulf, Marcus and Aurelius trailed along behind. As they passed the woman she stepped up and whispered to the Saxons.

'They do know this is Derby, don't they?'

'We haven't told them,' Aurelius said. 'Let them find out for themselves.'

The woman nodded. 'They idiots, then?'

'They are, yes.'

'Oh, good. I'd heard Normans were, but it's nice to know.'

'We're looking for Brother Hermitage,' Edgulf said.

'Oh, yes?' the woman asked with interest. 'You going to murder one of the Normans?'

'It's a thought.'

'Brother Hermitage will find you out,' she cautioned.

'I know all about Brother Hermitage and murder,' Edgulf was serious. 'He's still at the workshop?'

'Far as I know.'

'Not gone off on any investigations?'

'I saw him in town only yesterday. Wandering about looking at things like normal. Well, not normal for normal folk, normal for him.'

'Right,' Edgulf nodded. 'I suppose we'd better go and tell the Normans we're in Derby before they find out for themselves. They'll only get cross.'

They quickly caught up with Fortmain.

'We got it out of the woman,' Edgulf said. 'This is Derby.'

'This is Derby?' Any hope of the Norman not getting cross was quickly lost. 'What do you mean, this is Derby? How could you not know this is Derby? Are you playing games with me?'

'Not at all. It's like I said, we didn't come from the south last time. And we had carriages. I've never been on this road before.'

'Where's the monk, then?'

'He'll be at the workshop.'

'What workshop? A monk's workshop?'

'No, no, the workshop of Wat the Weaver. That's where he lives.'

Fortmain went horribly quiet. Then he started shaking slightly, which was a worry.

'The workshop of who?' he asked very slowly and very deliberately.

'Wat the Weaver?' Edgulf made it sound like a timid question.

'This monk, the King's Invigilator...,'

'Investigator.'

'Don't correct me. This monk lives with Wat the Weaver?' Fortmain seemed caught between anger and disgust.

'That's right.' Edgulf tried a light laugh. 'Funny, isn't it?'

'No, it is not funny. There is nothing funny about Wat the Weaver.'

'Wat the Weaver, eh?' Aurelius said with uncomfortable interest. 'You've erm, you've heard of him, then?' she asked the simple question but it somehow sounded positively inappropriate.

'Oh, I've heard of him,' Fortmain said in a very unfriendly manner. 'Why didn't you tell me this before now?'

'You didn't ask,' Edgulf said honestly.

'How am I supposed to ask if he lives with Wat the Weaver? I'd end up asking if everyone lives with Wat the Weaver.'

Edgulf's response; if it's that important, perhaps you should, was on his tongue but he managed to keep it there.

Fortmain appeared to be thinking seriously, a look that did not sit well on his face. 'How many people in this workshop?' he asked.

'No idea,' Edgulf said, wondering how on earth he was supposed to know. 'We've only just got here.'

'But you've been here before.' Fortmain now sounded as if he thought Edgulf was involved in some conspiracy against him. Tricking him into coming to the workshop for just this moment.

'Well, yes. But we only saw Wat and Cwen and Hermitage.'

'Who's Cwen?'

'Another weaver. Young girl, really.'

'He has young girls weaving?' Fortmain had moved on to horror at the goings-on of Wat the Weaver.

'She seemed to be more sort of, in charge really,' Edgulf offered.

'Just the three of them then?' Fortmain cast a glance at his men as if reminding himself how many he had. As it was three, it didn't seem a difficult total to recall. 'And four of us.'

'There were apprentices as well, I believe. And a weaving master of some sort.'

'So, there could be more.' Fortmain considered this information carefully.

'Unless they've all gone out,' Edgulf said.

Fortmain seemed to think this a serious suggestion but put

it to one side. 'We need to find out how many they are. What is the disposition of their forces?'

'Disposition of their forces?' Edgulf asked with some surprise. 'It's a weaver's workshop, I don't think they do disposition of forces.'

Fortmain did not reply.

'Are you thinking of attacking the workshop? The workshop full of weavers and the king's monk?' As he said this, he thought that it sounded like the perfect target for Fortmain's band; if they couldn't find a convent; one where all the stronger nuns were out at market.

'Wat the Weaver,' was all Fortmain said with a nasty growl.

'Just go and knock on the door,' Edgulf suggested.

'We need a scheme,' Fortmain ignored the perfectly sensible suggestion.

'Do we?' Edgulf asked. 'To get Wat the Weaver to come to his own door?'

Fortmain was so deep in thought he appeared not to hear anything. 'You came here about some murders, didn't you?'

'Oh, erm, well, yes.'

'So you can knock on the door. We'll lie in wait.'

'Lie in wait?'

'That's it. You go up there as if you've just arrived to see the king's man. These other two can go with you, then they'll think it's just a band of harmless Saxons.'

This was not how Edgulf had planned to approach Brother Hermitage. He wanted to get him alone, not have an audience standing by. He had also assumed that Marcus and Aurelius's interests in Derby would not involve the King's Investigator or Wat the Weaver. There was no getting rid of the Normans though, and the truth of his purpose was bound to come out now that he was here.

He supposed that he couldn't keep it hidden forever but hadn't really prepared himself for the revelation. There was no telling how the Normans would react and things might not go well. Nevertheless, he had come this far with his mission, he would not turn away now. Let the fates bring him what they may.

'I'll go alone,' he said. 'Even less suspicious, one man on his own in the evening.'

Fortmain considered this for a moment and then nodded once.

They had entered the main town of Derby now and the horses walked slowly up the main street, carefully observed by all who were out and about on their daily tasks.

The small gathering at Ern's alehouse watched the passage as well. Everyone kept still and quiet, in case the Normans decided to do something Norman to them all. The fact that three Saxons were accompanying the invaders was unfathomable, as they didn't look like captives.

Breath was released when the mounted party kept going on up the street, one of the Saxons announcing that their destination was "this way".

Once they were out of earshot, conclusions were quickly drawn. Brother Hermitage. No one else brought strange people to town. Wat the Weaver had brought strange people to town in his day, but they were strange in a different way.

A lively debate soon began about whether having the King's Investigator in town was a protection from trouble or a source of it.

Fortmain and the band continued up the northern road until the turn off for the workshop. The building was quickly spied, and the Normans drew to a halt.

'Right,' Fortmain said. 'On you go. And no tricks.'

Edgulf wasn't clear what tricks he could perform, but he was happy that the Normans were staying this far back. At least he could deal privately with Brother Hermitage. Even if they rushed over at the first opening of the door, it would be several moments before they reached him. Time aplenty.

The sun was dipping on the horizon, casting an orange glow over the scene as Edgulf dismounted his horse and stepped up to the front door.

He took one deep breath; his resolution having been girded during the last yards of his journey.

He knocked heavily and spoke the words he had prepared all those days ago.

'Brother Hermitage,' he cried. 'I have come to do a murder.'

Caput XIV: A Touch of History

Hermitage left mistress Wassa to her newfound hope and wandered back up towards the smithy. He needed to talk to Cwen, but that could wait. His new concern was Athlot's wealth.

The suggestion that a man could fall off a ladder and die was perfectly reasonable. The idea of an old man doing it was a little more peculiar but not impossible. The thought of a rich man doing it was quite ridiculous.

If Athlot still had his wealth he would have paid a craftsman to attend to his roof. Yes, he may well have been a soldier and been used to looking after himself, but why risk climbing a ladder at his age when he could afford to pay someone else to do it.

If there was a hiding place somewhere in or around his hovel it needed to be found. If the money was gone, there was motive for murder. If it was still there, he would have to think again.

Which took him on to Athlot's history. It now seemed perfectly reasonable that he had been in the service of King Aethelred. Wassa confirmed that he had been a soldier and had only arrived in Derby forty years ago, which would be somewhere in the reign of King Cnut.

If Athlot had served Aethelred during his exile in Normandy, he may well have been known to the duke. Hermitage was happy to enumerate the kings of England, but his knowledge of Norman history was pretty sparse. He knew that William's father had been called Robert but that was about it.

Had Robert been duke when Aethelred was there? Ignorance of historical details was far more frustrating than not knowing where some coins were hidden.

Had Aethelred been trouble to the Normans? Was Athlot involved somehow? If so, were the memories of the Normans so long that they would come looking for him?

He was sure that the smith would have mentioned if a group of Normans turned up to push Athlot off his ladder. And, as he had thought earlier, if Normans wanted revenge, they would make it far more obvious. What was the point of doing someone harm if all those nearby couldn't be terrified at the same time?

The question was, how to find out? Most of the books he had amassed were religious texts. There were several histories, but they were devoted entirely to England, which was understandable.

They did cover foreign kings and people, but only when they invaded England, which was admittedly quite often. Most of those were Danes of some sort. Sweyn, Cnut, Harold Harefoot. There hadn't been any Normans until there were the Normans. And they were here right now.

Oh, that was a thought. It was a ridiculous one, and he tried to tell himself not to even pursue it beyond the smithy, but he was the King's Investigator. Perhaps he could ask the king?

No, that was simply ridiculous. He was not going to go anywhere near any of the Norman nobles simply to look further into the question of whether Athlot had fallen off a ladder.

But maybe they had their own histories he could consult? He knew where his own volume that referred to Aethelred was, but then he knew where all his volumes were. He would consult that to see if there was any mention of Athlot. Then he would have to think where to get hold of a Norman history. Nottingham, perhaps? Or, even if there were no book, he could talk to Gilbert of Nottingham, see what he might know.[The Tapestry of Death and A Murder of Convenience; major roles for Gilbert.]

He was back at the smithy now and the thought of searching for hidden coin instead of researching history was a real disappointment.

'Back again?' Grimulf complained as he saw Hermitage approach. The boy was sitting on the step of the smithy, throwing small bits of stone into the road. A complete waste of time for a smith's apprentice, as far as Hermitage could see,

'I simply need to look at Athlot's home more closely.'

'You're not going to move in, are you?' Grimulf asked anxiously.

'No, no, I am not going to move in.'

'Just make sure you don't.'

'I couldn't move in,' Hermitage pointed out. 'We don't know who the place belongs to. Did Athlot leave it to anyone? Did he even own it in the first place, or was he a tenant? Doubtless, the new Norman lord will have his say.'

Hermitage felt quite guilty as he considered Grimulf's fallen face.

'Talking of which, did you ever see any Normans visiting Athlot?'

'Normans?' Grimulf clearly found the question quite unbelievable. 'Why would Normans visit Athlot?'

'That's what I want to find out.'

'There haven't been no Normans round here. If I'd seen one, I'd know.'

'I'm sure you would. Any strangers at all? Did Athlot ever have meetings with people from out of town?'

'Not that I saw, but then I wasn't watching him, was I? Not my job to look after him.'

'They'd have walked right past your door,' Hermitage said.

'Well, I didn't see them.' Grimulf obviously felt he was being accused of something.

'Grimulf!' the smith's voice barked from inside. 'Where are you boy? Get the wheel.'

Grimulf jumped up and ran quickly into the smithy. He emerged a moment later dragging the cartwheel behind him, which he hauled out onto the ground in front of the building where he lay it on its side. He then fetched a number of blocks of wood which he placed under the rim of the wheel so that the whole thing lay horizontal.

'Quick now,' the smith called.

Grimulf ran back inside and a moment later reappeared with the smith, the two of them carrying a metal hoop between them with long tongs.

The metal was clearly very hot as it steamed and spat as it was brought out.

Hermitage watched with interest. He had seen this done before but it was always an interesting process.

Carrying the hoop over to the wheel, the smith and Grimulf lowered it until it sat around the edge of the wheel rim.

The smith now took a hammer from his belt and looked to Grimulf. 'Where's your hammer?'

Grimulf ducked back into the smithy again and emerged with his own hammer, to be greeted by the disappointed shaking of the smith's head.

Together, the two of them hammered at the hoop until it slipped over the rim of the wheel and came to rest on the blocks of wood.

'Water,' the smith called.

Once again, Grimulf disappeared and returned with a leather bucket of water, which he handed to the smith.

The man now walked around the wheel, dousing the metal hoop with water, which almost immediately turned into clouds of billowing steam. Grimulf followed him, tapping the metal hoop to make sure it was centred on the wheel.

Seemingly satisfied with the work. The smith stepped back with the bucket in his hand.

'We'll let it shrink onto the wheel of its own accord now,' he explained to Hermitage. 'Honestly, Grimulf,' he gently chided the boy. 'Sometimes I wonder if you want to be a smith at all. You've got to pay more attention to the job.'

Grimulf ducked his head in apology and took the bucket back into the smithy.

Hermitage took the opportunity to repeat his questions. 'I was asking if Athlot ever had any visitors from out of town. Normans, particularly.'

'Normans?' the smith sounded surprised at the idea. 'No. Never saw Normans. Nor no strangers.'

'Never any visitors?' Hermitage pressed.

'Oh,' the smith recalled. 'He did have a fellow come by, but it was years back. Soon after I came to take over the smithy.'

'When was that?' Hermitage asked.

'When?' the smithy frowned at the tricky question. 'You mean what year?'

'That's it.'

'What year is this?' The smith asked by way of reference.

Hermitage sighed. 'Was it before the Normans?'

'Oh, yes. Definitely before the Normans, because I remember them arriving. That wasn't long ago.'

'No,' Hermitage agreed. 'It wasn't. And did you speak to

this visitor?'

'I did a little. We sat out together one evening.'

'Did you get any idea who he was?'

'Can't recall his name, but they obviously knew one another from way back.'

'Old soldiers together?'

'Aye, could be.'

'And was this visitor a Saxon, or did he talk strangely?'

'No, definitely a Saxon. From down Lesecestre way, I think he said.'

'And did they get on well? Was Athlot happy to see him?'

'Funny you should ask that,' the smith said thoughtfully. 'They was happy enough when we was talking, but he up and left the next day. All quickly like. And they was shouting at one another as he went.'

'What were they shouting?'

'This is a long time ago,' the smith complained.

'Try and think, it could be important.'

'It was something about how the stranger had told Athlot there wasn't time anymore and that he could make his own mind up. It wasn't the stranger's problem anymore.'

'What wasn't a problem?'

'Don't know. But whatever it was, it wasn't his.'

'And he never told you who he was? You never exchanged names?'

'Never.' he shook his head in apology. 'Although, wait a moment.' He clicked his fingers. 'I did overhear a name when he and Athlot were talking outside. Eadric.'

'Eadric?' Hermitage was disappointed that he now had a name and it was no help at all.

'That's what was said.'

'And you never saw this Eadric again?'

'No.'

'How did Athlot seem after his visit? Was he angry, upset?'

'He did stomp about the place for a few days, but soon settled again.'

This was very interesting and could possibly be connected to Athlot's fate, but Hermitage had not the first idea how. Had this Eadric come to warn Athlot of something? And did that something come to pass? It probably wasn't a warning about taking care when climbing ladders.

At least he now had another name he could add to his research. Was there an Eadric involved in Aethelred's court? Perhaps one of his own books might be informative on that.

'This has been most useful, thank you,' Hermitage said. 'I just want to check one more thing at Athlot's and then I shall head home to review my texts.'

'Right you are.' The smith clearly thought that sort of thing was best left to monks.

Back at Athlot's hut, Hermitage could see that there was really very little to look at. The simple room was bare and there was no sign of disturbance on the floor, indicating anything buried.

The space outside was small, just enough for a few vegetables for one man, and if Athlot did have money, he would have been able to buy his food anyway. That was another thing. Did Athlot spend widely in the town? Did he really have money, or was that just a tale? He spent on ale, according to Wassa, but what was the truth? This list of things to check was becoming too much for Hermitage.

He walked around the hut twice and could see no obvious hiding place for a hoard of coin.

The fateful ladder was still there, and he put it more neatly on the ground against the wall of the hut. He patted the thatch as he made to leave and wished that it could tell him its tale. What secrets it would know!

It was only later, as he was drawing near to the workshop that he reprimanded himself quite explicitly. Of course. The coin could have been hidden in the thatch. It would explain what Athlot was doing up the ladder. He wasn't fixing his roof; he was getting his money.

He turned and scurried back to the hut once more and this time got the ladder up and examined the thatch as best he could. Fortunately, it was not a large roof, but the daylight was starting to fade. He may have to return to this tomorrow. And he'd set his heart on going to Nottingham tomorrow to see if Gilbert had any Norman history books.

In his rather cursory search, he found no coin, nor an obvious hiding place, but then hiding coins in roofs wasn't really his area of expertise.

He would have to come back in the morning.

Wandering back to the workshop, he tried to make a list of all the things he had to do and then put it in some sort of order. At this rate, it could be a month before he had all the information he needed, let alone come to a conclusion about what might have happened to Athlot.

The simple fall from the ladder was now a more realistic proposition. If the man did have his money in his roof, of course, he would have been up a ladder. And he was ninety, which made him more likely to fall.

His involvement with Aethelred and the Normans, any connection to Wassa's husband and the bequest, his mysterious visitor Eadric; none of it could have anything to do with his death. He might simply have fallen off a ladder.

Hermitage told himself to simply accept this and stop looking for murder. But he had to know. There must be certainty in this somewhere and he had to get it. If it was the ladder, fine, but it still might not be.

Shaking his head at the imponderables of life, he pushed the door of the workshop open and closed it behind him.

Wat and Cwen were by the main fire in Mrs Grod's cooking area, it being mercifully free of Mrs Grod herself, who had gone back to wherever it was she went at night.

They were saying nothing and seemed very content to sit side by side and gaze into the flames. Hermitage didn't know whether to join them or not. Perhaps they were best left alone.

Wat glanced over. 'Find any killers?' he asked amicably.

'No,' Hermitage said as he moved up to the fire and warmed his hands. 'In fact, my day's investigation has shown that there might not have been one at all.'

'That's nice,' Cwen said in a dreamy sort of voice that he'd never heard her use before.

'I started by being told that old Athlot fell off a ladder and ended the whole day concluding that he may well have fallen off a ladder.'

'No murder at all, then,' Wat said. 'You should be pleased.'

'Yes,' Hermitage agreed. 'I should, but I need certainty. I'm not sure I have that yet.'

'Never mind,' Cwen hummed. 'Have a good night and go looking for it in the morning.'

Hermitage nodded. He could do with a peaceful night to think about all the things that still had to be discovered and to determine whether any of them really needed doing at all now. Perhaps the morning would come with the firm conclusion that there had been no murder at all.

Just as he was preparing to leave Wat and Cwen, there was a heavy knock on the door.

'Who's calling at this time of night?' Wat complained.

Hermitage faced the door and heard a vaguely familiar voice.

'Brother Hermitage,' it cried. 'I have come to do a murder.'

Caput XV: Introductions

Nobody moved.

Hermitage looked at the door as if wondering why it was talking to him.

Wat and Cwen looked as if wondering why he wasn't answering the door when it was obviously for him.

'Someone better see who it is,' Cwen said. 'I don't think they're going away.'

'Ah, yes,' Hermitage agreed without moving.

'Come on.' Wat stood and walked towards the door. 'Sounds like there's only one.' He took Hermitage by the arm and led him to the door. Lifting the large bolt, he pulled on the handle and opened the door.

Standing in front of them was indeed a single figure. A young man and one Hermitage recognised but could not immediately understand.

He knew who this was, but could not, for the life of him, work out what he was doing standing at this door. He should be miles away and the contradiction froze him to the spot.

Eventually, after a few moments of no one saying anything, he had to accept that this person really was here. 'Bart?' he asked.

'Brother Hermitage,' Bart bowed his head.

'Erm, what are you doing here?'

'It is as I said,' Bart replied, glancing back over his shoulder into the darkness, 'but it's got a bit complicated.'

'As you said?'

'I have come to do a murder,' Bart confirmed with a smile.

'To do a murder?' Wat asked as Cwen drew up at his side.

'It's Bart,' she said.

'We know.'

'What's he doing here?'

'Come to do a murder, apparently,' Wat explained.

'Oh, right. Anyone we know?'

'I have come to do a murder with Brother Hermitage,' Bart explained.

'I think we'd have to stop you,' Wat said, clearly not seeing any sign that Bart was a danger to any of them. 'You can't go murdering Hermitage. Why would you want to anyway?'

'No, no,' Bart insisted. 'Not murder him. Do a murder with him.'

'Do one with him? He's really not the type.'

'Investigate,' Bart explained enthusiastically. 'I've come to investigate.'

They all frowned at him now. 'You want to investigate a murder with me?' Hermitage asked.

'That's right,' Bart nodded and smiled.

'Why?'

'The Gudmunds have gone,' Bart said.

'Gone, gone where?'

'The Normans got them.'

There was no obvious way any of that made sense. 'I think you'd better come in and tell all,' Wat said, holding the door wide.

'Ah,' Bart hesitated. 'As I said, it's got a bit complicated. I'm afraid I'm not alone.'

Wat peered out into the gloom. Then he backed away slightly as figures appeared.

'Wat the Weaver,' a Norman voice called out, and it was not a friendly one.

'Hello?' Wat replied hesitantly.

A Norman soldier came forward and stood on the threshold, Bart helpfully standing to one side.

'I am Fortmain,' the Norman announced with grim certainty.

'Fortmain, eh?' Wat replied uncertainly.

'And you shall pay.'

'I shall pay? Pay for what? You being Fortmain?'

'Exactly.'

Wat looked around to see if anyone else had any idea what this man was talking about. 'Have we met?' he tried.

'Certainly not,' Fortmain spat. 'Don't be disgusting.'

'Do I know you at all?'

'I should think not.'

'But I still have to pay?'

'Of course.'

Three more Normans now appeared at Fortmain's side, and there were two other shapes farther back; one of whom seemed to be walking with difficulty.

'This is him,' Fortmain announced to his companions. 'This is Wat the Weaver.'

The other Normans noted the name but didn't seem quite as excited by it as Fortmain.

'And he brought ruination.'

'Did I?' Wat asked politely.

'Don't pretend you don't know.'

'I won't,' Wat assured him. 'I won't pretend anything at all.'

'As if the name Fortmain means nothing to you,' Fortmain scoffed.

'If I said it didn't, I suspect you wouldn't believe me.'

Fortmain drew his sword, quite quickly and effectively this time.

'Oh, now, wait a moment,' Wat said with some urgency, backing away into his hall. 'Bart,' he called. 'What's going on?'

'Who is Bart?' Fortmain asked fiercely.

'Erm, that is?' Wat waved a hand in Bart's direction.

'That is Edgulf,' Fortmain corrected.

'Is it? We know him as Bart.'

Fortmain darted a hard glance at Bart who shrugged.

'Bart, did you bring this Norman?' Cwen stepped in front of Wat. 'Or has he just followed you to make Wat pay for something or other?'

'He sort of caught us,' Bart explained. 'And when I said I was going to the King's Investigator, he said he wanted to come along and offer his service.'

'And make Wat pay?'

'Well, no. I hadn't mentioned Wat at all until we got here. And then he got very cross.'

Cwen addressed Fortmain. 'He's not going to be making Wat pay for anything,' she said with supreme confidence. 'Is he, Hermitage?'

'Oh, er, no,' Hermitage said, thinking it wise to agree with Cwen.

'You see,' Cwen explained to the Norman. 'This is Brother Hermitage, the King's Investigator. The one you want to offer service to. He's a close confidante of the king, Le Pedvin, de Sauveloy and all the other horrible names. And Wat the weaver is under his protection. So, if you want to go back and tell King William that you've killed one of his investigator's men, that's up to you.'

Hermitage thought this a brave approach. He strongly suspected that William would have to be reminded who they were and wouldn't be in the least annoyed if they were all murdered. He'd also never thought of Wat as one of his men.

But Fortmain hesitated.

'Look,' Wat offered sincerely. 'I really don't know who you are or what I'm supposed to have done. But if we sit down, perhaps without swords, you can explain.'

Fortmain's glance skipped from Wat to Hermitage as he tried to resolve his dilemma. Fortunately, the urge not to annoy the king appeared to win and he lowered his sword.

Wat breathed out with relief.

'This is only a chance for you to explain yourself,' Fortmain insisted. 'If that's possible.'

'Any explanations from anyone about anything would be welcome at the moment,' Wat said.

Cwen gave the Norman one last warning glance and then stepped aside to let him pass.

'Have you got any ale?' one of the Normans asked as he walked in and gave the place a rapid appraisal.

'Erm, yes, I suppose so,' Wat said. 'Why don't we all go upstairs, and I'll have some brought up.'

'And some bread,' one of the others added.

'Er, bread yes.'

'And cheese.'

'Right.'

Cwen nodded to Wat to go and sort out the supplies. 'Don't want him deciding to kill you after all,' she hissed.

'It's not fair,' Wat muttered as he went. 'I shouldn't have to feed the people who want me dead.'

The final Norman entered the building and two more figures followed on.

'How many people are out there?' Cwen asked, clearly expecting quite a crowd.

'Only us,' Marcus announced. 'Marcus and Aurelius.'

'The Roman emperor?' Hermitage asked, knowing for certain that these two people were nothing to do with Rome.

'That was it,' Bart said with some relief. 'I knew I'd heard it somewhere.'

Cwen nodded at Marcus but gave Aurelius the kind of glance that was usually saved for people who were going to try and steal your clothes while you were wearing them.

'And she's with you?' she asked Bart.

The young man sighed. 'No one's with me, really. I wanted to come here on my own, but things got in the way.'

'Several of them, it seems,' Cwen noted. 'Well, I suppose you'd better all come in. Let's make an evening of it.'

'Is that a fire?' one of the Normans asked, looking down the hall.

'Yes,' Cwen replied. 'We use them to keep warm and cook things.'

The sarcasm went over the head of the Norman. 'We'll take our food and ale down here,' he said.

His companions seemed to agree that this was a much better idea than listening to Fortmain for any longer than they had to.

'Please yourself,' Cwen directed the rest of them up the stairs and followed herself.

Once in the upper chamber, the organisation was not straightforward. There weren't enough seats for everyone, but Cwen took the one by the empty fireplace and indicated that Fortmain should sit opposite, being the most Norman person in the room.

Hermitage took the window seat while Bart was happy to sit on the floor.

Marcus and Aurelius circled the space like a couple of dogs looking for the best spot before Marcus perched next to Hermitage and Aurelius sat on the floor with Bart.

Bart looked at her, took a gentle sniff and then moved a couple of feet away.

'So, Bart,' Cwen began. 'You said the Gudmunds were

gone?'

'That's right. The Normans came and took the estate. A lot of people ran away.'

'But some stayed to fight?'

'Erm, no, not really. Perhaps I should have said they all ran away. Apart from Lady Gudmund, of course. She was just very cross and was going to give the Normans a piece of her mind.'

'These Normans?' Cwen looked to Fortmain.

'No, some different ones.'

'And you took the chance to leave the Gudmund's service?'

Bart nodded.

'And call yourself Edgulf?'

'Well,' Bart looked rather awkward. 'No one uses their real name these days, in case the, erm, Normans come looking for someone particular.'

'But Edgulf?'

'He was a member of the family.'

'I remember,' Cwen said. 'And not a very nice one.'[The 1066 to Hastings includes Edgulf not being very nice.]

'I just thought that it was a better name to use. People might be a bit wary of me.'

'So, you're not called Edgulf?' Fortmain checked.

'No,' Bart confirmed.

Fortmain simply shook his head as if unable to fathom the idiocy of Saxons.

'And I doubt these two are called Marcus and Aurelius,' Cwen added.

'We are now,' Marcus said.

'You left the Gudmunds and set off for here?' Cwen returned to Bart.

'That's right. With the Gudmunds gone, I had to think

what I was going to do. I mean, I've got no useful trade. Fetching and carrying for the Gudmunds was hardly a craft. And I'm too old to take one up now, aren't I?'

Cwen nodded that there was no getting away from that.

Hermitage could see the young man's dilemma. If he wanted to make something of himself in a craft, he should have started when he was about six.

'And after all that business with Lord Gudmund and Brother Hermitage, I knew that there could be more interesting things in life.'

'Investigating murder?' Hermitage asked, unable to believe that anyone would think that interesting.

'Exactly.' Bart was positively enthusiastic. 'Working out who did what. Who's lying to who. I'd never enjoyed myself more.'

Hermitage could only shake his head in worry for the poor boy. Surely, he could become anything he wanted, within reason. A merchant, a tradesman, a dung gatherer? Anything but an investigator.

'And I knew that although Wat and Cwen helped with things, they were already weavers. I thought you might have a vacancy?'

'A vacancy?' Hermitage asked.

'For an apprentice.'

'An apprentice?'

'Apprentice investigator. It's got to be quicker than becoming a carpenter or a smith. Not that I'm any good at them anyway.'

'But,' Hermitage tried to follow. 'There's no such thing as an apprentice investigator.'

'There you are then,' Bart held his hands out. 'I can be the first.'

Hermitage didn't know where to begin. It seemed harsh to tell this lad that he didn't want an apprentice, but he didn't. Perhaps if he explained the true horrors of investigation. it would put him off and he would decide on something more wholesome.

Wat could be heard clattering about downstairs serving the Normans and would be up at any moment to deal with the more serious problem of Fortmain's intentions.

'We had better talk later, young Bart,' he said.

Bart grinned.

'But I really don't think this is possible.' Hermitage tried to let the boy down gently.

'Let me get this straight,' Fortmain said. 'You're not called Edgulf and you haven't come to the King's Investigator with a murder at all?'

'Well, not exactly. But I'm keen to learn all about them.'

Fortmain pointed hard at Bart. 'We are here to be in service to the king's man, and there's no room for you.'

Hermitage wished someone might consult him about all these plans. Telling Normans that he didn't want them could be a lot more problematic than Bart alone. And why did everyone suddenly want to be in his service?

Perhaps this was the moment to live up to his name and announce that he was going off to become a hermit. It had always been an attractive life, now it felt like an essential one.

Wat made his way up the stairs and Hermitage thought that resolution to all these problems would have to wait. At least he might have some time to think what the resolution might be.

'Ale and bread and cheese,' Wat announced glumly. He cast his eyes around the room and frowned at Marcus. Then he looked at Aurelius and nearly dropped the lot.

'Hello Watty,' Aurelius smiled in that alarming manner she had.

'Hello, Watty?' Cwen repeated. 'Wat, do you know this, erm, woman?'

'Does he know me?' Aurelius enquired as if the answer was plainly, yes.

'Oh, God,' Wat moaned. 'There's a Norman who wants to kill me, and now things have got a whole lot worse.'

'Explain.' Cwen instructed.

'What's to explain, eh Watty?' Aurelius asked.

'Give it a try,' Cwen urged seriously.

'Me and Watty go way back,' Aurelius said with confidence.

'Oh, really?' Cwen said in that scary manner she had.

'Oh, yes. What would you call me?' She considered the question and then clicked her fingers. 'That's it. I'm his wife.'

Caput XVI: Aurelius's Tale

'She is not my wife,' Wat said firmly.

'I am.'

'You are not.'

'We were married,' Aurelius told the room.

'We were not.'

'Yes, we were. Don't you remember? There was a priest and everything.'

'He wasn't a priest,' Wat said.

'What do you mean, he wasn't a priest?' Cwen asked with horrifying intensity. 'Who wasn't a priest?'

'Oh, God,' Wat moaned. He staggered over to the window seat and Hermitage stood to make way for him.

'Who is this woman' Cwen demanded.

'I'm Rachel,' Aurelius announced.

'She's not Aurelius?' Fortmain asked. 'Are any of you who say you are? Are you even Marcus?' He asked.

'If you like.' Marcus smiled.

'I'm waiting for an answer.' Cwen stood and went over to glower at Wat from closer range.

Wat took a breath. 'A long time ago,' he began.

'You married me,' Rachel said.

'You. Shut up,' Cwen instructed. 'You, carry on,' she told Wat.

'A long time ago, I was doing some business down Holbeach way, out in the fens, you know. A small sort of place but the local lord was well provided for and had money to spend.

'He was a lovely old boy. Could have been ninety himself. Funnily enough, he served with Aethelred's army.'

'In Normandy?' Hermitage asked.

154

'Don't think so,' Wat said. 'Not if the way he talked about Normans was anything to go by.'

'Could we perhaps get back to the explanation for your marriage?' Cwen asked.

'Right, yes. Anyway, I took this lord some tapestry and he was well pleased and fetched me money to pay. All well and good so far and I was ready to leave.

'Oh no, the lord says, stay the night. Well, never one to turn down wine and food, I agreed. Foolishly, as it turned out.

'The next morning, I make my leave and am heading up the road, when his men come and drag me back. Apparently, a good portion of his coin has been taken in the night, and they accuse me! Me?'

'All makes sense so far,' Cwen said heartlessly.

'I am not a thief,' Wat said. 'I never have been. I may take advantage of people in business, but I would never simply take anything. It's too stupid. Thieves get caught.'

'You were,' Rachel put in.

Cwen glared at her. 'The next shut up will come with a lump of wood attached.'

Rachel held her hands up in mock surrender.

'And who should be there in the house but one Rachel, a servant of the mistress.'

Rachel smiled sweetly.

'Well,' Wat warmed to his tale. 'They put me in the lord's lockup while deciding what to do. But they have a problem. I don't have the coin.'

'Interesting,' Hermitage commented.

'Exactly,' Wat agreed. 'They couldn't find any of it on me or in my pack. No one had seen me sneaking about in the night, in fact, I'd had so much wine I slept on the floor by the fire with the dogs. And they didn't wake.

'Then, who should come and see me but Rachel.'

'Who you knew from the night before,' Cwen accused.

'No,' Wat said. 'I was told who she was when she brought wine, but that was it. I never spoke to her or had anything to do with her. You know what the business is like. We have to mix with money, not their servants.'

'So why did she visit you?' Hermitage asked, his investigative nature getting the better of him.

'She said that she had seen me take the coin and was prepared to swear it to the lord.'

'But she hadn't?' Hermitage checked.

'No, she hadn't. Because I didn't.'

'Then, why…,' Hermitage asked slowly before it dawned on him. 'She took it.'

'She did,' Wat agreed.

Rachel was shaking her head confidently at this nonsense.

'And she had been planning to take it for months, but she was stuck. She couldn't get the coin out of the house on her own and it was in the middle of the fens. And of course, being a servant, she wouldn't be allowed to leave anyway. She needed an accomplice, willing or otherwise.'

'You.'

Wat nodded. 'I think everyone else in the house knew what she was like and wouldn't go near her.

'And then she dropped the true horror.' He took a breath as if the memory were painful. 'She said I had a choice. Either she would swear that I had taken the coin and had buried it somewhere, or I could marry her.'

'That seems to be rather an extreme option,' Hermitage commented.

'A wife cannot give evidence against her husband,' Wat

pointed out. 'If I married her, she wouldn't be able to say a word against me. And if she was married, she could leave her mistress. She'd take the coin from where she'd hidden it when we left.

'Or, I could refuse to marry her and she would tell the lord that I must have hidden it somewhere. Then, she'd keep it for her next opportunity.'

'But,' Hermitage frowned. 'Why would anyone think you wanted to marry a servant you'd only met the night before?'

'Why do people usually marry people after one night?' Wat asked.

'Love?' Hermitage suggested.

'Love!' Cwen gave a hollow laugh. 'Men and women, Hermitage, think about it?'

Hermitage thought about it. 'Oh, my,' he said.

'Quite. But this is nonsense,' Cwen went on. 'Even if you were married, the coin was still missing. The lord is hardly going to let the pair of you walk out.'

'Oh, she was going to arrange for some of it to be found. A trail leading off into the fens. Some local robber must have sneaked in. Meanwhile, she has her escape route with the rest of it. And I had a strong suspicion that her new husband might end up in the bottom of a marsh once she was out of reach.'

'So, you are married,' Cwen concluded.

'If a drunken druid waving some leaves about and rambling on in Celtic constitutes a marriage.'

'Which it doesn't,' Hermitage said with authority.

'She doesn't look like she got away with a hoard of coin,' Cwen gave Rachel a disparaging look. 'Or if she did, she's spent it and has come looking for more. Is that your game?'

Rachel gave a disinterested shrug.

'Things didn't quite go according to plan,' Wat said with a wry smile. 'The lord took some persuading, but Rachel laid the tale on as thick as a bog. The trail of coin was found, and we were told we could go. Well, we were told to get out, but it was the same thing.

'But this lord was good business. He'd paid me a very fair price, which he now took back, but I could see that Rachel would be getting her fingers into everything.'

'What did you do?' Cwen asked slowly.

Wat shrugged. 'While Rachel was gathering her own possessions and one or two extra possessions that weren't hers, I found the coin.'

'You found it?' Hermitage asked. 'But you must have had it, ready to leave.'

'I did. But I made out that I'd found it outside, dropped in the marsh. Careless robbers in that part of the world. I gave it back to the lord.'

'Oh, Wat,' Cwen smiled.

'I don't know what made him happier, getting his money back or getting rid of Rachel.'

'I bet she wasn't happy,' Cwen said.

'That is putting it very mildly indeed. I was lucky to escape intact. And I got as far away as possible and made sure I never went back there again. All this was before I set up in Derby, so she wouldn't have known where I was.'

'And now she's heard of you and come here thinking she's going to get more money out of you because she's your wife.'

'I am his wife,' Rachel said. 'And he has to look after me.'

'Ha!' Cwen barked. 'You're no more his wife than, erm, Hermitage. And you needn't think you're getting a penny.'

Rachel's face took on a very dark expression as she seemed to see a foe in Cwen who might be her equal.

'And,' Cwen continued. 'You needn't think we're even going to pay you anything to go away. If you think you can cause trouble, you don't even know the meaning of the word.' She threw her look at Marcus to make sure it was understood that he was included in this.

His look said that he thought this scheme was never going to work, and he'd been right.

'Great heavens,' Fortmain spoke. 'Is this how you Saxons behave? It's appalling.'

'She is not a good example,' Cwen said. 'And I think she and her friend are probably ready to leave now.'

Rachel appeared to be fighting a strong desire to get up and do some fighting. Somehow, she managed to control herself while she stood up and went to the stairs as if this had been her plan all along.

'Come on, you,' she barked at Marcus, who followed his instructions.

At the top of the steps, she brushed down her hideous rags and looked at everyone in the room. 'This isn't over,' she said.

'It's over,' Cwen corrected.

'You think I came all this way just for him?' Rachel sneered at Wat. 'He was just a little treat. You wait. You'll see. When I come back, you'll be begging to welcome me in.'

'Only if you come for Hermitage to conduct your funeral,' Cwen bit back.

'Oh God,' Wat sighed once more once they'd gone.

'Don't worry,' Cwen reassured him with a pat on the shoulder. 'You've met my mother?'[A Murder for Mistress Cwen; mother included.]

'Well, yes,' Wat sounded confused.

'After her, Rachel will be a piece of pie.'

Hermitage worried that it wasn't going to be that easy.

This Rachel obviously had some other plan and if being Wat's wife was an example of her plans, he dreaded to think what the next one would be.

Caput XVI And A Half: Fortmain's Tale

'Well,' Wat said with heavy resignation. 'As we're making an evening of it, I suppose we had better find out what I've done to the Fortmain family.' He gave Fortmain an overly polite nod. 'At least I knew what I did to Rachel, this is going to be a revelation.'

'Fortmain family, pah!' Fortmain said as he stood.

'Don't say you're using a different name as well?' Wat asked. 'This could all get very confusing.'

'I am Fortmain now, but I wasn't.'

'I think that's what using a different name means,' Wat said very quietly.

'I had to become Fortmain because of you,' the Norman added the pointing finger to his accusation. 'My father was Fort en Bras, it means strong in arm, now I am just Fortmain, strong hand.'

Hermitage could see that there was a remark on Wat's lips; probably a clever and unhelpful one.

'Does that name mean anything to you?' Fortmain asked.

'Fortinbras?'

'Fort en Bras,' the Norman corrected.

Wat looked thoughtful but then raised his head with recognition on his face. 'Not Fortinbras of Caen?'

'Ah, you do know what you've done.'

'Well, no,' Wat said. 'But I did know a Fortinbras of Caen.'

'And you did business with him.'

'Yes, I suppose I did. Quite good business as I recall.'

'You didn't marry his servants as well?' Cwen asked.

'Shut up,' Fortmain instructed her.

'I haven't seen him for years,' Wat complained. 'How can I have done him any harm? How is he, by the way?'

'Dead,' Fortmain explained.

'Ah.'

'My father was a great man,' Fortmain said. 'Well thought of by Duke William and high in rank. I should have inherited his estates upon his death.'

'I take it you didn't,' Wat said.

'Of course, I didn't,' Fortmain said angrily. 'Upon my father's death, the duke himself came to visit with his men. Naturally, there was discussion of inheritance and any dues that were owed to the duke.'

'Dues?' Cwen asked.

'If I were to take over my father's estate, I would pay dues to the Duke.'

'Lucky duke.'

'It is perfectly normal. The duke may have had it in mind to pass the land to someone else, it was his gift, after all. I would pay my dues and the land would come to me.'

Fortmain sat heavily now as if the memories were becoming more painful. 'Quite properly, the duke's men appraised my father's possessions to judge the level of payment. They visited the land and the farms and assessed their value.

'Next, they considered our home, modest though it was, and all was going well.'

Nobody said a word as the tale seemed to be drawing to its conclusion.

'Finally, treasure.'

'Treasure?' Hermitage asked.

'Coin, jewels, gold. In part, this was to see if my father had amassed more than was reasonable; had he been out pillaging what was not his? The other purpose was to see what could be paid. There was no point the duke asking for a thousand

162

pounds of silver, we weren't that rich.

'Right at the end, just when we thought everything was to be settled, one of the duke's assessors considered my father's chamber. Just to see if there was anything there that he kept close because of its great value. A fine crucifix, perhaps? A jewelled knife.

'At the back of the chamber was a simple door. It was kept locked, and I had never been allowed through. Father said it was simply an old tower room that was no longer safe. The floor was rotten and if I went in, I would fall to my death.

'Well, I tried to warn the duke's man, but he seemed to think it was some sort of trick or deception and so wanted the door opened. Even my mother tried to stop him for safety's sake.

'We had to search high and low for the key but couldn't find it. Eventually, one of the duke's men at arms was told to force it open. And we were all there,' Fortmain hung his head.

'My mother, my sisters, even my aged aunt stood and watched as the door to that fateful room was opened.'

Hermitage was thoroughly intrigued. This was such an interesting tale that he was leaning forward to hear what the conclusion was going to be.

'And what did we find?' Fortmain asked.

Wat answered. 'A number of tapestries.'

'A number?' Fortmain was appalled by the understatement. 'A swarm. A gaggle. A whole world of tapestry. And not just piled up on the floor, oh no. On the walls. On display. Just hanging there.'

'Difficult,' Wat admitted.

'Difficult?' Fortmain almost screeched. 'Difficult?' My aunt fainted away. My younger sister screamed and ran off and my mother couldn't speak. My older sister took far too great an interest, and we had to drag her out and shut the door. But it was too late, wasn't it? The duke's man had seen.'

'A few tapestries,' Wat tried to make it sound inconsequential.

'A lot of tapestries,' Fortmain corrected. 'The like of which no one ever imagined even existed.'

'Oh, a lot of people imagined,' Wat said.

'Well, they shouldn't. And because of that, my father's reputation was destroyed. The duke was advised to pass the estates elsewhere, and the Fort en Bras family was as good as banished.'

'That is a bit much,' Wat sympathised.

'And then it got worse,' Fortmain moaned.

'Oh dear,' Wat was grimacing at how much more there was to come.

'To try and recover our good name, I took the few men bound to me and went to the aid of the duke.'

'That sounds good,' Wat encouraged.

'In Cabourg itself,' Fortmain said. 'There was a skirmish going on and we rode to the duke's rescue.'

'Excellent.'

'Unfortunately, there was a bit of a mix up in the melee and one of the duke's men was killed.'

'These things happen.'

'But it wasn't on my sword,' Fortmain was anxious to make this clear.

'Easy mistake to make.'

'And I presented the body of his supposed foe to the duke.'

'Ah.'

'And it's all your fault.' Fortmain rose again.

'That can hardly all be my fault.'

164

'Hardly your fault?' The Norman clearly couldn't believe what he was hearing. 'How is it hardly your fault? You made the disgusting things that ruined the whole family.'

'Lots of people make them,' Wat said. 'Briston the Weaver, Alaric of York. I've even heard there's a whole workshop doing nothing but, somewhere in the low countries. If your father hadn't got them from me, he would have got them from somewhere.'

'But he did get them from you. And you encouraged him. If you hadn't sold him the revolting, shameful things, he might never have found anything the like.'

'Look,' Wat said quietly. 'I'm not trying to avoid my responsibility. I did make them, it's true, but I don't anymore, I've stopped all that, haven't I, Hermitage?'

Hermitage nodded. 'He has.'

'It's too late,' Fortmain said.

'And it has to be said,' Wat started slowly. 'Your father did go to some lengths for particular works. Did you see one with a group of ladies in armour? Well, in a few bits of armour?'

'I did not examine them!'

'Oh. Well, that was a special request. Even surprised me a bit. Do you even know how many there were, exactly?'

'Most certainly not.'

'But a lot.'

'Too many.'

Wat looked thoughtful. 'I know I supplied quite a few, but not enough to fill a whole tower.'

'From floor to ceiling!' Fortmain added to the horror of the scene.

'Ah well, in that case, the ones he had were not all mine. He must have got some from other makers. Are you going to go round everyone and make them pay?'

'That would be good, yes.'

'And what will it achieve when you're done? Will it get your estates back?'

'It might,' Fortmain said. When I tell the duke that I have rid the world of this scourge, he will probably reward me.'

'He has seen my work himself, you know.' Wat said.

'Oh, really?' Fortmain did not believe this.

'He has. And not long ago, either.'[Murder Most Murderous; and revealing]

Hermitage didn't like to add that once William had seen one of Wat's tapestries, he threatened to beat him to death with it.

'I still think that if I can tell the duke that I found the man who made the awful tapestries my father had, and killed him, it will be well received.'

'But you have found me and know that I am making no more of these works. I am now in the service of the king, indirectly, and he knows of me. I'm sure all that will count for something.'

'Let's be clear,' Cwen stepped into the middle of the room. 'You are not killing him,' she instructed. 'You want to offer service to the King's Investigator and the King's Investigator does not want you to kill him.'

'That's right.' Hermitage thought it important to agree at this point.

'In fact, he instructs you not to kill him. Don't you, Hermitage.'

'Definitely.'

'So, you have a bit of a dilemma.'

'A what?' Fortmain asked.

'It's one of Hermitage's things. He has them a lot. You can kill Wat which might get you in the king's favour, or it might

166

not. Or, you can obey his investigator, which certainly will get you in favour.'

Hermitage wasn't at all sure about that assumption.

'And if an investigation comes along that you can help with, that will be even better.'

'I'm going to help with investigation,' Bart said.

Cwen interrupted before Fortmain could speak. 'I am sure that there will be plenty for everyone to do when an investigation comes along.'

Fortmain and Bart simply looked daggers at one another.

'Of course,' Cwen went on, 'there might not even be an investigation. Not soon, not ever. Perhaps Hermitage will never again be asked to investigate a murder.'

Hermitage thought that would be nice.

'In which case you'll both be wasting your time. If not the rest of your lives.'

Bart and Fortmain looked a little put out by this.

'I mean,' Cwen went on, 'you're not investigating any murders at the moment, are you, Hermitage?'

Hermitage could only look non-committal.

'He thought there was one earlier, but that was only alehouse gossip, wasn't it?'

'Erm,' Hermitage said. 'Alehouse gossip.' He repeated the expression, hoping that it would be sufficient.

'So, you see, nothing to do here. No point loitering.'

Cwen looked at Hermitage for confirmation of this conclusion. 'Hermitage?' she asked suspiciously, obviously able to spot that he was squirming in the face of this falsehood.

He tried to tell himself that it wasn't even really a falsehood. He hadn't come to any firm conclusions about anything, but it wasn't strictly true to say that he wasn't investigating. And he always liked to be strictly true; even when it was the most stupid thing to do.

And he was already worried about the number of things he had to do regarding the death of Athlot. Perhaps a bit of help might be useful?

Bart, he might be able to make use of, but Fortmain and his Normans? What use were they going to be?

'What are you up to, Hermitage?' Cwen asked.

'Nothing,' Hermitage said honestly. 'I am not up to anything at all. I simply went into town and discussed what Ern said this morning. Next, I went to the smith and looked at old Athlot's home. Then I found out some things about him and well, one thing led to another.'

'And what was the other?'

'I'm not saying it's certain, or even that it's likely, but I suppose that it might be possible, looking at all the information as a whole, that Athlot's death could be of interest to a number of people.'

'Pardon?'

Hermitage shrugged. 'Someone might have killed him.'

'Oh, Lord,' Cwen covered her face with her hands.

'There you are,' Fortmain crowed. 'We can be of service to the king's man.'

'I'm going to be his apprentice,' Bart insisted. 'I shall do whatever is required.'

'You shall stand aside, Saxon,' Fortmain instructed. 'This is Norman business.'

'I'll wager this Athlot was a Saxon,' Bart retorted.

'There is enough for everyone to do,' Hermitage said quite loudly, wanting to avoid any conflict, as usual. 'There are a number of things to find out from different places.'

Fortmain and Bart sniffed at one another, each assuming

that theirs would be the most important.

'But we can do no more until morning,' Hermitage said. 'Although I can consult my few books on history for any useful facts.'

'Useful facts?' Cwen asked with disbelief. 'In history?'

'I'll explain more later.'

'And I suppose you lot expect to sleep here,' Wat complained to the others.

Fortmain replied. 'We can take your hospitality or your life?'

'Let's get you comfortable,' Wat stood and smiled.

'Really, Hermitage,' Cwen hissed at him as they all made for the stairs. 'Perhaps we can get you an apprenticeship with a master of keeping your mouth shut.'

Wat gave a little chortle of agreement.

'And you'd better not make any more noises tonight,' Cwen said. 'You're in enough trouble already.'

Wat nodded but wore his mischievous grin. 'I'd better not tell Fortmain about his mother's preferences in tapestry, then.'

Caput XVII: The Investigator's Plan

'There's Normans,' Mrs Grod gave a loud and accurate report the next morning as she stood gazing into the cooking area.

Wat came quickly to her side, mainly to prevent any harm coming to the Normans.

'We'll soon get them out,' he assured her, stepping forward to rouse the Normans. 'They wanted to sleep by the fire.'

'My fire,' Mrs Grod explained.

'Of course, it is. Come on, come on. Everybody up.'

The Normans woke and looked about them, clearly trying to remember where it was they went to sleep.

Wat was trying not to remember that the reason they were sleeping so long was the huge amount of his ale they'd drunk the night before, and that was before they moved on to his wine.

Eventually, he managed to herd them all together and move them past Mrs Grod, who watched them go as if her ingredients were making a run for it.

'Let's go upstairs,' Wat said. 'I'll find the others.' He ushered the four men up the stairs and out of the way. The last thing he wanted was for the apprentices to find that they were now a lodging house for Norman soldiers.

'How are we going to get rid of them?' He asked Hermitage urgently as he Cwen and Bart headed for the steps a few moments later. 'They think they're in your service now. If you give them things to do, they'll move in permanently.'

'I know, I know,' Hermitage fretted. 'But what else could I do? There was no indication that they would leave if I said there was nothing.'

'You didn't give them a chance,' Cwen pointed out.

'We don't want them,' Bart said confidently. 'I can do anything that's needed.'

'That's fine then. We'll just ask the nice Norman soldiers if they'd mind leaving now, shall we? And you're another problem,' Cwen continued. 'We can't have people turning up saying they're Hermitage's apprentice and thinking they can live here.'

'I can look after myself.'

'No one pays for investigations, you know.'

That did seem to give Bart pause.

'The king doesn't send a purse to his investigator every year.'

'Then what's the reward?'

'The reward is getting to do what you're told by the king. Or any other Norman nobles, come to that.'

'Fortmain would love it,' Wat observed.

'That he would,' Cwen said very thoughtfully.

Before they started up the stairs, Cwen gathered them for quiet instruction. 'So, Hermitage, you have a plan?'

'I do, I believe. The death of Athlot has a number of interesting features...,'

'Not about that. A plan to get rid of the Normans?'

'Oh, er, no, not really.'

She tutted. 'Give them something they can report to the king.'

'Erm,' Hermitage couldn't see how he could something up.

'It doesn't matter what it is. Just come up with something that they can take news of to the king.'

'About Athlot?'

'About anything, for heaven's sake. We need them out of

here.'

Hermitage knew what he wanted to find out, but only now saw that some of it might actually be of interest to the Normans.

'There is a question over whether Athlot had any involvement with King Aethelred in Normandy.'

'We had a King Aethelred in England,' Bart offered helpfully.

'It's the same one,' Hermitage said.

'Oh, right,' Bart looked confused.

'Good,' Cwen said. 'And whether he did or he didn't, it needs reporting to the king, and who better to do it than Fortmain or Fortinbras or whatever his name is.'

Hermitage could see that that might work. It seemed a bit dishonest, which would be a problem, but he had to actually deal with one problem at a time, instead of simply worrying about them all simultaneously.

The upstairs chamber was positively crowded as Hermitage topped the stairs. All the Normans were up here and the four of them as well made it hard to see past the person standing in front of you.

'Here, Hermitage,' Cwen said. 'Stand on the chair.'

He didn't like to stand on chairs. Partly, it was concern at the misuse of furniture, but mainly, it was because the last time he stood on a chair and addressed a group, it was in a monastery and the monks had all thrown things at him.

At Cwen's bidding - and pushing and shoving - he found himself on the chair and the room fell silent. All faces looked to him for their instruction, which he really didn't like.

'Ahem, yes, good. Well,' he began decisively. 'Thank you all for coming.' No, that was wrong as well. He tried closing his eyes so he couldn't see all the people staring at him, but that only made him dizzy and he worried he would fall off the chair.

'Athlot,' Cwen prompted.

'Athlot, indeed.' He gathered his thoughts.

'Well?' Cwen asked after the gathering of thoughts had taken rather longer than expected.

'Yes. Old Athlot of Derby is dead,' he announced. 'Although that's a question in its own right.'

'He's not dead?' Wat asked. 'Not much of a murder.'

'Shut up,' Cwen instructed.

'No, no, he is definitely dead,' Hermitage confirmed. 'He has been buried in the churchyard, after all. Although I suppose we'd better check that as well. Anyway, where was I? Oh yes, Athlot is dead, although he is not of Derby in the proper sense. He was not born here, only arriving some forty years ago. Arriving with some wealth, it seems.

'Now, it is widely believed that he was ninety years old, and it could well be that he simply fell off the ladder and died.'

'What ladder?' Bart asked.

'Oh, didn't I mention the ladder? Yes, there was a ladder. And some thatch on his roof. Athlot was found at the bottom of the ladder, and he was covered in thatch. Perhaps he simply fell off while repairing his roof.

'But that does not sound right. For one thing, the roof was very low and could easily be reached without a ladder. And it was in good condition and didn't seem to need repair.

'So, how did Athlot die? Did he simply fall next to his ladder of old age? Erm, that's him, not the ladder. Or could there be any reason for his death other than a natural one? Did anyone have a motive, that's the question?

'And so we look into Athlot and what do we find?'

'We look into him?' Bart didn't sound very keen on that at

all.

'His history,' Hermitage explained. 'Is there anything in Athlot's life that would explain a threat to his life?'

'Oh, right.' Bart was happier.

'And two main questions have arisen. The first is that he was a man of some wealth. He came to Derby all those years ago with money and does not appear to have worked since. He spent a lot of time in the alehouse, according to Wassa.'

'The smith's mother?' Cwen asked. 'What's she got to do with it?'

'That is a very good question.' Hermitage was getting quite carried away with this thinking out loud and had almost forgotten all the people in front of him.

'Athlot's home was behind the smithy, and I was directed to Wassa as she might know something of his arrival in town. I understand she's lived here all her life and is fifty now.'

'Fifty, ha!' Cwen gave a short laugh. 'More likely she knows something of the Romans' arrival in town.'

'Shut up,' Wat instructed.

'And,' Hermitage continued. 'Wassa told me that Athlot had been a bad influence on her husband, who had left the family farm to the town, instead of Wassa herself. Which is the first thing we need to investigate.'

'Why?' Cwen asked. 'Does her farm have anything to do with Athlot?'

'Not really, I just said I would help.'

'Very kind of you.' Cwen did not sound impressed at this kindness.

'But,' Hermitage held up a finger. 'Wassa's information does leave the question of Athlot's wealth. Where is it?'

'Don't know,' Bart said full of enthusiasm.

'No, we don't.'

'Oh.'

'I could see no sign of it at Athlot's home, which was very humble. However, mistress Wassa's home is very comfortable, despite the fact she has no farm.'

'She killed him and took the money,' Bart said.

'Not necessarily. She said she is paid by the town for the farm's produce.

'So, the first, erm, what can we say, area for investigation, is Wassa and her farm. Cwen, I wondered if you could do that? I suspect it may need a strong word. Find out from the headman if the farm really was left to the town, or whether the widow has simply been cheated out of her inheritance. And, if she is not getting money from there, where is it coming from?'

'Find out if the headman is a cheat,' Cwen repeated her instruction. 'Got it.'

'At the same time as that, we need to find out where Athlot hid his wealth. I wondered whether it might be in his thatch, which would explain the ladder. But it was getting dark and I really didn't know what I was looking for.'

'Hiding places for money,' Wat said. 'That would be me.'

'Thank you, Wat. Now, finally, there is the question of Athlot's origin.

'He told many tales about being with King Aethelred, apparently, and that might have included the time in exile in Normandy.

'Could it be that he made enemies of old? Enemies who could get at him now that the Normans rule England?'

'A ninety-year-old?' Wat questioned.

'We Normans like revenge,' Fortmain explained.

'And the name Athlot means nothing to you?' Hermitage asked.

Fortmain shook his head. 'Nothing.'

'Very well. I plan to journey to Nottingham to speak with Lord Gilbert and to see if he has any histories of Normandy that might shed light on the matter. My own books were no help at all.'

'There's a surprise,' Cwen muttered.

'That's where Fortmain and the Normans can help.'

Fortmain stood up straight and proud but the other Normans didn't seem quite so enthused.

'So,' Hermitage said. 'Are we all clear?'

Most people nodded, only Bart was frowning.

'What about me?'

'Well, erm, perhaps you go with Wat?'

'It's not much of an investigation, looking in some thatch.'

'This is just the sort of thing it is,' Cwen said. 'Looking for things, finding people, little details. Isn't that right, Hermitage?'

'Erm, yes, it is.'

'I can be more use than that,' Bart said. 'When did this Athlot die?'

'When?' Hermitage asked.

'Probably just after he hit the ground,' Wat suggested.

'I mean what day. What time of day?'

'Well,' Hermitage hesitated. 'I don't know exactly. In the last week, that's for sure.'

'There we are then. I can find out exactly when he died and who was there at the time.'

'Can you?'

'Who found him?'

'The smith.'

'Very well.' Bart warmed to his task. 'I shall question the smith and discover exactly when the body was found.

Obviously, he's the main suspect, what with being the first one with the body.'

'Oh,' Hermitage said. 'I suppose he might be. Although I don't know what his motive might be. He seems a nice fellow.'

'How many homes are there in Derby?'

'How many?' Hermitage couldn't see what this had to do with anything.

'Over a hundred,' Wat said.

Bart seemed taken aback by such a vast number. 'Nevertheless, I can go to every home in town and ask them if they killed Athlot.'

'And if they say, yes?' Cwen asked lightly.

'Then we have our killer,' Bart announced proudly.

'You idiot,' Cwen said. 'They aren't going to say, yes, are they? We wouldn't need to investigate at all if killers were honest.'

Bart considered this. 'Then I can ask everyone where they were at the time of the death. Did they know Athlot? When did they last see him? Did they have any business with him? I can see if they behave strangely.'

'A lot of people in Derby behave strangely,' Wat said.

Hermitage couldn't help but think that all of this actually sounded quite sensible and thorough.

'It'd take you forever,' Cwen interjected. 'Over a hundred houses.'

'I probably wouldn't need to do all hundred,' Bart said. 'The chances of the killer being in the last house must be pretty small.' He frowned. 'Although come to think of it, you always find the horse in the last stable you check, don't you.'

'My gosh, you're right,' Cwen said. 'I wonder why that is.' She shook her head in bemusement.

'It could be helpful, Bart,' Hermitage said. The young man's ideas were reasonable, and in any case, he couldn't think of anything else for him to do, apart from follow someone around.

Bart beamed at his usefulness. 'Erm, there is one question though,' he said carefully.

'What is it, Bart?'

'This Athlot is dead, yes?'

'Well, perhaps that's one thing you can do; check with the priest, but yes, he is.'

'And is he going to be happy with us investigating him?'

'He's dead,' Hermitage didn't quite understand.

'Exactly. I wouldn't want dead people objecting.'

'Lord Gudmund didn't object when we investigated his death,' Cwen pointed out.

'Yes, but he wouldn't bother me, would he? I was only a servant. If I'm an investigator, there might be objections.'

'From the dead?' Cwen asked, her incredulity quite clear.

'You don't get haunted, then? By all the murdered people?'

'No, we do not get haunted.'

'Ah, that's a relief. It was one of my big worries.'

'Of course, it was.' Cwen rolled her eyes at Hermitage. 'Perhaps you'd better think about whether this non-existent apprenticeship is really for you.'

When they had all got to the bottom of the stairs, Fortmain took Hermitage's arm and drew him to one side.

'We are to Lord Gilbert, then?' Fortmain checked.

'That's right. Do you know him?'

'Know the name, but never met. And he's in Nottingham?'

'That's correct.'

Fortmain nodded. 'And this Nottingham, it's, erm, not in Scotland, is it?'

Caput XVIII: Into The Thatch

Wat, Cwen and Bart headed for town straight away, leaving Hermitage and the Normans to sort themselves out.

'This shouldn't take long,' Wat said.

'Finding money in a haystack? Not for you, I shouldn't think,' Cwen replied.

'And you be nice to the headman,' he instructed.

Cwen gave it a moment's casual thought. 'Probably not,' she said. 'I don't know how Wassa's got involved in all of this. She's always had ideas above herself. '"Her son's the smith",' she mocked. 'She probably just thinks she's entitled to more than she's already got.'

'We're going to the smith, yes?' Bart checked.

'Well, Athlot's home, which is behind the smithy,' Wat said.

'Good. I can question him about the circumstances of Athlot.'

'Dead, mainly.'

'Yes,' Bart agreed. 'But how and when? Those are the interesting questions. Were there any marks on the body?' He snapped his fingers as a new thought occurred to him. 'Had he been shot?'

'Shot? Where did that come from?'

'People die when they get shot. That old man in Gotham was shot to death.'[More from The 1066 To Hastings]

'He was,' Wat agreed. 'But we all noticed. And mentioned it at the time, I seem to recall. If Athlot had been shot, someone would have said that he'd been shot.'

'Not if they hid the fact,' Bart persisted.

'And covered over the hole and removed all the blood,' Cwen added.

'I shall ask the smith,' Bart said.

'You do that.'

They arrived at the road into town now.

'Right, I'm for mistress Wassa,' Cwen turned left. 'Wish me luck.'

'I wish her luck. And the headman,' Wat said.

Cwen gave him a cheery wave.

'Come on then, Bart,' off to the smithy.

Just as Hermitage had found them, Grimulf was outside the smithy, cleaning off some tools now, while the smith could be heard inside, hitting some metal with some other metal.

'Ho, Grimulf,' Wat called.

Grimulf looked up and saw who it was. 'Not so loud,' he pleaded.

'Don't want to be seen with your old friend Wat the Weaver?'

'You are not my old friend,' Grimulf hissed.

'That's not what you used to say,' Wat winked.

'And who's this?' Grimulf turned up his nose at Bart.

'This is Bart. He wants to ask the smith some questions.'

'Where's Brother Hermitage, then? He asks the questions.'

'He's gone to Nottingham to talk to Lord Gilbert.'

Grimulf seemed to be quite impressed by that. 'The smith's inside,' he explained over the loud noise emanating from the smithy.

'You don't say,' Wat commented. He nodded that Bart should probably go in, which the young man did.

'I'll need a word with you afterwards,' he said to Grimulf as he passed.

'Need what you want,' Grimulf sneered at the back of Bart who could only be about his own age.

'Now then, Grimulf,' Wat warned kindly. 'This is King's Investigator's business, so you help young Bart.'

Grimulf did not look in the mood to help anyone.

'Or I might just remember the last time you visited my workshop and the sort of thing you were looking for.'

Grimulf looked hurriedly up and down the lane to make sure no one was close by; or even far away.

Wat gave him a wink. 'Now then, I'm off to look at Athlot's place.'

'Not you as well?' Grimulf asked in a worried tone. 'What is it about his hut? It's no use to anyone. It's stuck behind the smithy. It should go to someone who needs it.'

'I don't want his hut,' Wat said. 'I just want to look at it. I know Hermitage was here before, but I need to look in the light.'

'That's what those other two said.'

'What other two?' Wat asked slowly.

'Man and a woman, early this morning. Well, I think she was a woman. Dressed like a witch.'

'They didn't give their names, I suppose?'

'Something foreign.'

'Marcus and Aurelius?'

'That was them.'

'Oh, bloody hell.' Wat left Grimulf behind and slipped quickly around the side of the smithy to where Athlot's hut sat. Or rather, where it used to sit.

'Oh, no.' Grimulf had come around after Wat and now surveyed the scene.

Athlot's home had only been mud and sticks and straw, and, strictly speaking, it still was. Only now it was a lot less hut-shaped.

'What have they done?' Grimulf wailed.

181

'They've taken it apart,' Wat said. 'Looking for something, I suspect. And I don't think they found it.'

'Looking for what? And why knock the place down? It'll take ages to put it back up again.'

'The question is, how on earth did those two know to be looking in the first place?'

'What makes you think they didn't find it?' Grimulf asked disconsolately as he stepped forward to kick through the wreckage.

'The whole place has been taken apart. If they'd found what they were looking for, they'd have stopped, and they didn't.'

'And what, exactly, were they looking for? And why didn't they ask, we might have known?'

'Athlot was pretty wealthy, yes?' Wat asked.

'Well, yes, I suppose so, He didn't do any work and always had money for ale and food. Still lived in this old place, but said it made him comfortable.'

'Comfortable, eh?' Wat mused. 'A wealthy man living in a hut behind the smithy. Anyone would think he was hiding.'

'Hiding from what?'

'People who wanted to come and take his house apart.' Wat nodded towards the pile of house on the floor.

Grimulf nodded to himself. 'You think they were after his money?'

'Can't think what else would make people go to this trouble.' He turned to Grimulf. 'Did you ever see him with money?'

'Saw him pay for ale, I suppose.'

'I mean a lot of money. A chest or a large purse full.'

'No,' Grimulf shook his head. 'And if I'd seen a chest or large purse full of money, I'd have remembered.'

'Makes you wonder about his death though, doesn't it,' Wat said.

'You mean he was killed for his money?' Grimulf sounded positively alarmed at this.

'It's possible. It's also possible that whoever killed him then found the money. Or they found the money and then killed him. Doesn't matter, really. Marcus and Aurelius didn't find it. Perhaps it had already gone. And how would they even know to come all the way to Derby to look? Perhaps they knew he was dead as well?'

Wat appraised the space that now held the bits of Athlot's house. 'It was a simple hut?'

'It was. Nothing to it at all. One hut, fire, few vegetables and that was it.'

Wat ran a hand over his head. 'Think about the money,' he said, mainly to himself. 'If Athlot had lived here for forty years and not done a stroke of work, he must have had a good store of money. More than could be hidden in some thatch, or the wall of an old hut.'

Grimulf looked bemused by the problems of hiding large sums of money.

'Did he ever go anywhere else?' Wat asked. 'Did he make regular visits anywhere?'

'Hardly left at all,' Grimulf said. 'Down to the alehouse and back was about it. But then, I've not been here long. You'd have to ask the smith.'

Wat stepped forwards and kicked over a few bits of the house. He bent and lifted what must have been part of the back wall away and peered at the ground underneath. 'No sign of burial,' he muttered.

'They buried him in the churchyard,' Grimulf said helpfully.

'And I'm sure our dear priest would have noticed if he was weighed down with coin.'

Wat stood again. 'I don't think there's anything else to be gained here.' He looked up at the sky. 'Hermitage has probably left for Nottingham now, too late to let him know. Perhaps I'd better talk to the smith.'

Grimulf had come forward now and was rather hopelessly lifting small pieces of hut, most of which crumbled in his hands. Even the wattle had been broken in most places.

'Did you see Marcus and Aurelius leave?' Wat asked.

'No, but I was in and out of the smithy. Might have just simply missed them.'

'Or they crawled out without being noticed. We need to find them. How long ago were they here?'

'Just after dawn. We were waking up the fires.'

'They've had too long,' Wat said. 'God knows where they've gone now.' He looked at the ruins once more. 'I can't see any clues here as to where to go next, but I'll warrant Aurelius won't have left town, not if she thinks there's a chest of coin here.'

Grimulf was still picking through the mess.

'She clearly didn't come to Derby for me,' Wat said. 'Or not just for me. But if Athlot stayed hidden in his hut and never left town, how could she possibly know he was here? And know that he had money? I think there is a lot more to old Athlot than any of us know.'

He had no answer to these questions but thought that perhaps Bart could tell more. After all, he was the one who had brought the wretched pair here in the first place.

There was no more to be done here, so he turned back towards the path.

He could go no farther as the smith stood there, holding

Bart by the scruff of his neck, his feet only just touching the ground. The young man was wriggling slightly but mainly looked flushed as he couldn't breathe properly.

'Is this one with you, master Wat?' the smith enquired.

'Erm, in a manner of speaking.'

The smith threw Bart forward where he staggered into Wat's arms. 'Then you need to learn him some manners.'

Wat tried to look politely enquiring.

'I'm a friendly fellow,' the smith said. 'Everyone knows that. But if strangers,' he pointed at Bart, 'come into my smithy accusing me of murder, I have to act, don't I?'

'Oh yes,' Wat agreed.

'I didn't accuse you of murder,' Bart coughed. 'I was merely asking.'

'Asking if I killed Athlot,' the smith said, his anger rising again.

'I'll, erm, take him away,' Wat said with a smile and a nod.

'What have you done to Athlot's house?' the smith now asked as he looked past Wat and saw the pile of bits behind him. 'It wasn't like that before.'

'Haven't done anything to it, have we Grimulf?' Wat asked, anxious that the smith didn't leap to any conclusions.

'Look at it,' Grimulf moaned. 'It's ruined.'

'It was the other two,' Wat said.

'What other two?'

'They call themselves Marcus and Aurelius.'

'The Roman emperor?' the smith asked, quite surprisingly.

'No, no. Two strangers. A man and a woman. Her real name's Rachel. Don't know about him.'

'And what are two strangers doing destroying Athlot's home?'

'Looking for money, no doubt about that. But how they

knew to look in the first place is a mystery.' Wat said. 'Athlot must have had money. Quite a lot of it.'

'He had a bit,' the smith acknowledged, still looking stunned at the state of the hut.

'Must have been a fair bit. He'd lived here for forty years and never did any work. Never earned any wage. Never bartered anything?'

'I suppose not.'

'Yet he always had coin to spend in the alehouse.'

'I suppose he did.' The smith did seem to see the peculiarity in this.

'And you never saw a chest or a large purse?'

The smith shook his head. He looked sadly at the remains of a home. 'The things people will do for a chest of coin, eh?'

'Some would knock down the whole of Derby to get a chest of coin,' Wat said. 'He didn't, erm, leave anything with you? To look after?'

'Money?' The smith sounded a bit disgusted by the idea.

'Well, yes.'

'No.' The smith seemed very sure of this. 'Kept himself to himself, mainly, and lived a simple life.'

'Apart from having a good sum of money somewhere.'

'Well, he never told me where it was. Or even talked about it. We'd just discuss the normal things; the weather, the town gossip, that sort of thing. And his old days of course, with kings and the like. Just as I was telling Brother Hermitage.'

'And he never displayed any wealth. No jewels or gold, that sort of thing?'

'Jewels or gold?' the smith laughed. 'Never.'

'Well, we're no further forward,' Wat sighed. 'Apart from knowing that Marcus and Aurelius are on the trail.'

Wat had a thought and walked over to the back wall of the

smithy. He peered left and right, up and down, to see if there was any sign of anything being hidden away. Nothing.

'You think he stuffed gold and jewels in my smithy?'

'It's a thought.'

'You worry too much about money, master Wat,' the smith cautioned. 'Always have done.'

'In this case, someone might have killed Athlot for his money, so I think the worrying is justified.' He gestured to Bart that they could leave now.

As they did so, the smith reached out and gave Bart a light clip round the ear.

'Is that your idea of investigation?' Wat asked when they were clear of the smithy. 'Walk into the smithy and accuse the great big smith of murder. The one with all the hot pieces of metal to hand?'

'I didn't accuse him. I just asked.'

'You just said, "excuse me, but did you kill Athlot"?'

Bart considered the ground. 'Not exactly.'

'But pretty close.'

Bart shrugged.

'Well, don't do it again. People who haven't killed anyone can get upset by questions like that. Big, strong people are best not upset.

'And if they have killed someone and you ask, they might kill you next.'

'How are we supposed to find out who did it?' Bart asked.

'We wait for Hermitage to say, Aha.'

'Aha?'

'That's it. We spend hours and days sometimes, wandering around finding things out and asking questions. Not questions like, did you kill so-and-so? Then, just when things are at their worst, Hermitage says "aha", and tells us who did it.'

'Why does he wait until then?'

'He doesn't, it just comes to him. That's why he says, aha. It's as much a surprise to him as it is to everyone else.'

'Anyone can say, aha,' Bart observed.

'But he only says it when he knows.'

Bart considered this. 'Then he will have to tell me how he does it. It sounds like it's a key part of the job.'

'Good luck with that. I don't think he knows himself.'

'Then how am I to become an investigator?'

'That, young Bart, is a very good question. You were lucky this was just the smith. You talk to a Norman noble like that and you won't need to worry about being an investigator because you'll be the dead body.

'And if you do come across Marcus and Aurelius, I wouldn't ask them either. She'll do the same as a Norman, only not so quickly.'

Caput XIX: Head Of Trouble

'**A**h, you've come to get my land back.' Mistress Wassa welcomed Cwen to her home and looked as if she'd been sitting by the door waiting. 'Brother Hermitage said you would.'

'Let's not get carried away,' Cwen said, ducking to enter the single room.

She looked about and saw that the place was, indeed, very comfortable. And this for a woman who had no trade and did not work. At least, Cwen had never seen or heard of Wassa doing anything useful around town.

'Let's get everything in order before we go simply accusing people of anything.' Cwen was usually quite keen on simply accusing people of things, but this time it was on behalf of someone else. She would like to know the truth before jumping in.

'It's as I told the brother,' Wassa said. 'My husband, Chad, bequested our farm to the town, or so I've been told. It wasn't a big place, but it was ours. Chad had fought for the king many years back and got the land as reward.'

'Which king?' Cwen asked seeing a possible connection to Athlot.

'Brother Hermitage asked that. Funny question really. It was Edward.'

'Edward?'

'Of course. Harold wasn't king for two drips of an udder. And William's new, isn't he?'

'I suppose he is. Chad didn't fight for Aethelred then?'

'Who?'

'King Aethelred.'

'King Aethelred?' Wassa asked with a broad smile. 'There's

189

never been a King Aethelred, you silly. Who told you that?'

'Hermitage.'

'Ah, monks.' That seemed to be sufficient explanation for the fabrication of kings.

'Was he very old, your husband?'

'No older than me,' Wassa said.

Very old then, Cwen thought.

'But he would have been about fifty when he died.'

Perhaps Wassa couldn't count higher than fifty.

'I tell you, it was a good job Brother Hermitage came along. He reckons that if there's no bit of writing that says this, then it's not right. That headman has been having the run of the farm when he shouldn't.'

Cwen took the seat by the fire. 'And you don't have any writing.'

'I don't.' Wassa sounded as if she wouldn't have that sort of thing in the house.

'And you don't know of any?'

'I do not.'

'So,' Cwen was warming to her task. 'We only have the headman's word that this arrangement is right. And how does Athlot fit in?'

'Athlot? Brother Hermitage asked about him as well. Don't know why everyone's so interested in that old fool all of a sudden.'

'Old fool?'

Wassa grunted. 'He was a bad influence on my Chad like I said to the Brother. Led him astray, he did. It was all right for Athlot, he had money and could afford to waste his days and nights. My Chad couldn't. And he shouldn't have.'

'So,' Cwen spoke thoughtfully. 'Athlot, with all his money, distracted your husband from his work.'

'That he did.'

'Then, you were told that Chad had left the farm to the town.'

'Unless I married again.'

'So, why didn't you marry again? If there was a farm to be had, someone would have been very keen. You should have been fighting them off.'

'You would think it.' Wassa said. 'And there was one fellow started courting me. Young Blednot. Very keen, he was.'

'I see.'

'Of course, I knew it was about the land, but I've never been blessed with children to inherit from me, so why shouldn't a wife take a young husband?'

'No reason at all. What happened to him?'

'He was coming round more and more and then suddenly he stopped. Just like that. No reason he ever told me.'

'Did you ask him?'

'That's not the sort of thing a lady would do,' Wassa said.

Cwen would have to think about that. It was exactly the sort of thing she would do. 'Did you never see him again?'

'Oh, I saw him around, but he avoided me.'

'Do you think someone scared him off?' Cwen asked carefully.

'Scared him off? What would scare him off me?'

Cwen didn't like to go too far with that question. 'Someone who didn't want you married.'

Wassa picked up on the suggestion straight away. 'Someone who didn't want me to get my farm. Who wanted to keep the earnings. That headman. The weasel.

'He put young Blednot up to not marrying me. And I shouldn't have had to marry at all. The land was Chad's, I was his wife, it should have come to me.'

Wassa sniffed and was looking on the verge of tears.

Cwen, despite having no great affection for Wassa, felt the injustice of this. She nodded once. 'I think we need to have a word with the headman.'

The way Cwen said, "have a word with", put hope in the air; not for the headman, obviously.

Wassa straightened her gown ready to leave, which Cwen noticed was a bit too good for a woman with no land.

'Hermitage said that they pay you?' Cwen asked.

'They do, as if that excuses them.'

'The headman gives you money?'

'He does. From the earnings of the farm. Obviously, there's the tithe to be done, but once that's out of the way the crops are taken to market and I get a share. A poor share, I'd reckon, with the town keeping the rest. With the headman taking the rest, more likely,' Wassa proclaimed. 'They cheat me out of my land and now out of my money.'

'Where is this farm?' Cwen asked. 'Have you ever been back there?'

'Oh, it's a way off,' Wassa said. 'It had to be the king's own land to give to my Chad, and this was the bit he got. It's down south.'

'Litchurch, way?' Cwen named a small collection of homes less than a mile away.

'Oh no,' Wassa said. 'It was down by the river crossing at Swarkestone.'

'Swarkestone?' That must be five miles away.'

'Aye, thereabouts.'

'And you went there every day?'

'Oh, bless me, no. We lived there.' Wassa was looking at Cwen as if weavers didn't know anything. 'Of course, we lived

192

on the farm, to begin with. Where else would we live? Can't look after the place and tend to things from five miles away. That would be daft.'

'I suppose so,' Cwen agreed. 'Then Chad died and you came here?'

'Not yet. The farm was doing so well, Chad said we should have a place in town, like well-to-do folk. So we built this.'

'And you came here?'

'We did. We even had some men to work the land. Chad reckoned as how we'd be nobles one day.'

'Nobles?' Cwen asked. Chad really was ambitious.

'That's it. We could get more land and have great estates.'

'Very impressive. But then Chad died.'

'Then he did. And the headman came and told me about the farm and how it belonged the town now.'

'That must have been a shock.'

'It was, I can tell you. I wasn't sure how I was going to manage the place on my own, but as you said, a new husband should have been easy to find.'

'How long ago was this?'

'Oh, be about two years now, I reckon.'

'And you've never gone back?'

'Five miles?' Wassa asked. 'Why would I walk five miles when I don't have to?'

'To see the old place again?'

'Pah,' Wassa dismissed that. 'Most of my married life was spent bent over those fields. Once we'd got men to work the land, why would we bother? Who'd want to be out in a horrible field when you've got a nice hearth to sit by.'

'But...,' Cwen began and stopped again. 'The farm. All this fuss is about them taking the farm away from you and you trying to get it back.'

193

'Yes, but I don't want to dig it myself, do I? It's mine, that's the point. And I could sell it if I wanted.'

'Sell it?' Cwen was thinking that this was not worth the bother. If Wassa didn't want the farm back to work it, why bother trying to get it for her?

'Why don't you get on and sell it, then?'

'Because it's not mine. Or so the headman says.'

'This is all very peculiar.' Cwen thought it was all going well beyond peculiar.

'You don't own a farm that you want to sell, but the headman is giving you money? Why would they give you anything at all? If the farm really was left to the town, they could have thrown you off and told you to sort yourself out. I've heard of the headman doing worse to people.'

'I suppose it's because I could still get the land back if I married again.' Wassa suggested.

'That's possible, I suppose. But it's still very, very odd.'

'Or it could have been something Chad said. Either that or they know they're in the wrong and are trying to make amends.'

'Hm.' Cwen couldn't see how this was working. 'I've known the headman be in the wrong many times, and he's never tried to put any of those right.'

She had no time for the headman and wouldn't be at all surprised to hear he was cheating a widow out of her inheritance. What was very surprising was to hear of him being kind or helpful to anyone.

Why did he appear to be doing anything decent at all? If there was money coming from the crops, the last thing that man would do would be willingly hand it over to anyone. He'd have a list of excuses and reasons why it couldn't be paid.

If Wassa became homeless and poor as a result, well, he wouldn't lose any sleep.

But, if there was one other aspect to the headman's character that must be in play, it was his cowardice. Yes, he was grasping and cheating and only interested in what was good for him, but confronted about what he was up to, he usually ran away or hid behind someone bigger. She could only think that for him to give money away, someone, or something, must be frightening the breeches off him.

'Is there anything else we need to know?' Cwen asked. 'Before we go and start looking for the headman?'

'What would you like to know?'

'Anything,' Cwen said with some exasperation. 'Anything about this business. The farm, Chad, this house, the money? It's all complicated enough as it is, but I thought I'd ask.'

'Can't think of anything.'

'Right, headman it is.'

The sight of Cwen marching down the main street with a very intense look on her face was usually enough to convince people that they'd got a lot of jobs to do indoors today. Faces would vanish and doors would be shut.

The sight of her marching with Wassa in her wake, and heading towards the headman's house, was enough to get the faces peering and the doors opening.

In fact, one or two hardy souls followed the pair, at a distance, to see what excitement was going to occur.

And hardy souls are usually followed by the less hardy, and so by the time of arrival at the headman's house, there was quite a crowd.

Cwen seemed to proceed as if she were the only person out today and knocked heavily on the headman's door.

'What is it now?' came from inside as the door was thrown

open quite angrily.

The first excitement of the day was the look on the headman's face when he saw what was going on outside. He only seemed to have eyes for the throng of townsfolk and was obviously trying to work out, very quickly, whether this was a good throng or a bad throng.

Only after a moment's appraisal did he drag his attention to the individual who had hammered on his door. That was the second excitement.

'Cwen,' he squeaked. 'Mistress Cwen, that is. Aha.'

'I want a word with you,' Cwen said.

Running away or hiding not being an option, the headman, tried to look for some of his authority.

'I see,' he managed to say quite sensibly. 'Is this town business?'

'Possibly,' Cwen said.

'Then the moot would be the right place and time.'

'Possibly not.'

'Or not.'

'It's about Mistress Wassa's farm.'

The headman seemed to have frozen in his own doorway. And it was a warm day.

'I see the topic is known to you,' Cwen said. 'Shall we come in, or would you like to discuss this on the street?'

'On the street,' a voice from the back of the crowd called.

'Come in, come in,' the headman said quickly and quietly. He held out an arm and indicated that they should pass inside. Once they had gone in, he gave the crowd a disappointed look and closed the door.

He then peered around the corner of a window to make sure that people were dispersing.

'What do you have to come shouting about that in the

middle of the town for?' he asked Cwen as he turned into the room.

'Not a problem, surely?' Cwen asked. 'There can't be a problem concerning Wassa's farm, can there? One that you don't want the town to know about? Never mind Wassa herself?'

The headman considered them both and seemed to be considering his options. He selected the one with the best chance of success and walked over to a chair that was set by the fire in the middle of the room.

He sat in this, buried his face in his hands and started to moan. 'Oh, God. Oh, God. I knew this day would come.'

'What day?' Cwen demanded. She gave Wassa a hopeful look that all would soon be well.

The headman dropped his hands and sighed.

'It was all their fault. I told them, but what could I do?'

'All whose fault?'

'Chad and Athlot.'

'I knew it,' Wassa snapped.

Cwen checked. 'This would be the Chad and Athlot who are now both dead and so can't explain for themselves?'

'It's true,' the headman pleaded. 'I should never have agreed.'

'Agreed to what?' Cwen asked.

Caput XX: A Horse, A Horse, Unfortunately

'No,' Hermitage said, bewildered by the very question. 'It's not in Scotland. It's only about ten miles away.'

'And Scotland's farther, is it?'

'Well, yes, of course, it is.'

'There's no of course about it. I'm Norman, how am I supposed to know where Scotland is?'

Hermitage thought that was an odd question from a man who seemed most anxious not to go there. 'I can assure you that Nottingham is not in Scotland. It will only take us a morning's walk. Scotland is much, much farther away. Hundreds of miles. It would take you weeks to get there.'

Fortmain seemed very relieved at this information. 'And weeks for anyone from Scotland to get here,' he reasoned.

'Well, yes. And England and Scotland have long had enmity towards one another over virtually everything. I understand that Edgar Aethling may have fled to Scotland.'

'Is that right?' Fortmain asked, clearly not having the first clue who Hermitage was talking about.

'So,' Hermitage moved on. 'Let us gather what we need and set off. We may be there by noon if we take a lively step.'

'We'll be there and back by noon,' Fortmain said.

Just for the briefest moment, Hermitage wondered how that was going to be possible. Unfortunately, the moment soon passed and he knew what would make it possible: horses.

The enmity between Scotland and England was nothing compared to that between horses and Hermitage. And it was all one-sided.

He had nothing against the animals. They were fine, magnificent beasts capable of so much. But they were best observed from a good distance. Whenever one got near Hermitage, it seemed to act upon some secret horse-knowledge and do its best to unsettle him. Either literally, by throwing him from its back, onto which he had been placed against his will, or by doing something surprising, like coming up to him.

In this situation, most people stroked the horse on the top of its nose or gave it something to eat. Hermitage knew that behind that nose were the teeth. They may not be the teeth of a dog or a cat, but they were big, there were a lot of them and they were far too close to his face.

'A horse, eh?' Hermitage asked, hopeful that the Normans had brought some new form of transport that worked without horses.

'And we can have one each now the others have gone,' Fortmain said brightly.

'I'm not, erm, not really used to horses,' Hermitage tried to explain. 'Monks being required to walk everywhere.' He knew this wasn't true but hoped the Norman wouldn't. And of course, he felt bad about the falsehood.

'You don't know how to ride?' Fortmain asked incredulously.

'Well, no.'

Fortmain sighed. 'I suppose you'll have to double up with one of the others, then.'

Hermitage didn't really know which was worse, being on a horse with someone, or being on his own. He concluded that it was the latter. If a horse got him alone, it would probably carry him off so the rest of the horses could deal with him.

Fortmain quickly summoned his men and issued the orders for departure. He chose one of his band to take Hermitage, and unlike most Normans he'd come across, this fellow did not violently object to having a monk on his horse. In fact, he was quite welcoming; which was a bit concerning.

'Come then, Brother,' the Norman said. 'Let's to the saddle. Ever ridden before?'

'No,' Hermitage said honestly. He never had ridden. He had been carried or thrown on a horse like a pack, but he'd never ridden. Riding sounded too much like being in charge of the horse, and he knew that would never happen.

The Norman mounted the horse and then held a hand down to pull Hermitage up.

Gathering his habit between his legs, Hermitage held his own hand up and before he knew it, was sitting on the back of the horse. The Norman had done this before.

'Hold on to the back of the saddle,' the Norman instructed. 'I doubt we'll be going at full gallop.'

Hermitage was confident that if they went at full gallop, he would no longer be on the back of the horse to worry about it.

'I'm Pinel,' the Norman introduced himself.

'Brother Hermitage.'

'Yes, I heard.'

Hermitage was pleasantly surprised to note that the Norman did not say that this was a funny name for a monk.

'My sister's a nun,' Pinel said.

Oh, Lord, Hermitage thought. Nuns and horses. His nightmares tonight would be well-stocked.

'Is she?' he said.

'Seems to like it,' Pinel observed.

At that moment, Fortmain issued the order to leave and the horses trotted off.

As Hermitage was thrown about on the rear end of the horse, Pinel twisted round and took his arm. Guiding his movements to match those of the animal, Hermitage found that the throwing and pummelling he took was considerably diminished. It was still nothing even approaching comfort, but it was better.

'I erm,' Pinel began hesitantly. 'I hear you do murders?'

'Oh, well, not do them, no. I investigate them.'

'Is that right?'

'Yes. It's from the Latin, vestigare, to track. I track murders, or murderers, to be more precise. I find out who did it if you like.'

'You find out who did it?' Pinel sounded quite disappointed.

'That's it.'

'What if they don't want to be found?'

'They seldom do, but they have to be found and brought to justice.'

'Really?'

'Absolutely.'

Pinel breathed out heavily. 'So, if someone close at hand killed someone else, you'd know who did it and bring them to justice?'

'I might not know, but I would try to work it out.'

Pinel muttered something under his breath in Norman French. Hermitage couldn't follow it, but it didn't sound happy.

'And are you, erm doing any of this finding out at the moment?'

'Possibly. It could be that a fellow called Athlot was murdered, but we don't know for sure. That's partly why we're going to Nottingham.'

'Ah,' Pinel brightened a little. 'His killer could be around somewhere, then?'

'Could be, I suppose, although he did die some time ago.'

'And you'd find him. This person who killed Athlot.'

'That would be the intention.'

'I see.' Pinel was silent for a few moments. 'Could you introduce, erm, point him out when you find him? Only I'd like to, erm, see what a killer looks like.'

'They look like the rest of us,' Hermitage said, thinking this was a morbid area of interest. 'If we find someone, I'm sure it will become known to all,' he said.

'I suppose that would do,' Pinel nodded to himself. 'This Nottingham place, then?' he asked as they rode along. 'Something to do with the murder? Is the killer there?' he asked with quite unseemly enthusiasm.

'Did Fortmain not tell you?'

'He doesn't tell us anything.'

'I want to talk to Lord Gilbert and examine any books he has on Norman history.'

'Was this Athlot killed that long ago, then?' Pinel was disappointed once more.

'No, no. But it's possible that he was in Normandy at some time in the past.' Hermitage didn't want to give too much away to a Norman soldier. If there was some connection to Athlot's death from sinister Norman forces, this man might be part of it.

He told himself that Fortmain and his band could not have had anything to do with Athlot as they had only just arrived in town with Bart. Still, a Norman was a Norman, after all.

'Do you know Lord Gilbert?' Hermitage diverted the subject.

'I don't know no lordships, me,' Pinel sounded quite pleased about it. 'We get there and I'll leave you to it. I expect those will be my instructions from Fortmain anyway.' This he did not sound pleased about.

They arrived in Nottingham faster than Hermitage had expected and he worried that he was getting used to riding on a horse.

As forecast, Fortmain instructed his men to wait and tend to the animals, while he accompanied Hermitage to the main keep of Nottingham castle.

Hermitage sighed as they approached the place. It didn't seem that long ago that he had been here dealing with a most convoluted and disgraceful affair.[A Murder of Convenience; an equal measure of both.]

At least Lord Gilbert himself was as reasonable a Norman as Hermitage had come across. A soldier at heart, he was happiest in and around others of his kind. Being lord of a castle seemed more of a burden than a triumph.

Hermitage froze as Fortmain approached the main door. He'd forgotten Aveline. How could he forget Aveline? Lord Gilbert's daughter was not a soldier's daughter at heart. He wasn't sure what she was at heart, but it wasn't anything nice. And she didn't like Hermitage.

But it was too late now, Fortmain had pushed through the door and entered the main hall.

It was a large space, flagged with stone and scattered with straw, which Hermitage didn't remember from last time. Torches hung on the walls, filling the place with an acrid smell while the light from small openings high in the wall gave little additional illumination.

A large figure looked over from the fire at the other end of the room, which was the brightest thing in here, and peered at the new arrivals.

'Brother Hermitage?' Gilbert called brightly. 'Is that

Brother Hermitage?'

'My Lord,' Hermitage gave a bow of the head as the two of them walked over to meet Gilbert halfway.

'Why Brother Hermitage,' Gilbert beamed a smile. 'What brings you to Nottingham. Not murder?'

'I fear so, my lord. Although possibly not. Well, hopefully not, I suppose I should say.'

'And who is this?' Gilbert asked, turning to Fortmain.

'Fortmain,' Fortmain announced with a bow.

'Fortmain? Gilbert didn't sound so happy now. 'Not Fortmain of Caen?' he asked suspiciously.

'My lord,' Fortmain bowed again.

'Really?' Gilbert clearly wondered at anyone admitting that.

'I have offered my service to the King's Investigator,' Fortmain said.

'Does the king know?' Gilbert asked.

'I have not seen the king for some time,' Fortmain replied as if delivering a report.

'And I think we know why that is,' Gilbert commented.

'My father..,' Fortmain began.

'Is probably best not mentioned,' Gilbert said. He considered Fortmain. 'But, if you're trying to do something useful, I suppose we mustn't complain.'

Fortmain knew enough to be quiet at this point.

'Your castle seems different, somehow,' Hermitage said as Gilbert brought them both over to the fire and ordered wine.

'It's Aveline,' Gilbert said.

'Ah, really.'

'Yes, she's gone.' Gilbert sounded inappropriately happy about this.

'Gone?' Hermitage asked with some horror.

'To Paris.'

'Ah, Paris.'

'Yes. King Philip wanted hostages from William. As a sign of good faith and fealty and so forth.'

'Really?' Hermitage had no idea how these things worked but had heard of hostages being exchanged, even between friends.

'Yes,' Gilbert didn't sound too sure about this arrangement now. 'And Aveline volunteered.'

'That was very noble of her.'

'Fortmain?' Gilbert asked. 'Did you hear anything of hostages for Philip?'

'No, my lord. But then, I am hardly in a position to know of such things.'

'I suppose not.'

Hermitage broached a question. 'You heard of the hostage request from, erm..,?'

'Aveline,' Gilbert confirmed.

'Ah.'

'But she has sent word that she is there safe.'

'That is good,' Hermitage tried to sound encouraging. If anything, he felt some sympathy for Philip.

'Anyway,' Gilbert dismissed the question. 'What foul deeds bring Brother Hermitage to my hall?'

'Only questions, really,' Hermitage said. 'There has been a death in Derby, and I am trying to find out if there is any question of murder.'

'At the king's request?' Gilbert asked.

'Well, no,' Hermitage admitted. 'A local fellow mentioned it to me, and I made some, what you might call preliminary inquiries.'

'You are too devoted to your calling, Brother,' Gilbert said.

Hermitage didn't need Gilbert telling him this as well.

'And who is the maybe victim?'

'A fellow called Athlot.'

'Athlot, eh. Good Saxon sounding name.'

'It means nothing to you?'

Gilbert looked into the fire and turned the wine goblet in his hand. Eventually, he shook his head. 'I know of no Athlot at all, never mind one in Derby. Don't think I've ever fought, captured or killed anyone called Athlot.'

'He was not always in Derby,' Hermitage pressed ahead in the face of this disappointing information. 'He was a fellow of great age and may have served under King Aethelred.'

'Good God,' Gilbert said. 'You are going back. How old was this Athlot?'

'They say he was ninety.'

'And you think he was murdered?' Gilbert sounded both horrified and surprised. 'Who would murder a ninety-year-old?'

'That is the question. There are indications that he had money, so that could be motive enough. And I also wondered about his service. It's possible that he went to Normandy with Aethelred.'

'And annoyed someone who wants revenge now that a Norman king rules England?' Gilbert got straight to the point.

'That is another thought.'

'If anyone is still alive, to remember,' Gilbert said.

'If he caused a great enough offence..,?'

'Families do keep track of these things,' Gilbert nodded his head toward Fortmain. 'But as I say, the name means nothing to me.'

'I wondered if you had any books?'

'Books?' Gilbert asked. 'Have we finished with murder now? He clearly wondered why Hermitage had suddenly changed the subject.

'Books of history. Books that might be a record of those years in Normandy.

Gilbert shook his head slowly. 'I've never been one for books,' he said. 'Aveline had some, but they went to Paris with her.'

'And none of your people have any?' Hermitage asked desperately, thinking that this journey had been a complete waste of time.

'No,' Gilbert had nothing to offer. 'Only tallies of supplies and the like. Oh,' he said. 'That's a thought. We could ask Silas.'

'Silas?'

'He's been around forever. Served my father. I wouldn't be surprised if he was ninety as well.'

'And where will we find this Silas?'

'Usual place, I expect. Some hole in the ground.'

Caput XXI: Routine Inquiries

Wat stood in the middle of the town street and looked up and down as if expecting to see Marcus and Rachel.

'They won't have gone,' he said to Bart. 'Rachel spent months waiting for the moment to get her master's coin. She won't give up on a dead man's very quickly.'

'But if it wasn't in his home, where would it be?' Bart asked.

'Hidden,' Wat said from experience. 'But where, that's the question.'

'Could be anywhere.'

'No, it couldn't. You don't just hide coin anywhere, especially if you need to get at it regularly, which it seemed Athlot did. It must be nearby.'

'Perhaps they went on and found where it was hidden and have gone now?'

Wat didn't like to think about that awful prospect.

'We can still follow their trail,' Wat said, brightening at the thought. 'We can track them. Vestigare and all that.'

Bart nodded agreement to this but didn't have anything helpful to say.

'What was all that nonsense you were going on about in the workshop?' Wat asked.

'Nonsense?' Bart sounded a little offended at the suggestion.

'Yes, when you asked how many homes there were in Derby.'

'Oh, that. Yes, I was going to go and ask everyone if they'd killed Athlot. It was silly, I see that now. I only tried it on one person, and it didn't go very well at all.'

'Exactly,' Wat said. 'We don't go and ask about Athlot, we ask about Marcus and Rachel. After all, she's pretty noticeable. If you saw her walking down the street you'd remember.'

'I suppose I would.'

'There we are then.' Wat looked up and down the street again, this time with more intent. 'That place is nearest the smithy.' He pointed to a good-sized dwelling set right on the road. 'Home of the Alodie family, if I recall. Oh, perhaps we won't start there.'

'It doesn't look like anyone's at home.' Bart said.

'No, and there's a reason for that. We'll try farther down the street.'

'That smithy's boy said that they arrived at dawn, yes?' Bart asked.

'He did, yes.'

'And it won't have taken them long to knock down Athlot's house, so they'd have been gone again pretty quickly.'

'I suppose so.'

'Then we need to ask people who would have been up at dawn.'

'Everyone's up at dawn.' Wat pointed out. 'Why would you not be?'

'But not everyone is out and about. Yes, people get up with the light, of course, they do. But some have tasks in their homes first. Others are already up and at work. Yet more are on the way. No point getting to a field before dawn, you wouldn't be able to see what you were doing.'

Wat could see the sense of this. 'It would be a waste of time asking people who wouldn't have had a chance of seeing them.'

'That's it.'

'Right.' Wat considered the dwellings and buildings of Derby for where a good place to start might be. 'The leatherman.'

'Leatherman?'

'He wouldn't open until dawn, no customers. But he'd want to be ready. People might want belts or harnesses fixing before the day's work began. He'll do. And he's a nosy so-and-so.'

Wat strode off towards the leatherworker's shop.

The only differentiation between this place and anyone's normal dwelling was that the outside was festooned with belts and straps and all manner of bits of leather, waiting to be made into something useful. At least the skins he used were fully prepared for working and the place didn't stink like the tanner's.

The door was open and Wat leaned his head in.

'Ah,' a cry burst forth, followed by the brushy end of a broom. The leathermaker's wife appeared at the handle end. 'It's Wat the Weaver!' she hollered as if warning the town. 'Out, out. We don't want your sort here.'

Wat held his hand out. 'I am not here for me,' he pleaded. 'Brother Hermitage is investigating the death of Athlot and I just want to ask if you saw anything.'

'I've seen nothing,' the woman screeched. 'And I don't want to see anything from you, you demon.'

'Oh, come on now..,'

'What'll people say if they see you here. Go on, be off with you. You've got your own workshop, why aren't you in it instead of bothering honest people?'

'I only want to know..,'

'Is that Wat the Weaver?' another voice asked. This was the butcher, who appeared at the opening of his shop, about four doors away.

'Can you believe it?' The leathermaker's wife said. 'In broad daylight?'

'You see him off,' the butcher suggested.

'I am doing. And it'll be more than a broom in a moment.'

'Oh, for heaven's sake,' Wat sighed as he backed away. 'Bart, you ask them. And tell them you're with Hermitage, not me.'

With Wat retreating down the lane, Bart approached the leathermaker's wife with some caution as the broom was still at the ready.

'Good morrow,' Bart tried.

'Don't you good morrow me. You're with him.'

'I am Bart, the King's Investigator's apprentice. Brother Hermitage, you know?'

'You're one of them weavers. It's disgusting.'

'I am not, I assure you. I'm just asking if anyone saw a strangely dressed woman in the town around dawn.'

'He wants a strangely dressed woman now!' The leathermaker's wife twittered at the butcher, who tutted and shook his head at the state of the world.

'I just wondered if you'd see one, that's all?'

'Decently dressed women, that's what he ought to be asking for.' The leathermaker's wife gave one last wave of her broom and retreated indoors.

The butcher now tutted and shook his head at the state of the leathermaker's wife.

Bart risked an approach. 'I don't suppose you noticed a strange-looking woman around this morning?' he asked. 'There would have been a man with her.'

'Ah, well,' the butcher said. 'Now you're asking.'

'Erm, yes, I am.'

'There you are then.'

'And did you? See anyone like that?'

'Sounds as if you'd like to know.'

'Yes, I would.' Bart gave Wat a confused look as the weaver wandered back now that brooms had been withdrawn.

'How much?' the butcher asked.

'Quite a lot, actually,' Bart explained. 'You see it's to do with the death of Athlot.'

'He means, how much?' Wat clarified.

'Yes, I heard. And I was just explaining that I'd like to know quite a lot. Well, even more than that, really.'

'No,' Wat said slowly. 'How much are you going to pay him to find out?'

'Pay him?' Bart was lost.

'Yes. Apart from meat, the butcher is now selling you the answer to your question. He's just waiting for you to tell him how much you're willing to pay.'

The butcher nodded thanks to Wat for the clear explanation.

'But what if the answer is that he didn't see anyone?'

'I don't think he'd be asking for your money if he didn't have a better answer than that.'

'I'm not sure this is right,' Bart said. 'How can we trust the answer if it's paid for?'

'Tell you what,' Wat came closer. 'Let's try another approach.' He nodded to the butcher as if they were about to engage in some formal debate.

'The butcher will tell us whether he saw anyone this morning, or I will tell the leathermaker's wife who he asked for a tapestry of a few years back.'

The butcher managed to look pale and angry and terrified at the same time. He appeared to consider his position, but not for long. 'They went down towards the church,' he snapped and turned back to his shop.

'There we are,' Wat smiled.

'I'm not sure that's much better,' Bart said.

'You know, I think you and Hermitage might get on after all. Come on, to the church.'

They walked on down the road in the direction of the church.

'What do you think they were going to the church for?' Bart asked.

'We don't know that they were going to the church. We only know that they were going in that direction. There's lots of things in that direction.'

Bart was very thoughtful as they continued.

'There's also Athlot's body and the priest who buried him,' he said.

'Oh,' Wat was interested. 'So there is. I wouldn't put it past Rachel to threaten a priest with something or other, but I think even she'd pull up short of digging up the dead.'

Bart looked quite appalled at the idea.

'Depends how much money we're talking about, I suppose.' Wat shrugged.

The church was quiet as they walked up towards it. There was definitely no sign of any digging, either to put someone into the ground or take them out.

'The priest here is, how can I put it? Not very priestly,' Wat explained. 'Even Hermitage is suspicious that the man might not even be a priest at all. And it takes a lot to make Hermitage suspicious. We'll be lucky to talk to him, let alone get any useful information.

'Mind you, if Rachel passed through, I'm sure he'll remember.'

Up at the main door, Wat gave a half-hearted push and was surprised to find that the door swung open.

'Not locked?' he asked the air. 'There must be something going on.'

He pressed forward on the door, and it swung right back on its hinges. Carefully poking his head around the corner, Wat called out into the dark interior.

'Hello? Any priests at home?'

There was no reply.

'Now that doesn't surprise me,' Wat said as he walked on in.

Bart followed close on his heels and they both considered the dank, dusty interior of the church.

Off in the gloomy distance, the altar was a simple affair but was the neatest spot in the place. This priest may not be much of a priest but even a bad one would not risk his eternal soul by neglecting his most sacred duties.

Bowing to the altar, as they had been taught, the two of them walked down the aisle, rapidly losing hope of discovering anything useful.

Only as they got as close to the altar as they were allowed, did they notice that the priest seemed to be taking his devotion to extremes, by sleeping at its foot.

The muffled voice and the wriggling of the arms and legs indicated that he may have been put here against his will.

'Rachel,' Wat said as he stepped up to release the priest from his earthly bonds. He also pulled the cloth from the man's mouth, which looked like it was supposed to go somewhere completely different.

'Where are they?' the priest snarled as he regained the power of speech.

'Gone,' Wat said. 'I take it this was a man with a woman

who looked like a witch. Marcus and Aurelius, although you could call her Rachel, if she knew you well.'

'I didn't catch their names,' the priest said angrily as they released his arms and legs. 'But they have desecrated holy ground.'

'She's like that,' Wat observed. 'Took some money, I imagine.'

'They stole from the church,' the priest was outraged. 'Can you imagine such a thing?'

'Must have been quite a sum,' Wat said. 'More than the week's donations to get you tied up.'

The priest now got back to his feet and looked around his church as if hoping that he'd spot them hiding in a corner.

'Find them,' the priest commanded.

Wat did not move. 'How much money are we talking about?'

'How much? What does that have to do with anything?'

'Quite a lot. If it was say three shillings, I'd think it almost certainly belonged to the church. Ordinary folk paying their dues. If it was more than that, I'd have my doubts about where it came from. And where it was going.'

'How dare you?' The priest gave a priestly glare. It seemed to bounce off Wat so he turned it on Bart. 'Who is this?' he demanded.

'This is Bart who is helping the King's Investigator.'

'Brother Hermitage.' The priest seemed to almost sag at the name. 'I might have known he'd be involved in this somehow. If something is going to go wrong in this town, you can be sure it's circled Brother Hermitage first. Isn't it time he moved somewhere else? Closer to the king, perhaps?'

'Brother Hermitage is investigating a murder,' Bart said quite officially. 'And it is the duty of all to offer him aid.'

'He can investigate another one when I get hold of the people who stole from me.' The priest looked like he was struggling not to ask the next question, but he couldn't resist. Even so, it was a weary and disinterested enquiry. 'Who's been murdered, then?'

'Old Athlot,' Wat said.

'Athlot?' The priest's tone was an odd one and Wat detected it.

'Yes, Athlot. Why is that of such interest to you?'

The priest tried to regain his composure. 'I have just interred the man. I didn't know that he had been a murder victim.'

'Neither do we, for sure.' Wat's eyes narrowed as disgraceful thoughts crossed his mind. That was the advantage of having naturally disgraceful thoughts, you could spot them in others. 'Did he have a good burial?'

The priest tipped his head towards the back of the church. 'He has a place of rest within the walls.'

'My, my,' Wat almost whistled, but there were some things even he wouldn't do in church. 'That must have cost a bit.'

'Athlot was well provided for.'

'Come on,' Wat said with some finality, folding his arms as he did so. 'If we're going to try and get this money back from Rachel, we need to know what's going on.'

The priest did not respond.

'And I don't think you have a chance of getting it on your own. If it's even yours in the first place. Or should I say the church's?'

For a man of the cloth, the priest looked to be horribly calculating for a moment.

'All right,' he said. 'The money was mine, I mean the church's. It was a bequest from Athlot.'

'A bequest?'

'That's right, It's perfectly reasonable for him to make a bequest.'

'It is, it is,' Wat agreed. 'No problem with that at all. I imagine it was quite a large bequest, what with Athlot being well provided for.'

'It was significant,' the priest admitted.

'And when did he make this bequest? Before or after he died?'

'Before, of course,' the priest snapped. 'He had been making it gradually for some considerable time.'

'Really?'

'Yes, really. Do not cast your own avaricious nature on the priesthood, Wat the Weaver,' the man patronised.

'I wouldn't dream of it,' Wat said. 'I'd cast it on you though. Why was Athlot bequesting nicely for some considerable time?'

'Why does any man? He was of great age and knew that his years could not be many more. He wanted to be sure that he was well received in the hereafter, and that prayers would be said for him down the years. And that his sins would be forgiven.'

'Hm. Any sins in particular?'

'You expect me to break sacred vows and reveal the confidences of another soul?'

'Yes please.'

'It could have a bearing on the murder,' Bart added.

'Well, I won't. All I will say is that Athlot saw himself as a sinner, as should we all, and was making his recompense.'

'And he started this a while ago?'

'He did.'

'All right.' That seemed to be all Wat was going to get out

of this man, but it was very interesting. 'We'll go and see if we can pick up the trail of Rachel. I take it this money was quite heavy?'

'It was in a chest,' the priest said. 'Quite a large one.'

'Good, that'll slow them down. You had better go and alert the headman, while we carry on looking.'

The priest paused briefly and then nodded agreement. He ushered them both out of the church and carefully locked the door behind them.

'Well, well, well,' Wat said when they were alone once more. 'Wasn't that fascinating?'

'I suppose so,' Bart didn't seem quite so fascinated. 'At least we know where Athlot's money went.'

'We do. Don't you think it odd that his donations to the church, which have been taking place for quite a while now, are still in this very church? Why hasn't the priest passed them on to his Bishop? Surely that's the proper thing to do.'

'I wouldn't know,' Bart said.

'No, neither would I, really,' Wat admitted. 'But I know a monk who would.' He mused further. 'I also think I know a priest who wouldn't be averse to helping an old man off a ladder if there was a chest of coin involved.'

Caput XXII: Ride In the Country

'I suppose you'd better see,' the headman wilted under the onslaught of the two women, one of whom wasn't really onslaughting at all.

'See what?' Cwen demanded.

'The land.'

'Wassa's land? It's five miles away. I'm not walking five miles to look at a field. You can tell me about it.'

The headman shook his head. If I told you about it, you wouldn't understand. You have to see it. We can take my cart.'

The headman's claim that all headmen had carts of their own provided and paid for by the town had never been challenged as so few people knew any other headmen. Nonetheless, there was always the suspicion that the headman had made this up; mainly because he made a lot of things up that were for his own good.

'Why do we have to go five miles in a cart to see a bit of land? Cwen persisted.

'Because it will all be clear,' the headman said. He tried to find a bit of courage. 'And I'm not going to tell you about it anyway, I'm only going to show you.'

Cwen looked to Wassa and shook her head in disappointment at the headman's idiocy.

'Hermitage has gone to Nottingham to find out about Athlot,' she said. 'I suppose we've got the time.'

'Time?' the headman asked.

'The time before Hermitage comes back and tells us who murdered Athlot.'

'Murdered him!' the headman almost fell off his chair. 'What do you mean, murdered him?'

'It turns out there's a lot more to Athlot than meets the eye.' Cwen enjoyed seeing the headman squirm. 'Connections to one of the old kings and Normandy, secret wealth, that sort of thing. Just what makes one person kill someone else.'

'But he was ninety years old. He fell off a ladder.'

'If Hermitage says that's what happened, fine. But if he doesn't, we'll have a killer on our hands.'

The headman did not look at all happy, which was good.

'Come on then,' Cwen instructed. 'Get your cart and let's go and have a look at this exciting field.'

Taking a lot longer about the task than would normally be the case, the headman hitched the town horse to the town cart, and they were ready to be off.

'It's quite a nice day for it,' Wassa observed. 'I'll be interested to see how the old place is coming along.'

'Of course, you will,' the headman grumbled.

The horse trotted along and Cwen could see that five miles would quickly go by.

'Wassa, then,' she said to the headman. 'Why didn't she inherit the land from Chad?'

'That was the agreement.'

'Agreement? What agreement?'

'The agreement that said she would not inherit the land from Chad.'

'Don't try and be clever with me,' Cwen instructed.

'It'll make sense when we get there. And I wouldn't believe everything that old Wassa says if I were you.'

'Who are you calling old?' Wassa demanded.

'You,' the headman made it clear. 'Funny how Athlot dies and you suddenly start claiming the land.'

'That land is mine. I've been saying it for years,' Wassa insisted.

'But happy enough to sit in your house and take the money until now. Didn't want to know what was going on, did you?' He mimicked Wassa. 'Don't tell me and then I won't know. And what I don't know can't hurt me.'

'I've been cheated of my inheritance,' Wassa insisted.

'Funny sort of cheating when you've had it three times over already. And I've never seen you coming to give anything back because you've had too much.'

'What is going on?' Cwen pressed.

'No point explaining,' the headman said. 'You've got to see.'

They trotted on in uncooperative silence, taking the main road out of Derby to the south. It was a busy trail, being the main route from the north on to Coventry and the south. The River Trent was crossable farther on where shallows allowed for a ford.

All manner of people walked the road along with the three on the cart. There were even people on horseback and a contingent of Norman soldiers heading away from Derby, fortunately.

Anyone looking remotely well-off or with goods was stopped by the Normans as they made their way. Luckily, the headman, Cwen and Wassa looked neither and so were left alone.

A few of the less well off tried to take a ride on the cart, but a shout from the headman and a look from Cwen saw them off.

'This land is near the road, then?' Cwen asked after they had gone on for quite a while.

'Exactly,' the headman said as if it explained anything.

'Make it easier to get crops to market, I suppose. Or drive sheep from grazing. How much land is there?' she asked

Wassa, only now realising that it was probably quite an important question.

'Oh, quite a few acres,' Wassa said proudly.

'Quite a few? How many?'

'Oh, well, it'd be about, erm, one hundred and two acres, three roods, fifteen perches.'

'That's very precise,' Cwen observed. 'And it's a lot of land to be gifted by the king.'

'He was a good man, my Chad.'

'Ha!' The headman did not seem to share the opinion.

The road was getting crowded now as they drew towards the river.

'Are we nearly there yet?' Cwen asked.

'We are,' the headman announced. He drove the cart off to the side of the road and through a gap in the hedge that led onto a low field of grass.

'Is this it?' Cwen asked. It didn't look very valuable, having no crops on it at all. Still, perhaps it was grazing this year. Well, it would have been grazing if there were any sheep.

The horse seemed very happy with their destination and kept trying to stop to try the grass.

The headman urged the animal on until they came to a bend in the hedging and the field dropped away farther to the river.'

'What the hell?' Cwen could not contain her shock.

'Told you you had to see it,' the headman said.

Cwen climbed down from the cart and considered the sight before her. The crowds of travellers were congregating and there was a buzz of conversation as people and livestock and carts made their way back and forth across the river at an almost constant rate.

There was only one question that she had to ask, even

though she thought it was one of the most stupid ones she would ever utter.

'Where in God's name did that bridge come from?'

'Nice, isn't it?' the headman asked.

Wassa was shaking her head in a very disappointed manner. 'This is shocking,' she said, her voice notable for its absence of shock.

Cwen tried to consider this in a purely disinterested manner and concluded that no, it was not nice. Not really. It was a bridge in that it spanned the river, but that was about it. Wooden piles had been driven into the riverbed and planks had been laid across them, but construction had stopped there. If anyone was of a mind, they could simply walk off the edge of the bridge into the water below.

And the water below wasn't even that far below. At its height, the bridge was only about six feet above the swirling current.

Cwen had to say the next words as well, even though they were plainly wrong. 'That should not be here,' she said in a very matter of fact manner; in the face of a very factual bridge. 'The only crossings here are one very rickety line of planks and a ford. It's Swarkestone ford, everyone knows that.'

'That's the clever bit,' the headman said.

Cwen wiped a hand over her face as she worked this out.

'This is Chad and Wassa's land and you've built a bridge on it.'

'That we have. Well, they have.'

'Who?'

'Chad and Athlot.'

'Ah.' Cwen now saw the scheme and the sense of it. 'And a good toll is being charged to cross the bridge that Chad and Athlot built.'

'Of course. Can't cross a bridge without paying a toll.'

'Quite right. And tell me, did the king know about the bridge that Chad and Athlot built? So he could take his tax?'

'Don't think he ever came this way,' the headman said.

'And they didn't bother to mention it to him,' Cwen concluded. 'You know, you were right. I did have to see it.'

'Told you.'

'Let's work it out further. You can't build a bridge without money. Not even a rather bad one like this. And Athlot had money.'

The headman said nothing.

'While Chad had the land in the right place.'

'Chad and Wassa,' Wassa put in.

'And of course, the town would need to keep quiet about the bridge and more specifically the toll. Wouldn't want them telling the king's taxman.'

'If you say so.' The headman certainly wasn't saying.

'And Athlot's money was much safer in a bridge than sitting around in a chest waiting to be stolen at any moment. And he would get money from the bridge every time someone crossed over.' Cwen stopped herself.

'I'm sorry,' she said more to herself than any of the others. 'How can anyone not notice a bridge? How did word not get to the king that someone had built a toll bridge over the Trent? This is a main thoroughfare.'

The headman shrugged. 'He was busy?'

'Busy? Kings are never too busy to miss their taxes.'

'It was just good timing I suppose. By the time it was built, Edward was dying and people were arguing over who was going to be king. Harold had a bit more to worry about than the odd bridge here and there, and then William arrives. As far as he knows there's always been a bridge here. The

Normans even pay their tolls like everyone.'

Cwen couldn't believe the sheer cheek and luck. 'They're going to find out, you know. The Normans are planning to count everything in the country. I don't think they're going to miss a whole bridge.'

'That's all right. It's here now. If we have to pay some tax, I suppose we'll manage.'

'Suppose you'll manage, ha. And what about the town? Didn't anyone there wonder who just put a bridge up on their road?'

The headman considered the sky and the trees. 'Perhaps they thought the king had done it.'

'You mean you told them the king had done it.' Cwen turned to Wassa. 'And you must have known all about this,' she said. 'How can you not know about a bridge on your own land? It's not like a rabbit warren in the bottom field.'

'Because she took great efforts not to find out,' the headman said. 'Never came back here, never asked where the money was coming from. Any time the subject came up, she'd put her hands over her ears and leave the room. Made sure that poor Mistress Wassa wasn't responsible for anything.'

He looked at her hard. 'And why do you think she never married again?'

'She said you drove away her suitor.'

'Yes, she would say that. Couldn't have a man coming along and taking her wealth, could she? How unfair would that be? A man inherit the land that's paying her so well? She frightened Blednot away. I don't know what she did to him, but he even left town.'

'It's my land,' Wassa said. 'That's the point.'

'You were happy enough to live in the house and take the money without even wanting to talk about the land until now.

Ah,' he drawled as he saw the change. 'Of course. Athlot is dead. Suddenly the land is very interesting again.'

Wassa tried to shrug as if that didn't matter, but it obviously did.

'So,' Cwen addressed the headman in her straightforward manner. 'Tell me everything about this arrangement.'

'Let's go down onto the bridge,' the headman suggested. 'You can have closer look.'

'I'm not sure I want to go on that thing,' Cwen said. 'If that's the result of Athlot's wealth, it can't have been as great as we thought. Why couldn't they build a proper bridge?'

'They're expensive things, bridges. And you don't want to go mad if you're trying to make a bit of money.' The headman nodded that they should all get back in the cart and he slowly drove it down the slope towards the bridge.

'The explanation?' Cwen prompted.

'Right. As you say, Athlot had money and Chad had land. Obviously, Athlot wasn't going to just give his money to Chad and Chad wasn't just going to give his land to Athlot. So they agreed to a share.'

'From what I know already that doesn't sound like them, but go on.'

'And they had to think what to do when one of them died. As neither had any children, the easiest thing would have been to simply leave their share to the other one. But they weren't keen on that.'

'Greedy in life, greedy in death, eh?'

'So, when the first one died, the running of the bridge would be taken over by the town, rather than the one still living. If it was Chad, Wassa here would continue to be looked after and Athlot would keep getting his share. Half Chad's share would go to the town to run the bridge.'

'If it had been Athlot, Chad could have kept his full share coming in until he died.'

'And when they're both dead?' Cwen asked.

'They never really made that clear. I don't think they cared if the other one was dead. Just didn't want him having more in life.'

'Charming,' Cwen commented.

'However,' the headman went on. 'The obvious thing is that they would want the town to carry on running the bridge and looking after Wassa.'

'Oh, no,' Wassa said. 'On the contrary. The bridge and the land should come to me as the last survivor. I get both shares and I might give something to the town.'

'But you never paid for the bridge,' the headman pointed out.

'Which is on my land,' Wassa retorted.

They had arrived at the bridge now and all got out again, the headman and Wassa sharing hateful looks.

'Ho there, Ursen,' the headman called up to the bridge house.

A bridge house was what a bridge should have so that the man who took the tolls could be under cover in bad weather and protected against any passing robbers who thought they'd quite like all the toll money.

In this case, the bridge house was a table. And not a very good table either.

Ursen the toll man looked down and appeared to be quite harassed.

'Oh, thank God you're here,' he called down. 'It's mad today. I don't know what's going on. Here, come and take this before someone helps themselves.'

While simultaneously taking tolls from travellers as they

passed by in both directions, Ursen kicked a sack at his feet. It was a big sack and it didn't move at all when he kicked it.

Wat would have recognised the sound; it was that of a large number of coins in pain.

The bridge users continued to pass and hand over more money, many of them complaining about how long it was taking and how a bridge really ought to have more than one toll-man for days like this.

The headman went over and slid the sack of coin off the bridge, staggering slightly as he took its weight.

'I can see why you wanted the cart,' Cwen said. Even she was quite impressed at the volume of coin being generated by this bridge. 'You could use the money to improve the bridge,' she said.

The headman and Wassa looked at her as if she were mad.

'Some of it,' Cwen clarified. 'You'll get nothing if the bridge falls down for want of repair.'

No, they still didn't get it.

'Anyway, I can see why there's now an argument over who gets the bridge.' She shook her head as Wassa stood very close to the headman while he handled the money.

'And,' Cwen said, looking at them both quite piercingly. 'I can see who might have an interest in Athlot's death. That's a sackful of motive for murder if ever I saw it.

'After all, why give a ninety-year-old man who lives in a hut regular sacks full of coin? What's he going to do with it? Much better in the hands of a headman or a smith's mother.'

'That's plain ridiculous,' the headman said, recovering from his exertions. 'If we wanted him dead, we'd have done it straight after Chad had gone.'

'Not if Athlot was still a healthy old man and an old soldier. I don't think Wassa would be much of a challenge to him, and you wouldn't ask someone else to say boo to a goose for you.

'Pushing an old man off a ladder though, that would be easy.'

'And we wait around for him to climb a ladder, do we?'

'Not necessarily. Could have been luck. You went to pay a call and there he was. One little push and there he wasn't.'

'That is an outrageous suggestion,' Wassa complained.

'Well,' Cwen said. 'We can tell Hermitage all about the bridge arrangement and see if it helps him work out who did do it.'

'I did not kill Athlot,' Wassa insisted. 'Although, I can see that the situation might raise some doubts.'

'Really?' Cwen was surprised by this response.

'Absolutely,' Wassa nodded. 'The whole business is a little suspicious, and those involved must be considered carefully.'

'I'm glad to hear you being so sensible about it.'

'Not a problem.' Wassa pointed at the headman. 'It must have been him.'

Caput XXIII: Silas The Drain

Hermitage didn't like to ask questions about things that made no sense. He would either look foolish, because they made perfect sense to everyone else, or he would be given even less sense in the answer, which always disturbed him.

'A hole in the ground, eh?' he said as nonchalantly as he could manage.

'Yes, he's always digging about somewhere,' Gilbert explained. 'Of course, he's getting a bit past it himself now, but he has some lads to help.'

'With the holes.'

'That's it. As I say, he's been with the family forever.'

Gilbert put down his wine, stood and strode off towards the door, naturally assuming the others would be behind him, which, after a moment's confusion, they were.

When Hermitage caught up, he had thought of an innocuous question that might help. 'And, erm, has Silas been doing holes all this time?'

'Absolutely,' Gilbert confirmed. 'There's no one like him in the whole of Normandy. We're lucky to have him really. I've even loaned him to the duke on occasion.'

'To help with his holes?'

'Exactly. Of course, Silas could have done greater things, but he seems happy so why change?'

'Why indeed.' Hermitage would just have to wait to see the hole and find out if there was any sense in this at all.

Gilbert led them out of the upper stockade and round the side of the hill upon which the castle sat. When they had got perhaps a quarter of the way around, they came upon works of some sort, which did involve a hole in the ground.

Hermitage considered the site. Foundations, that was it.

Silas was an expert in foundations. He knew from some of his books that this was an important and poorly considered area of construction. Apparently, a castle could fall down completely if it didn't have good foundations.

Hermitage wasn't at all clear what good foundations looked like, but he knew they involved holes in the ground.

'Here we are,' Gilbert announced. 'And here is Silas.'

Hermitage gave a bow to a very old but fit-looking fellow who stood on the edge of the hole, at the bottom of which two much younger men were working hard.

Silas had the look of a trade about him, with a grubby apron on his front and a measuring pole in his hand. Perhaps he was actually a mason who specialised in foundations.

'My lord,' Silas bowed. He raised an eyebrow at Hermitage but then dropped it into a frown for Fortmain.

'How goes it, Silas?'

'Excellently sire,' Silas forgot everyone and almost bubbled with excitement at his hole. 'Absolutely marvellous. We have found a good base of solid rock not three feet below the soil. The slope is near perfect, and the approaches will be straightforward. One of the easier jobs. Not like the Lincoln country, eh, sire?'

'If you say so.' Gilbert, while grateful for Silas's expertise, clearly did not share his enthusiasm.

Silas addressed Hermitage for no clear reason. 'The soil was very loose.'

'Was it?' Hermitage asked politely.

'No strength to it.'

'I see.'

'Brother Hermitage here is the King's Investigator, Gilbert said before Silas could expand further upon Lincoln country soil.

'Is he?' Silas asked. 'Vestigare, to track, eh?'

'Just so,' Hermitage said. Despite this fellow's fascination with the earth, his enthusiasm was infectious. Well, it was for Hermitage who was susceptible to enthusiasm.

'And what do you track, Brother?'

'Murder, I'm afraid.'

'Murder? My heavens. Who knew there was such a thing as an investigator of murder.'

'There wasn't,' Hermitage said with a sigh. 'But the king appointed me, so here I am.'

'And what brings the King's Investigator to old Silas? Not drainage, I imagine?' There was a wisp of hope in the question.

'Drainage?' Hermitage asked.

Silas held out a hand towards the hole. 'This will be a fine system. Full discharge from the whole castle and enough fall to see an outflow nearly four hundred feet away, straight into the river.' He was clearly enormously proud of the plan.

'Silas is the leading Norman expert on drains,' Gilbert explained with very little pride or enthusiasm.

'Ah, drains,' Hermitage understood now, which always made him comfortable.

'Of course,' Silas said. 'What else?' He now looked at his hole and a shadow fell over him. 'Nothing up to the standards of the ancients, though. Do you know, we have Roman drains that are still functioning as if they were built yesterday? Glorious, brick-lined thoroughfares, big enough for a man.'

'Cloaca,' Hermitage said. 'And the heathen God Cloacina.'

Silas almost bounced with glee. 'Cloaca, just so. I can see you are an educated fellow, Brother. Do you see, my Lord,' he burbled to Gilbert. 'The Romans had a God of drains.'

Gilbert looked moderately pleased for them.

'I have been in one,' Hermitage said.

'No.' Silas was struck with awe.

'It was to the east,' Hermitage said. 'One was found in an old monastery, and I had to use it as a means of, erm, escape.'[The Case of The Clerical Cadaver; right in the sewer.]

'The east, you say,' Silas was clearly more interested in the drain than the escape.

'We are not going east,' Gilbert said quickly and firmly.

'I have been to Rome, you know,' Silas confided in Hermitage.

Now Hermitage was impressed. To make pilgrimage to the holy sites of Rome was a constant dream. Even to be near the Holy Father would be enough.

'The Cloaca Maxima,' Silas breathed. 'The Great Drain.'

'Yes,' Gilbert interrupted the mutual reverie. 'Brother Hermitage did not come here to discuss drains. He wants to know of years past in Normandy.'

Silas shook his head sadly. 'In Normandy?' he asked. 'Very little serious work on a reliable drainage system.'

'And it's not about drains!' Gilbert snapped.

Silas looked to Hermitage with an enquiring expression. Clearly, if there was something more interesting than drains, he had yet to hear it.

Hermitage explained. 'I am dealing with the death of an old fellow in Derby with the name of Athlot. Do you know it at all?'

Silas at least gave the question serious consideration. 'No, I'm afraid I have never met anyone called Athlot. Nor heard the name.'

Hermitage sagged. He tried never to get his hopes up, but

having old Silas close at hand had seemed fortuitous. Might as well carry on.

'He claimed to have served under King Aethelred.'

'Ah,' Silas raised a finger. 'Now him, I do know.'

'And it is possible that this Athlot attended upon Aethelred during his time in Normandy.'

'The exile,' Silas said.

'Just so,' Hermitage's hopes stirred once more. 'Were you in Normandy at the time?'

'Of course,' Silas confirmed. 'You don't get a whole foreign court suddenly descending upon a small dukedom without serious expansion of the drainage system being required.'

Hermitage saw the scale of the problem; not the drains, the people. 'There would have been many people with the king.'

'Oh yes,' Silas said. 'An entourage, as we say. Of course, the king himself and one or two others stayed with the duke, Richard, it was. Other people were scattered all over.'

'And Athlot could have been one of them.'

'He could well have,' Silas confirmed.

'And was there any trouble?' Hermitage asked. 'Any falling out or arguments?'

'There was always trouble of some sort,' Silas said. 'You don't get two courts in the same place without some hot-headed fools taking arguments too far.'

'Anything serious?' Hermitage asked. 'Anything that might make revenge a possibility after many years?'

'Good Lord. It would be many years indeed,' Silas said. 'We are talking over fifty years ago. There can't be many alive who even remember those days.'

'But if some great wrong were done, or was even thought to have been done, the thirst for revenge may have been passed on from father to son.'

'And now the Normans are in England, you think they may have taken this revenge?'

'It does seem extreme,' Hermitage admitted.

'There have been Normans in England for many years,' Silas said. Living peacefully under King Edward. If some revenge were wanted, I'm sure it could have been arranged.'

Hermitage could feel the first twinges of persuasion that Athlot may simply have fallen off a ladder. If Silas, who was as old as the hills himself, had nothing to offer, there would be nowhere else to go.

'How old was this Athlot?' Silas asked.

'They say he was ninety.'

Silas nodded. 'He would have to be. And who would want revenge on a ninety-year-old?'

'You are right,' Hermitage breathed deeply. 'I am chasing at shadows that aren't even there. Athlot came to Derby many years ago with a good fortune. It is possible someone killed him for that fortune. It is possible he came by it dishonestly and someone wanted him dealt with. Or it is possible he was a ninety-year-old man who simply died.'

'A fortune, eh?' Silas gave a short laugh. 'There was only one fortune that went astray, but that was dealt with pretty promptly.'

'A fortune went astray?' Hermitage asked with a small flame of interest.

'It did.' Silas slowly lowered himself to sit on the side of the hill and indicated that everyone should find a spot while he told his tale. Gilbert and Fortmain looked around but decided they'd rather stand. Hermitage sat.

'Well,' Silas began. 'Old King Aethelred, as you know, had paid the Danes tribute in order to stop them attacking everyone all the time.'

'The Danegeld,' Hermitage said.

'That's it. So, when King Sweyn invaded England and Aethelred had to leave, that all stopped. And when Aethelred arrived in Normandy, everyone assumed that was it. The Danes were now kings of England.

'But then Sweyn went and died.'

'He did,' Hermitage agreed. 'Only a few months later.'

Silas nodded. 'But again, it was assumed that Cnut, his son, would become king. Until word arrived from England that is.

'The English nobles must have decided that they didn't think much of a Danish king and would quite like their old one back again.

'They sent a whole deputation to Normandy to negotiate getting him. I heard that they made Aethelred swear that he would rule them a bit more justly than he had before, but if he did, then he could come back and reign once more.

'Eventually, it was agreed and Aethelred set off against Cnut. The things kings get up to, eh?' Silas chortled. 'Funny to think that when Aethelred's son, Edmund died, Cnut ended up king anyway. What was the point of it all?'

'Things become clear when you reach my great age. The main thing being, what's the point of it all? Kings come and go with the wind. Drains, now. There's something that lasts.'

'The fortune?' Hermitage prompted.

'Which one?' Silas asked.

'The one that was lost,' Hermitage urged.

'Oh, right, yes. Now then, where was I? So, Aethelred sets off to deal with Cnut, but thinks that he ought to take some tribute with him, just in case the Danes can be paid to go away, instead of having to fight. Like they'd do in the old days.

'But he's in Normandy, he hasn't brought enough chests of

wealth with him to buy a whole Danish army, so he gets Duke Richard to lend him some. As soon as he gets back to England and is king once more, he'll pay the money back.'

'And he didn't?' Hermitage asked, aghast at the deceit.

'Oh, it didn't even get that far,' Silas said. 'Aethelred had a man, and not a very nice one if you take my meaning.'

Hermitage gave Silas an encouraging look to go on.

'Done all sorts of awful things for Aethelred, he had. Killed people, blinded some. Slaughtered a whole lot of Danes in earlier years, apparently. But he was married to Aethelred's daughter, so no one could tell him what to do. Behaved like he was the king himself, so they said.'

'And he wasn't called Athlot?'

'No. Definitely not Athlot. But we haven't finished with him yet. Duke Richard lends his fortune to Aethelred who gives it to his man to take over to England, in advance of their attack.

'Aethelred sets off for England with some ally from Norway, would you believe? Fellow called Olaf. They take London, drive the Danes back north and Aethelred is king once more.

'But of course, Cnut isn't happy about this and keeps harrying and attacking here and there. So, word is that Aethelred decides to start paying the Danegeld from his own purse. He sends for the fortune to give back to Duke Richard, as is right and proper, except then what's happened?'

Even the lads in the hole had stopped digging now to find out what happened.

'Aethelred's man has gone over to Cnut, taking the fortune with him.'

'No!' one of the lads in the hole exclaimed.

'True as you're in a hole,' Silas said. 'Well, naturally,

Aethelred and Richard are furious at this. I shouldn't think Aethelred's daughter was very happy, either. And they want the treason dealt with.'

'You said it was dealt with,' Hermitage observed. 'Presumably, they got him.'

'Not them, as it turns out,' Silas said brightly. 'This fellow was such a greedy, treacherous dog that he tried to cheat Cnut. Well, it's not sensible trying to cheat a Dane.'

'What did Cnut do?'

'He chopped his head off.'

'Good heavens,' Hermitage said.

'On Christ's Mass day,' Silas added. 'Which is not really a decent thing to do. And threw his body away as well, which isn't at all right.'

'And the fortune?' Hermitage asked.

'Never came back. Richard and Aethelred must have sorted out something between them, but I don't know that bit.'

'Maybe someone else got hold of it?' Hermitage suggested. 'It could be that our Athlot was involved in all of this somehow.'

'Could be,' Silas acknowledged.

'What was the name of Aethelred's man? The traitor who took the money?' Hermitage asked. Perhaps there was still a connection to be made.

'Eadric,' Silas said. 'Eadric the Acquisitive, they called him.'

Caput XXIV: Back in The Neighbourhood

'I must return to Derby,' Hermitage said when they were back at the castle, having thanked Silas for his tale and left him to more productive work; drainage work, obviously.

'You really think this Athlot was Eadric?' Gilbert sounded very sceptical. 'Silas said he had his head chopped off.'

'That's the tale,' Hermitage agreed. 'But tales can be wrong. After all, not even Silas was there to see it happen. And the smith in Derby reported hearing the name Eadric when Athlot was talking. I'd assumed the other person was Eadric, but maybe not.'

'Is it such an unusual name, then?'

'Well, no.' Hermitage had to admit that a lot of people were probably called Eadric. And only one of them was reputed to have had his head chopped off by King Cnut. As far as he knew. Perhaps Cnut chopped a lot of Eadrics' heads off?

'But it seems too much of a coincidence.' He stuck to the Eadric in question. 'This Athlot is the right age. He appeared in Derby about the right time with a fortune and has been hiding ever since.' He saw that bit was right.

Gilbert shook his head slowly. 'Do you know any men of fortune who live in small huts behind the smithy?'

'I suppose not,' Hermitage accepted, but then he didn't know many men of fortune.

Although come to think of it, he did. The king, Le Pedvin, Ranulph de Sauveloy, he assumed they were all pretty rich, having conquered a whole country. He couldn't see any of them living in a hut behind a smithy. Le Pedvin, perhaps, but that ghastly man seemed to disdain fortune in favour of killing people. He couldn't imagine Le Pedvin giving up killing people to live in a hut.

'People of fortune flaunt it,' Gilbert went on. 'And mostly, they expend a lot of their effort in trying to increase that fortune, even though they already have more than enough.

'Look at me,' he said. 'I'm happiest as a soldier on campaign and have little interest in acquiring a fortune; which I'm frequently told is one of my main faults; mainly by Aveline. If this Athlot was rich, his behaviour was all wrong.

'I can see a man hiding for a year or two, but this is a long time for rich Eadric to stay hidden. Even if he did survive having his head removed.

'Further, it sounds as if he betrayed everyone he came into contact with. The Saxons, the Danes, the Normans, everybody wanted him.'

'Hence the small hut behind the smithy in Derby. And a change of name to Athlot. I am positive that no king's men frequent the alehouse of Derby, so he could have stayed hidden. And if everyone thought he was dead anyway, who would be looking?'

Gilbert shook his head. 'Men of fortune again,' he said.

'What about them?'

'This Eadric was moving in the circles of kings. I have seen such men and their worst punishment is to be banished. They crave the power and might of kings, even if they only bathe in its glow. Remove them from that and they wither. Either that or they try to establish themselves as nobles somewhere and come to a very sorry end.'

Hermitage could see that. 'But he may have escaped removal of his head by the breath of a sparrow. He values his life and saw that it could come to an uncomfortable conclusion. And he was getting old by then. Not very old, but he had a few years behind him and as Silas said, life becomes clear. Mainly the importance of keeping it going.'

'Why would Cnut let him go at all?' Gilbert asked. 'He sounds most untrustworthy.'

'If he did.' Hermitage was quite excited about this version of events now.

'Eadric seems to have been quite capable of deceiving dukes and kings, as well as their daughters. It's quite possible he simply slipped away with the money. Cnut then spread the tale that he had chopped off Eadric's head to avoid looking like a fool. He even threw the body away so that no one could tell if he was really dead or not.

'All right,' Gilbert smiled and spread his arms, bowing to Hermitage's wisdom. 'Let's accept that Eadric escaped from Cnut with a fortune, hid in a hut in Derby and lived out the next years of his life in quiet obscurity. Why now? Why, after all these years, has someone come for Eadric? If no one knew who he was or where he was, who could find out?'

Hermitage thought about that. 'This visitor that the smith overheard. he came to warn Eadric about something. Perhaps that people were looking for him again. Or it could be an accident. Eadric simply gave himself away by mistake. After all, he is ninety, or was.'

'Gave himself away to who? I've never heard of any of this, and I'm a Norman commander.'

'I don't know,' Hermitage confessed. 'But I can try to find out.'

'As you will,' Gilbert accepted. 'But I don't know what the rush is. Athlot or Eadric is dead now.'

'And someone may have killed him. And that killer could still be in Derby, looking for the fortune.'

'Bit stupid to kill a man and then look for his fortune,' Gilbert observed. 'The other way round would be more effective.'

'The actual death could have been an accident,' Hermitage now realised. 'Push a ninety-year-old around and they may just die. By which time it's too late to ask them where their fortune is.'

'Please yourself,' Gilbert said. 'Fortmain here can accompany you back.'

Fortmain gave a short nod.

'And Fortmain,' Gilbert added. 'If all these convolutions are true, there could be a fortune to be found.'

Fortmain kept very still.

'A fortune that rightfully belongs to the Duke of Normandy. If such fortune were to be recovered, the man who did such service to his duke might find his own fortune restored.'

Fortmain gave another nod, but it had a touch of gratitude about it.

Gilbert hadn't finished. 'But a man who found a duke's fortune and decided to keep it, couldn't have a hut small enough or far enough away to save him.'

Fortmain swallowed and nodded now.

'I wait to hear the news,' Gilbert said.

The ride back to Derby was an awkward one as Pinel was desperate to know what was going on. Why had they ridden to Nottingham, what had they discussed and why were they going back? Had Hermitage found any killers at Lord Gilbert's castle and could he point them out?

Hermitage prevaricated as if he'd been asked to say exactly how many animals were in Noah's ark.

Helpfully, Fortmain rode close by at one point and told Pinel he was showing too much interest in what might be the duke's business. Prying into the duke's business was clearly not something anyone wanted to be accused of and so Pinel maintained a resentful silence.

Once back at the workshop, Hermitage got himself off the horse as quickly as he could and rushed in. He called around and even skipped up the stairs to find no one about.

In the kitchen area, Mrs Grod stood in command of her cooking and as Hermitage opened his mouth to ask, her head turned slowly to face him. He decided not to ask Mrs Grod.

In the workshop proper, the apprentices were hard at work. Even Hermitage could tell that it was not the same "hard at work" as when Cwen was in residence, but the looms were busy.

Hartle directed the apprentices from a chair by a small fire in which he appeared to be dozing.

'Hartle,' Hermitage called. 'Have you seen Wat and Cwen?'

'Eh, what?' Hartle jumped in his chair. 'Who?'

'Wat and Cwen, where are they?'

'Not here,' Hartle didn't sound disappointed by that.

'They haven't come back?'

'Back from where?'

Hermitage was frustrated that Hartle wasn't following until he realised that the man didn't know what was going on in the first place.

'Wat went to look at Athlot's hut and Cwen was going to Mistress Wassa.'

'Why?' Hartle asked.

'It doesn't matter why.'

'It'll matter to Mistress Wassa,' Hartle said in all seriousness.

'Oh, never mind. They're not here, then?'

'Yes,' Hartle confirmed, coming fully to his senses. 'Still not here.'

Hermitage gave up and ran from the workshop, followed by the gazes of the apprentices, who now slowed their work even further, while Hartle made himself comfortable again.

'They must still be in town,' Hermitage reported to Fortmain.

'Right.' Fortmain, who had dismounted, swung himself back into the saddle.

'It's not far,' Hermitage said. 'I'll walk, I think. Meet at the smithy.'

Fortmain nodded to his men, who mounted as well, and they all set off at a gallop into Derby.

Hermitage felt quite bad about imposing these men on the town, but the business was urgent now. There could well be a killer prowling the streets of Derby and anyone who got in their way, would not be safe. Which could include Wat and Cwen.

Where to begin though? If Wat had found anything at Athlot's hut, he could have been spotted by the killer who was lying in wait.

And he had sent Cwen straight into the house of Mistress Wassa. The Wassa who had got money from somewhere, possibly Athlot's home.

He told himself that Wassa was highly unlikely to have killed anyone. She lived a comfortable life and had done so for some time. Athlot had only just died this week. The connection was not there.

Anyway, Wat and Cwen could take care of themselves, he knew that. They could take care of themselves a lot better than he could take care of himself. And he had just ridden to a Norman castle and back in a day and had survived.

Everyone would be fine.

But, if the trail to Athlot's fortune had been discovered, the person following it would not easily be dealt with. If some secret servant of a duke or king had been seeking out Athlot, there could be real danger.

He increased his pace along the track and was soon back on the main road into Derby. A little farther and he came upon the gathering of Fortmain and the Normans, sitting on their horses alone in the street.

'Everyone ran away,' Fortmain explained.

Hermitage could understand that. And it was a sensible step to take.

'You wait here,' Hermitage said. 'I'll go and talk to the smith. In fact,' he added. 'Perhaps you could wait out of sight somewhere.'

'Out of sight?' Fortmain seemed to consider this the most dishonourable suggestion.

'Yes, erm, in case our killer is around, we don't want to scare him into hiding.'

Fortmain didn't look convinced but indicated to his men that they would take their animals off the track and lay in wait in the trees.

Hermitage hurried to the smithy and banged on the now firmly shut door. There was no reply.

'It's all right,' he called. 'The Normans have gone.'

There was a noise inside and the door creaked open a small amount.

'Gone?' the smith asked very quietly.

'I have sent them off,' Hermitage announced, instantly regretful at such boastfulness.

The door opened more and the smith appeared, looking cautiously up and down the road.

'What are they doing here?' he asked as Grimulf appeared at his side.

'It is a long and complicated tale,' Hermitage said, avoiding the confession that he had brought them. 'Have you seen Wat or Cwen at all?'

'Aye,' the smith said. 'Wat was here not long back with some impudent young fellow.'

'Bart?'

'Could be. Accused me of murder!'

'Ah.'

'Clipped his ears for him.'

'Excellent. And where did they go?'

'Don't know, but they didn't find what they were looking for.'

'It's knocked down,' Grimulf complained.

'Sorry? What's knocked down?'

'Athlot's hut. It's all gone.' Poor Grimulf seemed very disconsolate about this.

'Two people came and knocked it down,' the smith explained. 'Romans, they were.'

'Romans?' Hermitage really didn't want any more confusion in his life.

'Marcus Aurelius, apparently.' The smith didn't seem too put out at the thought of a dead Roman emperor knocking down huts in Derby.

'Oh, was it?' That was interesting. 'Are they the only strangers you've seen recently? Particularly anyone else taking an interest in Athlot?'

They both thought about this.

'Only that stranger years ago I mentioned,' the smith said.

'The one who said the name Eadric,' Hermitage prompted.

'That's him.'

'But you said he left.'

'He did.'

'And Athlot was fine afterwards?'

'Well, he wasn't happy, but he wasn't dead if that's what you mean?'

Hermitage nodded, but mainly to himself. Surely, he thought, Marcus and Aurelius, or rather Rachel, could not be secret servants of anyone. From Wat's telling of their history, Rachel had such a disreputable and dishonest nature that no one would trust her with a spare stick, let alone the location of a king's ransom.

Or maybe that was the point. This whole business seemed filled with disreputable and dishonest people. Rachel might be the perfect choice.

'What's going on, Brother?' the smith asked. 'Old Athlot dying should have been a straightforward affair. He was ancient and had come to his end. Now we've got strangers knocking down his house, Normans in the street and young boys accusing me of murder.'

'I'm sure he didn't mean to accuse you of murder,' Hermitage pleaded Bart's part. 'He misspoke, that's all.

'I shall miss-kick his backside if he does it again.'

'Of course, of course,' Hermitage tried to move on. 'I hope I will be able to explain everything in due course, but for now, I need to find Wat and Cwen.'

'Can't help you with that. Wat didn't even say where they were going.'

Hermitage sighed that he didn't even know where to start. How to find out where, in the whole of the town, Wat and Cwen might be? Just go and look, he supposed. Or perhaps ask. What was that ridiculous thing Bart had said? Ask every house if they killed Athlot?

He didn't need to do that, but he could ask who had seen Wat or Cwen. It was a strange sort of investigation to go knocking on peoples' doors asking them if they'd seen anything, but he had no other choices.

He raised his hand in goodbye to a suspicious-looking smith and a glum-looking Grimulf.

'Don't worry Grimulf,' he said. 'Now that Athlot's hut is destroyed, no one's going to want it. There is no son of Athlot. I'm sure it's just an empty piece of land.'

Grimulf didn't seem much cheered by that.

Caput XXV: Follow The Follower

Several of the residents of Derby were getting a little fed up with their day being disturbed by people asking questions.

The leathermaker's workshop was the first place Brother Hermitage found and he knocked politely on the door.

'Yes?' The wife appeared. 'It's that monk now,' she called to her husband who was presumably inside somewhere, doing something to some leather.

Hermitage didn't quite understand the sense of the alert, but he smiled and bowed as was proper.

'I was wondering..,' he began.

'We've seen no strangely dressed women.' the leathermaker's wife told Hermitage before he could go any further.

'I wasn't going to ask about strangely dressed women,' Hermitage said.

'Well, make sure you don't.'

'I was going to ask if you'd seen Wat or Cwen.'

'Eeek,' the woman screeched and ran indoors.

'What is it now?' a voice could be heard asking from inside.

'Now the monk wants to know about Wat the Weaver,' the woman complained.

'Oh, for heaven's sake. He's only a weaver.'

'Only a weaver, is he? Is that what you think? Well, that's just typical,' the female voice rose to such a pitch that Hermitage thought it best to simply leave.

'Looking for Wat and Cwen, then?'

He turned and saw the butcher standing outside of his shop.

'Ah, yes, I am.'

'I expect you want to know where they are.'

Hermitage couldn't immediately think of another reason for asking.

'Erm, yes, thank you.'

'Be worth your while knowing,' the butcher said with a wink.

'It would,' Hermitage looked expectant.

So did the butcher.

Eventually, the tradesman sighed. 'I don't suppose monks have any money anyway.'

'No,' Hermitage explained. 'We don't. Well, we're not supposed to.'

'They went down the road,' the butcher said. 'Wat, that is. And some boy. Haven't seen Cwen.'

'Did they say where they were going?'

'Towards the church,' the butcher sighed. 'Following the two strangers from this morning.'

'Two strangers, excellent. I say,' Hermitage continued. 'You haven't seen any other strangers around town perchance? People who may have even asked about Athlot, or even someone called Eadric.'

'Eadric?' We haven't got no Eadric in town.'

'Well, no obviously,' Hermitage stumbled. 'They would have been asking in error, of course.'

'Asking in error about someone called Eadric?' The butcher was having trouble with this.

'Something like that,' Hermitage said weakly.

'No,' the butcher confirmed. 'No Eadric. And in all my time here no one has ever asked about Athlot. Which is funny, when you think about it.'

'Is it?'

'Lived here years, he did. Told tales about his life but no one ever came to visit.'

'Really?' Hermitage asked without really paying attention. He was getting quite anxious to move on now.

'I mean,' the butcher was keen to explain. 'If you've got a fellow who's met kings and travelled the world, he has visitors, doesn't he?'

'Does he?' Hermitage's experiences of visitors were almost always bad.

'Of course, he does. Old companions come to chew the fat. People travelling past who know that old Athlot lives here and come to pay their respects.'

'Ah, yes,' Hermitage now saw that this was actually a useful bit of idle chatter.

'But not Athlot. No visitors. Lives in a tiny old hut. No one ever even asked for him. Poor fellow. I suppose he'd got so old that anyone he knew was dead.'

'Could be,' Hermitage agreed. 'And no one asked about Eadric, either.'

'Why do you keep going on about Eadric?'

Hermitage thought a bit of truth might help here. And he always had to tell either the truth or say nothing.

'I have recently heard tales of a fellow called Eadric who also dealt with kings and travelled the world.'

'And you think he might have been a friend of Athlot?'

'It's erm, possible,' Hermitage stumbled over the half-truth.

'Well,' the butcher concluded. 'I have never heard of a fellow called Eadric. Oh, tell a lie.'

'You do know of someone?' Hermitage asked in excitement.

'Cousin's younger daughter's boy down Coventry way. I think he's called Eadric. Or is it Ealdram?'

'Not the fellow I'm thinking of.'

'I reckon not. Not likely to have known Athlot.'

'Really?'

'He's only four.'

'Ah. Well, anyway, Wat went to the church, thank you very much.'

'You're welcome, Brother,' the butcher called after Hermitage. 'And I'll keep an ear out for any Eadrics and let you know.'

Hermitage thought about going and getting the Normans from the woods at this point but concluded they would be more trouble than they were worth. It was bad enough getting sense out of the people of Derby without waving Normans in their faces.

As he walked away from the butcher, he wondered why Wat would be going to the church. If Marcus and Rachel had gone that way as well, what were they up to?

Had they got what they wanted from Athlot's house and had headed south, passing the church on their way?

He longed to know what Wat and Cwen had found on their own missions. He should never have left them to go wandering off to Nottingham. One thing at a time, that was best, not three different things at once. Nothing could be achieved that way.

He approached Mistress Wassa's home now and it only took a moment to confirm there was no one there. Where had everyone gone?

Not much farther down the road, the church loomed over him. The church with the priest inside, the priest who didn't get on with Hermitage. He looked at the tower and tried to take his courage. All he had to do was ask. Wat had headed for the church, so Hermitage had to stop and enquire there.

Walking up the path was easy. Considering the door was

no problem at all. He closed his eyes and knocked. He knew there was no point simply trying to walk in. It was not time for any service and so the priest would have the place securely shut. With him inside it.

All too quickly, there was a horrible grinding noise and the door opened a crack.

'Who is it?' the priest demanded in a fierce whisper.

'It is I, Brother Hermitage.'

'Ha!' The door was now thrown wide. 'I might have known,' the priest said, his hands on his hips. 'Have you got my money?'

That was such an unexpected question that Hermitage couldn't immediately think how to answer. 'Well, no,' was the best he could come up with.

'Where is it, then?'

'Erm, I don't know.'

'That weaver went off to get it, why hasn't he brought it back?'

'I think you'll have to explain,' Hermitage said as gently as he could. The priest seemed to be in a particularly angry state just at the moment. He seemed to spend a lot of his time in an angry state and was probably well practised.

The priest peered around, clearly seeing if Hermitage was on his own.

'Come in here,' he instructed.

This really was an unusual day.

Hermitage stepped into the church and the door was quickly shut behind him.

The priest still had the look about him of someone who was looking about him for something to take his anger out on, even in his own church.

'The money,' he said.

'What money?' Hermitage asked with his most harmless voice and expression.

'The money the woman took.'

'A woman took some money?' Hermitage could only assume that this was Rachel they were talking about. No one in Derby would come and take money from the church.

'From the church!' The priest exclaimed.

'Well, quite. Appalling. No doubt about it. She stole the offerings?' Hermitage asked. He could see that this was an awful sin and upsetting, but the priest seemed to have gone completely to pieces over a few coins. The people of Derby knew they had to pay their dues to the church, but they weren't very generous about it.

'No, not the offerings. The money.'

'There was more money?'

'Of course. The chest of money Athlot gave.'

Hermitage stopped and gaped. 'Athlot's money was here? He gave it to you?'

'That's it.' The priest grasped Hermitage's habit and clutched it in his hands as if shaking it would make his money drop out. 'And the madwoman came and took it.'

'Erm, why did Athlot give you his money?' Hermitage asked as calmly as he could in the circumstances.

Thankfully, the priest released Hermitage and took to simply striding up and down; angrily. 'He was paying for his eternal soul's salvation, there's nothing wrong with that, is there?'

'Well, erm, no, I suppose not.' Hermitage knew that the church's own teaching said that this was perfectly fine, but he had his own doubts. Doubts he naturally kept to himself.

'And he gave you a lot of money? I mean, he donated a lot to the church for his salvation?'

'Aye. He had been doing so for some time.'

'He obviously thought his eternal soul needed a lot of salvation. And all this money was still here?' Hermitage asked, puzzled at why such a generous payment had not been passed on to the appropriate church authorities.

'It was, for the time being,' the priest sounded rather evasive. 'But then this mad woman turned up.' The priest clicked his fingers in Hermitage's direction. 'The weaver said you were looking into Athlot's murder.'

'Well, possible murder. It's still not certain.'

'The madwoman could have killed him as well as taken his money.'

Hermitage shook his head. 'She wasn't here when Athlot died. She was out in the east.'

'You don't know what mad women can do,' the priest said.

Hermitage was pretty sure they couldn't be in two places at once.

'Did she say she was Rachel?' Hermitage asked. 'Or Aurelius.'

'No, there was only one of them. But she had a man with her.'

'Marcus, yes. The two of them came and took Athlot's money. How did they know it was here?'

'They said they were going to start here, where he was buried, and then tear the town apart until they found it.'

'And you had it.'

The priest gave a slightly nervous nod. 'But they weren't happy. Said there wasn't enough. Where was the rest? They kept asking. I said there was no more and that this should be enough for anyone.'

'How much was there?' Hermitage asked.

'A good chest full. That was enough, wasn't it? I mean,

how greedy can some people be?'

Hermitage was wondering the same thing. 'Yes, yes, quite enough,' he said.

No, he thought at the same time. It wasn't enough. If this really was King Aethelred's Danegeld, it should be enormous. He had heard of ten thousand pounds of silver being one payment alone.

He was no great expert on money, but he knew that ten thousand pounds would not fit in one chest. Not unless it was a very big chest indeed, in which case no one would be able to move it.

'But they took it anyway,' the priest complained. 'Didn't stop them searching the rest of the church and tying me up though.'

'They tied you up?' Hermitage considered the priest who was definitely not tied up.

'Wat and some young lad came along and found me.'

'Ah.' Now Hermitage was making some real progress. 'And where did they go?'

'Said they were going to try and track the madwoman.'

'I see. Which way did they go?'

'South, I think.'

Hermitage considered that and wondered about it. South was Norman country. It would be best not heading there with a chest full of coin. But north was not much better these days, what with King William being particularly angry with the north for some reason.

Rachel and Marcus had accompanied Bart from the eastern marshes, perhaps that was where they would head. Back towards Hereward and the resistance to Norman rule.

But then, he couldn't think of any ruler who would let strangers wander about with chests full of coin uninterrupted.

And he found it hard to believe that Rachel would be returning the treasure to its rightful owner.

'They said I should tell the headman,' the priest continued.

'A wise suggestion. If these people are out there with stolen money, a local force may be required to capture them.'

'But I couldn't find him.'

'He was gone?' Hermitage knew that the headman seldom went anywhere. He much preferred people to come to him.

'He was. And his horse and cart with him.'

'Oh, dear,' Hermitage fretted. 'Everyone is gone. I was looking for Mistress Wassa and can't find her. Wat and Cwen are gone, as are Rachel and Marcus, and now the headman.'

'How are you going to find them?' the priest asked, making it quite clear that most of this was Hermitage's fault, and so he was the one who had to sort it all out.

'Me?' he asked.

'Yes. You're the mighty King's Investigator. From the Latin, vestigare, to track, as you insist on telling us all the time. Well, get on and track something. Make yourself useful for once.'

Hermitage thought that there was no need to be rude, he was doing his best. And he didn't even want to be investigator in the first place.

'And when you've found them, you can bring my money back.'

'The church's money,' Hermitage corrected.

'Yes, yes,' the priest snapped.

Despite the abuse, Hermitage saw that some tracking really was needed. He had no idea where everyone had gone or even where to start looking or how to go about it.

He could carry on asking at houses up and down the street

to see if anyone had been spotted. But there had to be a quicker way than that. If Rachel had gone with the money, she needed to be stopped quickly. And he had a very good idea who would be very good at something like that.

'If you'd just like to wait here for a few moments,' he said. 'I'll go and get someone I think may be able to help us.'

Caput XXVI: A Coming Together

Wat and Bart's enquiries along the road in Derby were most productive. A strange woman and a man carrying a large chest were hard to miss, and very easy to talk about.

In fact, the main challenge in this pursuit was getting the people of Derby to shut up about the strange woman and the man carrying a large chest.

A single household's speculation about what they were up to could have taken a whole day and the two of them had to drag themselves away quite rudely on occasion.

The general impression was that the two were heading south. At one point, it was reported that they had got a hand cart from somewhere and were wheeling the chest along the road. This was worrying as Wat and Bart's supposedly simple questions were getting longer and longer answers, which were slowing them down.

When one woman swore on her husband's grave that Marcus and Rachel had been flying on the back of a great eagle, they decided they would simply keep heading south and stop asking questions.

The woman's veracity was further brought into question when her husband appeared and asked her to stop swearing things on his grave.

'They must be trying to make it back to the fens,' Bart said as they walked on, looking on the ground for signs of a hand cart. As this was a busy road, signs of carts were all over the place. 'This was the road we took to get here.'

'Bit of an odd direction to get to the fens,' Wat said.

'We avoided Ely,' Bart explained. 'Hereward, you know.'

'Yes, I do know Hereward,' Wat said. 'I met him once and I completely agree that he's best avoided.'

'You met him?' Bart was impressed.

'Don't be impressed,' Wat said. 'The man's not everything he's made out to be. In fact, he's not any of the things he's made out to be, but I suppose as long as people believe, where's the harm?'

'He hides in the fens and does great battle with the Norman foe,' Bart sounded like he was reciting a song. 'Not that battling the Norman foe does the rest of us any good,' he complained.

'Hides in the fens, yes, definitely. I'd be a bit more cautious about the great battle bit if I were you.

'Anyway, if Marcus and Rachel do want to head back to the fens, and avoid Hereward, where are they going to go with their wealth? There will be no place to hide with it. The likes of them can't suddenly appear as rich merchants. And the Normans will take anything they have a fancy to. Chests of coin being quite popular, I imagine.'

Bart had no answer to that.

'How did they even know about it in the first place?' Wat asked. 'Athlot's wealth wasn't even well known in Derby, let alone the fens. Did they say anything to you?'

'No. Only that they had an interest in Derby.'

'Were they coming here anyway?' When you met them?'

'I think so, now you ask. They said we should stick together on the journey for safety But I think that was only after I'd said I was coming here for Brother Hermitage.'

'And you didn't mention me?'

'No. Nothing until we got here when Fortmain got all excited.'

'And Rachel realised whose workshop she was going to. That is a bit of a relief, actually.'

'How so?'

'I'd hate to think she'd deliberately come looking for me. That woman is trouble.'

'It is a long way off to know of someone's fortune,' Bart said. 'And the two of them were clearly living a poor life. They tried to sell me King Harold's thumb so that I would be invisible to Normans.'

'Ha,' Wat laughed at the idea. 'She's certainly dressed for the part now. My, her fortunes have changed. From stealing her mistress's fine gowns to wandering the country as a witch.

'Do you know anything about Marcus?' Wat asked.

'Not a thing. He's obviously the one to draw the people in, then he springs Rachel on them, after which he takes the money.'

Wat nodded. 'And if they do sell Harold's thumb, they move on to sell another one in the next town. Good job kings have lots of thumbs.'

They were well out of Derby now, but the track was still well-used and there was no telling if their quarry had passed this way.

'They're probably making for the bridge,' Bart said.

Wat frowned at this. 'Nottingham? It's a more sensible route to the east, but why would they be coming this way?'

'No, no,' Bart looked confused. 'The bridge this way.' He gestured down the road.

'Swarkestone bridge?' Wat asked. 'That thing's barely a plank over the river big enough for one at a time. There's a ford if that's what you mean.'

'I think I know a bridge when I walk over one.'

'I'm sure you do but tackling that thing with a chest of coin is more than I'd risk.'

'It was a bit rickety,' Bart admitted. 'Didn't seem quite level in places.'

'You were lucky it was up at all.' Wat spoke in the manner of a father being forced to explain to his son where new rabbits came from. 'It is a sensible place for a proper bridge, but not the one that's there.'

'Fortmain better ask for his toll back, then.'

'What toll?' Wat asked in some exasperation.

'The toll he paid for us all to cross the bridge.' Bart replied with even more exasperation.

'You'll see,' Wat said confidently as they walked on.

'Yes, you will,' Bart replied.

'It must have been dark,' Wat said. 'It's a plank.'

'A big plank,' Bart replied.

'Whatever is there, Marcus and Rachel will be trying to cross with their chest of coin. It'll be a tricky thing to get through the ford and they might need to organise a larger cart. That should slow them down a bit.'

'Although wheeling theirs over the bridge shouldn't be so difficult.' Bart explained. 'And they'll have enough coin to pay the toll I would think. We can only hope that the bridge is busy to delay them.'

Each of them gave up trying to persuade the other until they broached the last hill before the river and looked down upon a very busy scene indeed.

'Where in God's name did that come from?' Wat asked.

'It's a bridge,' Bart explained.

'I can see that it's a bridge. What's it doing there?'

'What do bridges usually do?'

'It shouldn't be there. It should be some planks on stepping stones. Why is there a bridge?'

'Well, it was here when we arrived, and it's still here now, so I suspect it's not one of those magic bridges that disappears at sunrise.'

'I don't understand,' Wat sounded positively lost. 'You can't just have bridges.'

'You've not been this way for a while?'

'I suppose not. Gone east and north quite a lot but haven't come south for a year or two. Sent some of the apprentices and I suppose they said they crossed the river here, but I assumed that was on the plank.'

'I said it looked quite new. And that it didn't look like it would be here much longer,' Bart said. 'It's not exactly a wonder of bridges.'

'That it isn't,' Wat accepted. 'Looks like someone stuck it up overnight and was surprised to see it still standing the next morning.' He rubbed his chin. 'Hence the toll.'

'Oh yes,' Bart confirmed. 'A penny.'

'A penny,' Wat whistled at the high price. 'And this used to be a ford you could cross for free.'

Bart nodded down towards the river. The water mostly flowed smoothly, but in places around the bridge, it swirled menacingly. 'Looks like they dug up the ford while they were building the bridge.'

'Quite right too,' Wat said. 'Don't want people walking around your bridge for free when they can give you a penny.'

'No sign of Rachel,' Wat commented when he had got over the shock of there being a bridge where there shouldn't be.

There was quite a crowd coming and going over the bridge, as well as queueing on either side to make their journey. Rachel would have been easy to spot among the non-witch people going about their daily business.

'Unless she's covered herself with a cloak or something?' Bart suggested.

Wat growled. 'Just the sort of deceitful thing that woman would do. How are we going to spot her?'

Bart scanned the view from their vantage point to the bridge and beyond to see if there was anything out of the normal.

'Seems to be a bit of a disturbance down there.' He pointed to the field off to the left of the bridge on the near side of the river.

'It's all we've got,' Wat said. 'Come on.'

They hurried down the slope towards the river and a quite active gathering of people who seemed to have found something of great interest.

'She'd be a fool to draw attention to herself,' Wat said as they approached. 'And if there's one thing Rachel is not, it's a fool.'

They got closer now and came to the edge of quite a crowd of people who were gathered in a thick circle around one particular spot. Whatever was going on here was clearly of more interest than crossing the river.

Travellers with packs, families and even merchants with small carts of produce had abandoned their journeys to come and see whatever this was.

But then, these were probably the same people who would stop whatever they were doing to gather round in a circle simply because some other folk had gathered before them. Whatever was going on in such a circle had to be interesting.

Wat and Bart pushed their way in, to some objection and suggestions that they should wait their turn.

Perhaps this was Rachel. A cart of coin would certainly be enough to create a circle of interest anywhere, field or not.

When they got to the middle of the circle, the situation was clear and relatively uninteresting.

There were no merchants fighting over some disputed cargo. There were no young bloods, threatening to kill one another as a result of some perceived insult.

There were not even any animals fighting simply because they were animals who fought.

Instead, there was a very mature woman sitting on the ground against the hedge with her arms folded firmly in the manner of one who is refusing to be moved.

Standing in front of her, arms equally implacably folded, was a man who looked down upon her as if she were making a fool of herself.

The crowd had not yet started taking bets on who was going to come out of this on top.

Still in the circle, but some distance from the site of the main conflict, an exasperated looking Cwen stood by a cart.

'They yours?' Wat asked stepping over to her.

'Oh, hello,' Cwen said as if she'd just met Wat in the vegetable patch. 'Hello Bart,' she nodded. 'The headman.' She held an arm out to indicate the headman.

'I recognise him.'

'And Mistress Wassa.' The arm went out to Mistress Wassa.

'So it is.'

'Are having a small dispute.'

'It's getting bigger by the moment,' Wat observed as travellers with too much time on their hands came over to join the outer edges of the circle.

Cwen acknowledged this with a tip of the head.

'And the nature of the dispute?' Wat enquired.

'Well, for a while they were each accusing the other of murdering Athlot.'

'Were they?' Wat was interested.

'At root is a problem which you may have noticed on your way here,' Cwen said conspiratorially. 'There's quite a substantial bridge over there.' She tipped her head in the right direction.

'I thought I saw something. Bart and I were only just discussing the question.'

Bart looked thoroughly confused by this odd conversation.

'Well,' Cwen explained in the manner of the best town gossip. 'Mistress Wassa here reckons that this is her bridge. While the headman maintains that it is his.'

'When there's only supposed to be a plank. Quite a dangerous one, if I recall. And a ford.'

'Exactly. Mistress Wassa has stated that she is not going to move from this spot until the headman accepts that this land is hers, and as a result, so is the bridge.'

'As are all the tolls from said bridge.'

'Precisely.'

'Has the headman realised that if this is Mistress Wassa's position, he can simply walk away and leave her here? In the field, on her own, with no food.'

'He has not,' Cwen said. 'But then realising things is not one of his strengths. By the by, what brings you here?'

'Ah, much more interesting. We are on the trail of Rachel and Marcus.'

'Tracking?' Cwen asked.

'Just so. And we have followed her this far. She appears to have taken a chest of coin from the church, previously the property of one Athlot of Derby.'

'Well, well,' Cwen said with interest. 'The King's Investigator will be pleased with our progress.

'I can report that a lot of Athlot's fortune was spent building this bridge.'

'He was robbed,' Wat observed.

'And the profit from the tolls has been going to Athlot,

Chad and Mistress Wassa, with the headman taking a portion for the town. All instead of the king, which is the normal arrangement.'

'Funny how none of that has been spent on the town,' Wat observed.

While this friendly discussion was going on, Bart climbed up onto the cart behind Cwen and was surveying the crowd and the bridge.

'Over there,' he called. 'On the bridge.'

The crowd turned as one to face the bridge.

'Rachel, Marcus and the cart,' Bart cried.

The gathered travellers, obviously thinking that this whole thing was some sort of entertainment, headed over to the bridge to watch the performance of Rachel, Marcus and the Cart, whatever it was.

'We have to stop them,' Wat said, trying to push his way through the crowd and back towards the bridge. 'If they get to the other side, they could disappear into the woods and make the job ten times harder.'

Cwen and Bart joined Wat but the crowd was still thick and stopped them making fast progress.

Rachel was now onto the bridge and past the toll man and was worming her way through the throngs. She had put a cloak on over her bizarre dress, but the wildness of her hair gave her away. That and the fact that Marcus was with her, and they were pushing a valuable-looking chest on a hand cart.

'We can still catch her,' Cwen urged, barging someone aside to get a bit of free space.

They were all free of the entangling people now and had a clear run to the bridge. But Rachel was halfway across. Even if they got to the bridge straightaway, Rachel would be across before them.

As hope of success receded, the attention of the whole area, field, bridge and all was dragged to the crest of the hill, where a shining force of horsemen appeared, armed and hot in their pursuit.

'Good God,' Wat said, looking at the horsemen, or rather at one in particular. 'Is that Hermitage on a horse?'

'No,' Cwen said thoughtfully. 'I think it's a horse with Hermitage on top.'

Caput XXVII: Mind The Gap

The Norman horsemen swept down from the hill as only Norman horsemen could sweep. They thundered, they pounded, they drummed the earth with their might, and somewhere amongst it all, a monk squealed.

Hanging on to the back of Pinel for dear life, Hermitage, eyes firmly closed, could tell they were now going down a hill. There seemed to be a lot of cheering and shouting at the same time, but he had to assume it was not a horse race.

'She's on the bridge,' he heard Wat's voice call out. He momentarily felt elation that their mission was heading for success. Wat was found and Rachel was obviously just ahead. Surely, they would catch her.

Momentarily, his momentary elation left. 'Did they say, bridge?' he asked Pinel in a voice more quiver than voice.

'Aye,' Pinel called back, sounding much more excited at the prospect. 'That horrible-looking wooden bridge ahead.'

'A horrible-looking wooden bridge?' Hermitage asked. 'On horses? At this speed?'

'It won't be a problem,' Pinel called. 'You worry too much.'

Hermitage knew that he worried too much. He didn't need to be told that he worried too much. Just at this moment, when he was on the back of a horse riding at full gallop onto a horrible-looking bridge, he thought the expression, worrying too much, was completely inadequate.

He heard the clatter of the hooves as they moved from the nice solid ground to the planks of the bridge. He briefly wondered about the fact that there wasn't a bridge on this road and that they must have come the wrong way, but he didn't think accurate directions were his main concern at the moment.

There was lots of shouting about him, presumably from the travellers on the bridge who were objecting to the passage of the Norman horses. He objected to the passage of the Norman horses, and he was on one of them.

'We'll have her now,' he heard Pinel cry.

He could only hope that they would have her very soon indeed, after which everyone could stop moving.

The clattering of hoof on plank continued, but at least it slowed slightly. The cries of the crowd diminished as well, presumably because the worst of the onslaught was over.

Then, to his ears, the slowing of the hooves and the quiet of the people began to sound more like an ominous silence.

In the midst of the ominous silence, he heard a most definite creak, almost immediately followed by a splintering noise.

'Ah,' he heard Pinel say perfectly calmly. 'The bridge might be about to fall down.'

From the shore, the sight was quite magnificent. A band of horsemen had pounded onto the bridge without so much as breaking step. People had scattered, many of them taking to the shallow water, where they stood shaking their fists at the Normans.

At the commencement of all of this, Ursen the toll man followed the instructions he had been given for such occasions. He grabbed the money and ran.

Once on the bridge, the horses had to slow as there was simply no room for them all to proceed at full pace. Whether it was the arrival, or the slowing was irrelevant; the bridge began to sway.

It was quite a peculiar sight, a whole bridge full of people and horses swaying above a river.

Some people thought they had gone mad as they saw part of the world stay still, while a bridge-shaped bit of it moved about.

The cracking and splintering sounds soon made it clear that the world had not gone mad, it was only a bridge falling down.

As the movement of the bridge increased, most of the people on it simply struggled to keep their balance. Those near the edge decided that resuming use of the ford was best, but many found that quite a bit of the ford had been taken away and they plunged into the cold river.

The horses, surprisingly, didn't seem too disturbed. Perhaps having four legs instead of two made things like this less noticeable.

The person of most interest on the bridge, Rachel, was most intent on holding on to her hand cart and its cargo and she clasped herself to it as a mother to her newborn.

Unfortunately, most newborns do not weigh twice as much as their parent, nor are they equipped with wheels with which they can move rapidly on sloping bridges.

The cart and its heavy load of a chest full of coin had no choice but to make for the water. Despite Rachel and Marcus hanging onto it for dear life, the journey was inevitable.

The bridge tipped, the cart rolled, Marcus and Rachel went with it and they all quickly found that chests of coin don't float.

Once one side of the bridge had collapsed, the other quickly followed suit and the result was that the whole thing simply dropped a few feet into the water below, where it sat in the shallows.

The horses looked around seemingly confused about where all the water had suddenly come from.

Hermitage started breathing again. 'Can I get off now?' he asked, his voice breaking into small pieces.

'The horse or the bridge?' Pinel asked.

'Oh, both?'

He felt the horse move slowly this time and chanced an opening of his eyes. 'Oh,' he said. 'The bridge looks a lot lower closer up.'

Pinel guided his horse slowly off the bridge and once they were on the shore, he helped Hermitage off.

Hermitage stood for a moment, surveying the extraordinary surroundings before his legs told him they weren't going to do standing up anymore and sat him on the ground.

'Hermitage!' Cwen called as she came rushing up. 'That was an incredible sight.'

'Was it? I wasn't looking.'

'The horses and the bridge and everything. What were you thinking?'

'Thinking,' Hermitage muttered to himself. 'Yes, I'll do that next time.' He forced himself out of the daze he had fallen into. 'There was no one in Derby, so I had to find you.'

'No one?'

'Well, you and Wat and Bart and the headman and Mistress Wassa. All gone. I heard you went south but couldn't follow fast enough, so I went for Fortmain.'

'And his horses,' Cwen pointed out. 'And you've been all the way to Nottingham and back as well?'

'Yes. It's been a bit of a day.'

Wat joined them now with Bart at his side.

'This investigation business is more exciting than I thought,' Bart enthused. 'Do you always have chases for the missing treasure and bridges collapsing and people in rivers?'

'No,' Hermitage said. 'This is unique. It has never happened before and I pray it will never happen again.'

'Where is the lovely Rachel, by the way?' Wat asked, looking over towards the bridge. 'Oh, there she is.'

They all looked over and saw Rachel and Marcus walking round and round in the water, obviously trying to locate the spot where the chest of coin had gone down.

Rachel walked in one circle which clearly incorporated a large hole in the riverbed, into which she vanished. Marcus quickly jumped forward and thrashed about himself until he had hold of her by her hair, with which he dragged her back to safety.

She expressed her opinion of this behaviour loudly and with agitated gestures, to which Marcus responded in kind.

Into the conflict rode Fortmain, who took Marcus by the scruff of the neck, while one of the other Normans grabbed Rachel. Insistent demands that they be released and let go were ignored. and the two of them were dumped on the riverbank, where a small crowd gathered to look at them.

The Normans then returned to the river, where Fortmain directed his men to scour the riverbed in quite an organised manner. Four abreast, they walked backwards and forwards beside the fallen bridge.

Every now and then, one of them would fall into a depression in the riverbed, but then they stopped, gathered themselves and actually dived down under the water to search below.

After a surprisingly short period of this, one of the Normans cried out. His fellows went to join him and between them, they dragged the chest from the water.

'That's mine,' Rachel cried.

'Not only is it not yours,' Fortmain called over. 'It never

was and never will be.'

A new cry now disturbed an already disturbing day. A piercing sound, like a buzzard on high calling to its mate, swept down over the ground and got everyone's attention.

Hermitage turned and saw two people approaching. Neither of them looked at all used to running, but they were trying their best.

From one of them, the extraordinary noise was issuing forth.

'What have you done to my bridge?' Mistress Wassa wailed with a volume that seemed bigger than her body.

'Your bridge?' The headman asked fiercely. 'What have you done to the town bridge, that's the question?'

'Whose bridge?' Hermitage asked.

'It's a long, convoluted and very greedy tale, Hermitage,' Cwen explained.

'Why is there a bridge here at all?' he asked.

'Was there a bridge,' Wat corrected. 'It's gone back to being a wobbly plank now.'

'It's all to do with Athlot's fortune,' Cwen said. 'And it could be to do with his murder as well.' She looked hard at the headman and Wassa.

'I did not kill Athlot,' Wassa insisted.

'And I didn't kill him as well,' the headman added.

'I think we'll let the King's Investigator decide who killed him.' Cwen sounded very official.

They both looked at Hermitage who wasn't feeling very decisive.

'You see,' Cwen said to him. 'We found out quite a lot while you've been off having a nice talk with your friend Gilbert.'

'How did you get on?' Wat asked.

'Me?' Hermitage's senses were getting themselves back in order, but confusion was taking over now.

'Yes. Nottingham. Gilbert. Remember?'

'Of course, of course.' He now sorted himself out and stood, trying to take in the complete chaos about him.

'Did you find out about Athlot?' Cwen asked. 'Were the Normans after him?'

'I found out that he probably wasn't Athlot at all,' Hermitage said.

'Wasn't Athlot? Where was Athlot then?'

'I mean he was Athlot, but he wasn't. That wasn't his real name.'

'We seem to have a spate of people not using their real names,' Cwen nodded towards Rachel, who seemed to be too soggy and disheartened to even bother trying to get away.

Travellers on this side of the river, who had gathered in groups for the various excitements the day had provided, now seemed disappointed that things had quietened down, and were starting to remember what it was they were supposed to be doing.

A few were taking tentative steps onto the collapsed bridge, discovering that it was quite stable and could take their weight.

Once the first courageous few had made it all the way across without incident, the rest of the crowd started to resume their journeys. It was only necessary to step into the water where the bridge had actually sunk that far.

Packs were taken up and a general movement began.

Seeing this restoration of normal service, the headman looked around and spotted Ursen not too far off, guarding his day's takings.

'Get back there,' the headman called. 'There's people

crossing the bridge without paying the toll.'

'What bridge?' Ursen called back, obviously not too keen on resuming his duties.

'The bridge over the river.'

'There isn't a bridge over the river anymore.'

'All right, the bridge through the river. People are still walking on it, so they need to pay their toll.'

Ursen took a good hard look at the wreckage of the bridge, some bits of which had started to float downstream. He then considered the headman, surrounded as he was by several people who seemed to be talking about murder.

He also considered the group of Norman horsemen who were now approaching with their find from the river. As far as he was concerned, they were the ones who had caused his livelihood to collapse into the water and were not people to be argued with. He obviously decided that he didn't want to be a toll man anymore. Or if he did, it would be on a proper bridge that didn't fall down.

He came over, dropped his sack of takings at the headman's feet and headed back into town.

The headman huffed. 'You cannot get good people these days.'

'That's certainly true,' Cwen agreed. 'After all, no one is setting a good example.'

Fortmain now arrived, two of his men carrying the chest between them.

'We have recovered Aethelred's ransom,' he announced grandly.

'We've what the what?' Wat asked excitedly.

'It too is a long and greedy tale,' Hermitage said. 'And I'm not sure that is the same money,' he said to Fortmain. Seeing the chest close up, he was positive that this could not be

Danegeld. There simply wasn't enough.

'We have recovered Aethelred's ransom,' Fortmain repeated very plainly. 'And we shall return it to the duke.'

'I'm confused,' Wat said. 'That's the money from the church.'

'What money from the church?' the headman asked.

'The money Athlot gave to save his soul,' Hermitage said quite pointedly.

'Then it's our toll money,' the headman said. 'He can't just take it.'

'The four armed Norman soldiers with their horses can't take it?' Cwen checked. 'Is that what you're saying?'

The headman quickly realised that that was not what he was saying. 'But it's my money,' he whimpered.

'Mine actually,' Wassa put in, but she seemed equally reticent about insisting on its return.

'Is that more?' Fortmain asked, looking at the sack at the headman's feet.

'This?' he asked lightly. 'Oh no. This is nothing. Just a few coins from the bridge tolls, that's all. Nothing for you to worry about.'

'Then we shall take that as well.' Fortmain gestured that one of his men should do so. 'After all, the bridge belongs to the king, doesn't it?'

'Oh, erm, yes,' the headman agreed, unable to see any alternative.

'And we shall need a horse and cart to carry it all,' the Norman said, looking around the field. He spotted the headman's cart and waved one of the men to go and get it.

'Of course, you will,' the headman looked ready to sink to his knees.

'What about Rachel and Marcus?' Hermitage asked

Fortmain.

'Nothing to do with us,' the Norman replied. It was clear that he had already decided that his name was as good as restored and that he no longer needed to bother with common Saxons.

'And Athlot's killer?' Cwen asked with barely contained anger. 'Or are the Normans not interested in killers either?'

Fortmain looked at her. 'Not at the moment, no. And if what we've heard is true, the man is better off dead anyway. If someone hadn't killed him already, we'd probably have to. I could take his body to show the duke, I suppose, but that didn't go too well last time I tried it.'

Caput XXVIII: Who?

'What did he mean, Hermitage?' Cwen asked with some annoyance as they watched the Normans slowly wend their way over what was left of the bridge; her irritation was mainly caused by the low sobbing of the headman as he watched his money disappear.

'I think we had best return to Athlot's home before going into all the details. From what I have learned, his tale is a complex one, but there's something I need to see before I make any suggestions concerning his death.'

'We'd better bring them,' Wat nodded towards the sodden Marcus and Rachel. 'If they're not up to their eyes in this I'd be very surprised.' He took Bart and they went to fetch the two suspects.

Plodding back and looking very despondent about it, Marcus and Rachel joined the group as if they had nothing better left in their lives.

'Now you're going to learn something, young Bart,' Cwen said as they all started back towards the town.

'Is that right?' Bart asked brightly.

'Oh, yes.' She winked at Hermitage. 'This is the most important part of an investigation. You go back to the scene of the murder. You get all the people involved together and then you walk up and down in front of them.'

'Walk up and down.' Bart sounded as if he were taking a note so that he would know what to do when it was his turn.

'Then, after what can seem quite a while you say, aha! And that's that.'

'That's what?'

'You know who did it.'

'How?' Bart asked.

'Don't ask me. You'll just have to watch and see if you can spot the moment.'

'Take no notice of her,' Hermitage said. 'We just have to think through all the information we have and see what fits. When it does fit, it will be obvious.'

'Aha,' Bart said.

'Exactly.'

'And do you know who did it already?'

'I do not,' Hermitage said. 'I have a suspicion, but I need to hear what Wat and Cwen have discovered. Only then will everything fit. We hope.'

It was quite a procession that made its way back into Derby. The travellers from the south side of the river, who had been delayed by the collapse of the bridge, had come across and were now making their way north once more. The noise of their passage prompted doors to open and faces to appear.

The butcher and the leathermaker were only two of the tradesmen who appeared, smiling their welcomes to all of this passing custom.

Chatter concerning Mistress Wassa and the headman was quiet but intense. Pointing and laughing at the bedraggled Marcus and Rachel was much more explicit.

Hermitage led the contingent on to the smithy where the smith watched them arrive with considerable surprise.

'Can we warm by your fire?' Marcus asked with a shiver.

'Aye, aye,' the smith said, stepping back to let him and Rachel pass.

The others followed and the interior of the smithy was soon over-crowded.

'No Grimulf?' Hermitage asked, noticing that the boy was not here, mainly because there had been no moaning or complaint at this interruption.

'He's round the back,' the smith said.

'I think we had better join him,' Hermitage said, waving a hand in front of his face. 'It is very hot in here already, even without all these additional people crowding your workplace.'

Marcus and Rachel moaned they weren't dry yet, but Hermitage promised them they could come back in a few moments. The smith even put his tools down, interested to find out what was going on.

They all trooped around to the back of the smithy where Grimulf was busy clearing away the wreckage of Athlot's house. He looked up and his face fell to its usual shape of sneering disdain.

Hermitage gave him a nod of acknowledgement and indicated that everyone else should find a space.

'Well,' he said. 'We are back where it all began. And to think that if Ern had just said a murder, instead of the murder, none of this might ever have happened. I blame myself, I suppose.'

'You did it?' Wat asked. 'Hermitage, how could you?'

Cwen struck him, but quite lightly.

Hermitage pressed on. 'The question we had was whether Athlot had been murdered at all. Had the poor fellow simply fallen from his ladder and there was no reason for concern?

'It only seemed reasonable to confirm the situation, but that confirmation was hard to come by. The more questions were asked, the more difficult the situation became.

'Why was a ninety-year-old man up a ladder at all? And if he was, why did he bother when his roof was so low in the first place?

'And a simple question opened up a whole world of difficulty. From Athlot's own tales, he could have had dealings with King Aethelred and the Duke of Normandy. He came to Derby with wealth that was never explained. He lived a life of ease but in a tiny hut behind a smithy.

'Was there still a hidden treasure somewhere? Had someone found it and killed Athlot in the process? Was he being sought by Normans out for revenge? We set out looking for answers. I to Nottingham and Wat and Cwen here in Derby.'

'And me,' Bart put in.

'Ah, yes, and Bart.'

Bart looked at everyone to make sure they had registered his involvement.

'And what did you find?' Cwen asked.

'You first,' Hermitage said. 'I think I need to hear what you discovered.'

'Quite simple, really,' Cwen said. 'Athlot and Chad were in league with the headman and Wassa here to cheat the king out of his tax.'

This brought a brief furore of complaint, but Cwen ignored it.

'They used Athlot's mysterious wealth to build a bridge over the river from which they then all took tolls to live long and comfortable lives.'

Wat added, 'Until Athlot, probably thinking he was old enough to die soon and would quite like to save his soul, started giving his to the church. Our priest naturally keeping it as if it were his own.'

'Hence,' Cwen announced. 'Wassa and the headman are in very good positions to be Athlot's killers.' She clicked her fingers. 'Perhaps they were in it together and now they're trying to betray one another. Typical.'

More objections were silenced by Hermitage's raised hand.

'This is very informative.' He nodded to himself as he took all that in. 'And now I can tell you what I found in Nottingham.

'Athlot, was not, in fact, Athlot,' he declared. 'I strongly suspect his real name was Eadric. Eadric the Acquisitive, betrayer of kings.'

'Oh,' said the smith. 'That's nice.'

'Nice?' Hermitage couldn't believe his ears.

'Yes,' the smith explained. 'It's nice to have important people in town, isn't it? And to think he was behind my smithy.'

'Erm, yes.' Hermitage thought it best to simply shake his head and carry on.

'Eadric, or Athlot as we knew him, stole a fortune from the Duke of Normandy and King Aethelred.'

Wat whistled. 'That must have been a while ago.'

'It was. He further went on to betray King Cnut, who is reported to have chopped his head off.'

'He did well to make it to Derby, then.'

'Obviously, he escaped this fate,' Hermitage explained. 'As the report is only that, a report.'

'Soon after all this betrayal was going on, a fellow called Athlot arrives in Derby with a fortune.'

'Could be anyone, though,' the headman spoke up. 'He could really have been Athlot.'

'He could, but several things are against this. Why did he go to live in a small hut behind the smithy? As Lord Gilbert of Nottingham said, wealthy people like to enjoy their wealth. Athlot seemed to be hiding.

'Further, the smith overheard an argument where the name Eadric was used. I assumed it was Athlot who said it, but now I can see it was someone calling Athlot by that name.

'The smith said the words used were that there wasn't time anymore. But time for what?'

'I don't know,' the smith said. 'They didn't say.'

'Could it be time for Eadric, Athlot to make amends for his past ways? Was this some old confidante of Eadric's warning him that life was short and his judgement awaited him?'

'Oh.' The smith was impressed. 'Could be.'

'So,' Hermitage continued. 'Bearing all that in mind, it seems reasonable to conclude that this was Eadric and further, that someone might well want revenge for all the awful things he did.'

'After all this time?' Wat asked.

'Exactly,' Hermitage agreed. 'Lord Gilbert had never heard of these tales and he is a Norman commander. Only old Silas remembered the stories.'

'Who's old Silas?' Cwen asked.

'A fellow who has been digging Norman drains for many years.'

'Poor fellow. What did he do to deserve that?'

'It seemed to be his calling.'

'Called to the drains, eh?'

'His drains are irrelevant,' Hermitage tried to concentrate. 'The point is that he was old enough to remember the events in question.

'I have read histories, as you know.'

'We do,' Cwen confirmed.

'Including several of King Aethelred and his dealings with the Danes. And I have never come across any record of Eadric or a stolen fortune.

'It could well be that he had simply lived long enough to evade his pursuers.'

Wat put his hand up.

'Yes, Wat?'

'If this is the case, what are Marcus and Rachel doing here? They obviously came for the fortune and not for me at all. I was just a what-do-call-it.'

'Bonus?' Hermitage suggested. 'A good they might gain?'

'If you like. If no one else knew of Athlot and his fortune, how did they find out?'

'This is speculation,' Hermitage said, feeling most uncomfortable at the very idea. 'But they obviously did know, and they must have found out somehow. My thought is that lord you sold tapestry to in the fens.'

'Really?'

'You said he was old and had served with Aethelred. I can imagine that in those days, talk of Eadric's betrayals was common. It sounds as if this lord liked to talk about his earlier days and doubtless, Rachel overheard him.'

'But how would they know of Athlot and Derby?'

'Someone did,' Hermitage said. 'We know that Athlot had a visitor who came to warn him about his time running out. His secret was obviously not perfect.'

'Either your lord knew himself, or someone visited who did know. And again Rachel overheard.'

'Or she got it out of them, one way or another,' Cwen said with a revolting leer.

Hermitage nodded. 'That place is her only connection to those times. It must have been from there.'

'Well?' Wat asked Rachel.

'Do you think I'm going to tell you?' She sniffed at him.

'Please yourself,' Wat said. 'You got no fortune and you'll probably be dead soon from falling in the river.'

'However they knew, they can't have killed Athlot,' Cwen said. 'He was dead before they got here. 'Wassa and the headman it is then. Or one of them.'

More objections sprang forth.

Hermitage shook his head. 'I think not.'

'Oh,' Cwen was disappointed.

'Why now?' Hermitage asked. 'I was interested to hear what they were up to, but Chad died some time ago and the arrangement with the bridge, dishonest and deceitful though it was, was paying them both nicely. If they'd wanted Athlot dead, they could have done it long before now. If they were capable of it, of course.'

'That's more like it,' Cwen said. 'Even if they wanted him dead, I can't see either of them having the courage to do it.'

'It could have been you then,' the headman tried.

'Don't be an idiot,' Cwen instructed.

'So he just died?' Wat said. 'As ninety-year-old men do.'

'There's still the question of the ladder,' Hermitage said.

'Just left against his roof and that was where he happened to die,' Wat said.

'I think not,' Hermitage said in all seriousness.

'He was up the ladder?' Cwen sounded surprised.

'He wasn't.' Hermitage turned to one face in the group. 'Was he, Grimulf?'

Everyone looked at Grimulf.

'What are you looking at me for?'

'Because you were up the ladder.'

'Me?' Grimulf sounded disgusted at the idea. 'What would I be doing up a ladder?'

'Helping Athlot.'

'Old fool,' Grimulf said. 'I wouldn't help him.'

'Ah, but you would. And you did. The smith told me you were always round there helping him out with things.'

'Not me,' Grimulf said, doing his best impression of a

fearsome young man.

'I imagine that the youths of the town compete with one another for toughness and daring. You wouldn't want anyone to think that you were a kind, thoughtful lad who helped out your elderly neighbour.'

'I don't help no one,' Grimulf maintained his stance.

'I had conflicting tales,' Hermitage said. 'You told me you wouldn't help a moaning old man who kept going on about old times, while the smith said you were always round there helping out.

'Further, he would have me believe that you are a nice boy, who only puts on airs to sound fierce. Even though he is the only one who thinks so.

'Asked who to believe, I would choose the smith. And here you are, tidying up the remains of his home.'

'There was clearly no way that Athlot himself would climb a ladder. For one thing, he was very old and for another, he was very tall and could reach the roof on his own if he had to. You are still a boy. You would need a ladder.'

'This is nonsense,' Grimulf insisted.

'But you are a kind boy,' Hermitage pressed. 'Even if you want everyone to think you are brave and dangerous. It's perfectly natural.' Hermitage could only assume it was perfectly natural as he had never wanted to appear either brave or dangerous.

'But Athlot died. It's clear to me that you would not mean him harm, so what happened? Why did you not fetch help? Why did you leave the smith to find him? Did the ladder slip?'

'I didn't kill him,' Grimulf insisted, but the bravado had slipped.

'Of course not,' Hermitage agreed. 'You would never do

such a thing. But you were there when he died.'

Grimulf's head dropped and he slipped to the floor. 'He was complaining at me. He was always complaining at me,' he said.

'Go on,' Hermitage urged gently.

'A little bit of thatch had come off his roof and he wanted it put back. Well, I was doing it, but I'm not a thatcher, am I? He said I wasn't doing it right.

'I tried to do what he told me, but he kept moaning and telling me how useless I was. He was always doing that despite all the things I did for him.'

'Most unjust. And then?'

'Then he pushed the ladder.'

'Pushed it?'

'Yes. He gave it shove, telling me to get down because he could do it better himself and he was ninety.'

'And?'

'When he pushed, I was right on top of the ladder, leaning over and didn't have my balance. I hung on to the roof, but the ladder slipped. When I got down, there he was.'

'Oh, this is very serious,' the headman said.

'You need to keep your mouth shut,' Cwen said. 'You already owe the town an awful lot of money.'

'But you weren't responsible,' Hermitage said. 'It was an accident.'

'Who was going to believe that?' Grimulf asked.

'I do,' Hermitage said.

'And he is the King's Investigator,' Wat said. 'He does this sort of thing all the time.'

'Grimulf,' Hermitage said. 'It was an accident but still one you should have mentioned. You could have called for help but you didn't. Are you even sure Athlot was dead?'

'Oh, he was dead all right. If he'd been alive, I would have gone for help, of course, I would. But he was on his back staring and not breathing. And there was the great big mark on his head where the ladder hit him.'

'Then we must accept that he was dead,' Hermitage said. 'And he was a man of great sin, only trying to make amends at the end of his life.'

'And even that was with dishonest money,' Cwen pointed out.

'I would suggest confessing to the priest,' Hermitage said. 'But in these circumstances, I think you'd better give that a miss.

'Simply continue trying to do good. Don't worry if people think well of you. It does not mean that you are weak, but that you are strong. After all, the easy path is the one that everyone has trod before you.'

'What?' said Grimulf, turning up his nose.

Caput XXIX: Ever After?

'You never said, aha,' Bart complained when they were back at the workshop.

'It didn't seem appropriate in the circumstances,' Hermitage replied. 'Poor Grimulf. He must have been in a real worry since Athlot's death. And I believe his tale. He did not murder Athlot. If he had taken up the ladder and beat him to death with it, an "aha" would have been called for.'

'And the headman is in a real worry now,' Cwen said with glee. 'The next town moot is going to be a lively affair.'

'I gather Mistress Wassa is claiming that the shock of her husband's death made her lose her memory and she doesn't remember anything.' Wat grinned

'For two years?' Cwen asked. 'I think it's going to be back to work for both of them.'

Wat and Cwen were sitting comfortably together, and Hermitage had to remind himself that this whole sorry business had started with an uncomfortable dispute. And a largely pointless one at that.

He couldn't help but think that Athlot's pointless complaint had gone so far as to lead to his death. If he had been kinder to Grimulf, he might still be alive today. Or not. He was ninety, after all.

Or Marcus and Rachel would have found him and robbed him, which might have had the same effect. He wondered what had happened to them. They'd asked to go and dry by the smithy fire, and no one ever saw them again. It was probably for the best.

But Bart was still here. Was Hermitage really to have an apprentice investigator? Was one even needed? If it was, what on earth could be taught? To have an apprentice, you needed to be a master, and Hermitage fell at the first hurdle.

The death of Athlot had not really been a murder anyway. Not a real, horrible one like some of those Hermitage had had to deal with. Perhaps, when faced with the worst, including the worst the Norman nobility had to offer, Bart would decide this was not for him.

Hermitage could only hope. He wouldn't want to see a nice young man like Bart follow his own sorry path.

And if there was one apprentice investigator, where would it end? Before long, the world would be full of investigators, all of them looking for murders. It was unthinkable.

'Right,' Cwen said firmly as if she had just made up her mind about something.

They all turned to look at her.

'Bart,' she said. 'If you're going to stay you have to make yourself useful.'

'Who said he's going to stay?' Wat asked.

'I'm coming to you,' Cwen replied. 'Now Bart, what was it you said you did at the Gudmunds?'

'Just fetching and carrying, really.'

'Excellent. We could do with some fetching and carrying around here.'

'But..,' Bart began.

'You thought you were going to investigate murders?'

'That's right.'

'Well, we haven't got any at the moment. And when there are no murders, Hermitage continues his work on the lexicography of the Post-Exodus prophets.'

'You know!' Hermitage burst out.

'Of course, I do. I'm only teasing you most of the time. I have no idea what it means, but it's what he does. And as far as I can tell, it involves no fetching and carrying so that's what

Bart can do.'

Bart said nothing.

'Or head back to the east?' Cwen offered.

'All right,' Bart grumbled.

Wat was looking a bit stunned at these arrangements for his workshop being made while he was sitting there.

'Now then, Wat the Weaver,' Cwen said as if appraising Best Weaver in Show. 'Any other little secrets from you that we need to know?'

'Little ones? Probably. But it's hard to keep track of them all.'

'Big ones, then. Anyone else going to arrive one night claiming to be your wife?'

'Definitely not. One encounter with Rachel was enough to make me very cautious in that regard.'

'Excellent. Because something like that could put the whole workshop at risk. We saw what happened with Wassa and Chad.'

Hermitage was grateful for Wat's reassurance, but, it being Wat, he wasn't sure how reassuring it was.

'So,' Cwen went on in a very business-like manner. 'We need to safeguard against problems like this and I've come to a decision.'

'Oh yes?' Wat asked with a rather weary tone.

'Yes. I've decided that you can ask me if I'll be your wife. And I will.'

Finis - or is it...?

Post Scriptum

'Brother Hermitage,' Cwen said as she took him by the arm and drew him to one side after the noonday meal one day.

He gave her his best attention.

'It is to be my wedding soon.'

'I know.' Hermitage was overjoyed at the thought. It was wonderful that she and Wat were to be together under the eyes of God.

'And there's one thing I want you to promise me.'

'Of course. Anything at all.'

She looked him hard in the eyes and issued her clear instruction. 'I don't want it ruined by some murder.'

Continuandum...

Made in the USA
Las Vegas, NV
05 March 2022

45101971R00177